AFTER THE GALAXY

THE CRUCIBLE

MIRTH PUBLISHING
ST. JOHN'S

SCOTT BARTLETT

THE CRUCIBLE
© Scott Bartlett 2018

Cover art by: Tom Edwards (tomedwardsdesign.com)

Typography and interior formatting by: Steve Beaulieu (facebook.com/BeaulisticBookServices)

This work is licensed under the Creative Commons Attribution-NonCommercial-ShareAlike 4.0

License. To view a copy of this license, visit creativecommons.org/licenses/by-nc-sa/4.0 or send a

letter to Creative Commons, 171 2nd Street, Suite 300, San Francisco, California 94105, USA.

This novel is a work of fiction. All of the characters, places, and events are fictitious. Any

resemblance to actual persons living or dead, locales, businesses, or events is entirely coincidental.

Library and Archives Canada Cataloguing in Publication

Bartlett, Scott

The Crucible / Scott Bartlett ; illustrations by Tom Edwards ; typography and interior formatting

by Steve Beaulieu.

ISBN 978-1-988380-16-2

This one's for you - the reader.

LAMBTON CLOUD

1

"I need those slipspace coords, Cal," I say. "There's nothing more to it."

We're standing on opposite sides of the living room in the apartment Lambton gave me. Cal Pikeman, the Shiva Knight who turned out to be my father, grimaces. "This isn't open to debate. The slipspace coords for accessing the Shivan Cathedral are intended only for use by knights and their proteges. There are things you don't understand, and this is clearly one of them."

"If it wasn't open to debate, then I wouldn't know about it. The game is clearly changing, and it's changed even more since Fairfax killed you in the Core. Resetting the galactic Subverse isn't as easy as it used to be—and I know it was never easy. If you have a slipspace route that'll put us farther into the Core in two hops than Fairfax can hope to get in eleven, then we *all* need that information. Not just me, but the eight Troubleshooters that will be accompanying me."

But Cal's shaking his head vigorously. "The Shivan Cathedral can *only* be accessed by the Shiva and their protege. If I allow even a single uninitiated to go there, it risks discovery by the outside world. And that's unacceptable. The Cathedral is the brain behind all we do. It's too valuable."

"Then the entire quest is out of the question. There's no way I can take on the forces Fairfax has assembled without backup. And if our nine Broadswords have to take the slow way, he'll beat us to the Core by a long shot. Hell, Fairfax already has a big lead! We probably need this just to make up ground."

Cal raises a hand, finger jabbing toward the ground as he speaks. "You committed to embracing humility. You promised you'd defer to me."

"Not when it endangers the quest," I say, softening my tone. Look, Cal, I've bought everything else you've sold me. The training, the need to reset the galaxy, even the idea that there are worse things than letting the Subverse keep existing. We're on the same side. But I think you need to consider whether there might be times *you* need a little humility. Enough to realize that maybe you're wrong about this."

Cal stands frozen, hand raised, finger pointing at the floor. I guess I'm getting a taste of what it would have been like to actually be raised by him.

"Think on it," I say, turning toward the exit. "I have things I need to do."

Walking out, I realize I'm still not used to how heavy I feel down here. And when I open the door, stars gleam up through the floor of the corridor beyond—a little patch of nothing, to remind me where I am.

I step over the reinforced glass, toward the elevator waiting at the end of the hall. Lambton gave me an underground apartment, situated at the edge of the rotating tube that is Cylinder One: in other words, the very bottom of the gravity well. Maybe it's his way of reminding me that he's only helping with the mission in order to get back at Fairfax for wrecking his precious habitat.

At least the increased gravity helps me keep up my cardio.

Makes bone density less of an issue. Helps with muscle preservation. Always look on the bright side, right?

Of course, I keep up my daily calisthenics no matter the gravity level. But hey, a little extra gravity can't hurt.

When the elevator doors open onto the surface, it seems a brighter than I remember. Ah—looks like the construction bots have finally made some headway on fixing the section of sun tube the giant Kitane busted up before I put her down. They've mostly been working at night, with Lambton giving orders to slow and then stop Cylinder One's rotation, killing the gravity for a few hours after midnight so the bots can just float up there and get to work. The alternative would have been a gigantic scaffolding reaching halfway across the cylinder's diameter. Not quite as practical.

The upshot of killing the gravity has been everyone tethering themselves to their bunks before they go to sleep, just in case. No one wants to wake up floating above their dresser when the gravity comes back on. That's a good way to get a concussion.

There's been plenty to do since Fairfax retreated and headed for the Core. Repairs to the *Ares*. Drilling the Guardsmen who'll accompany me on the next leg of the journey—filling them in on what to expect. Continuing my training with an increasingly irritated Cal Pikeman.

And trying to figure out what to do with Dice.

As I amble along the path leading from the elevator, the bot steps out of the shadows of a comfort station's awning, striding purposefully toward me. Not the best way to walk to avoid drawing attention, but Dice has never known any other way to walk than purposeful.

He still has no Auditor monitoring his behavior, though I think he would have gone along with having another one installed. The thing is, I can't bring myself to do it. He's earned his freedom, as far I'm concerned.

Except, even though he has free rein to modify his own

consciousness, improve his intellect, install new capabilities—it still isn't freedom. Not really. Not if he has to stay on Cylinder One, or follow me wherever I go.

Because as smart as Dice is, he can't make himself slipspace capable. Without a ship of his own, he's stuck, forced to tag along with humans who do have ships. I won't have him go with anyone else, because I don't know what they'd do to him—especially once they discovered what he's become: the first bot in history with the potential to become a superintelligence.

But I don't really want him with me, either. Not if he doesn't want to be. And I know he doesn't.

That's why I'm giving him Harmony's ship—*Europa's Gift*. The same ship she stole from her grandfather, Daniel Sterling.

"Your daughter won't be pleased with this outcome," Dice says as falls in beside me, and we make our way toward the elevator that will bring us up to the zero-G landing bay at Cylinder One's center. The hole the *Ares* blew through the bay has been patched up with a temporary covering, so that no one falls out of it, but it'll be some time before Lambton gets around to assigning bots to permanently fixing it. There's too much else to do: the smashed-up sun tube, the shattered pipes of the main water filtration and recycling facility, the torched buildings, the wrecked bots littering the grounds. Sometimes, I get the impression Lambton blames me for all that, even though I'm the reason he has control of Cylinder One at all. I guess I did participate in its destruction, technically. I just happen to be the only one who stuck around afterward. So I get the blame.

"I know she won't, Dice," I say, glancing over my shoulder. Harmony tends to keep a close eye on everything—she has the technical prowess to hack whatever equipment she needs to conduct her surveillance. Everything has a back door, she likes to say. Somehow, though, I've managed to hide what I intend to do this morning. "The truth is, I'm killing two Kitane with one missile, here. Harmony's only used that ship to get into trouble. It's much better if she's with me."

"So you're setting one free and imprisoning the other."

I glance at him, but of course there's nothing to be read in his eternally impassive face and scarlet eyes sensors. "Basically. For now, anyway. Look, when Harmony's nineteen—maybe twenty—she can go adventuring all she wants. Twenty-seven's a good age. Anyway, when she's older, she can join *you*, for all I care. You can wander the galaxy together, hand in hand. But I want this business with Fairfax to be over before that happens."

"Well, please pass my apologies to Ms. Harmony. I rather like her, as she's always treated me well. But regardless of the circumstances, I thank you, Commander."

"Please. Call me Joe."

"Joe, then."

As Dice has worked on his own mind, tweaking here, upgrading there, I've started to notice a difference in him. He still calls me fleshbag, but he sounds more sophisticated than before. It's not just that his vocabulary's gotten bigger—though it probably has—it's that he uses words in a more subtle way. More shades of meaning, and you have to be quick to catch them all. I'm sure I never do. I'm not good with words.

"You're welcome, Dice," I say. "But the truth is, you deserve this. You saved me more times than I want to admit, and at least one of those times, you did it because you wanted to. That means a lot to me."

Bizarrely, I actually feel like I could get emotional, here, so I stop talking, since nothing horrifies me more than that. We walk in silence the rest of the way to the elevator, and on the way up, I compare the battered, pockmarked landscape to my memory of how it looked when I first visited. It still has a bit of a post-apocalyptic vibe to it from the fight, which is kind of cool.

The lift reaches the landing bay, and when the doors open we both push out, gently drifting toward the corner where *Europa's Gift* floats, moored to a pair of cleats projecting from the bulkhead.

The *Ares* floats opposite Harmony's ship—I flew it up here before Lambton ordered repairs to the landing bay breach, and bots have been working on fixing her up ever since, free of charge. They finished yesterday morning, and now she's as good as new—down a couple Javelin missiles, but otherwise charged up, refueled, restocked. At least Lambton threw me that bone, especially considering I'm not versecasting anymore and so I don't have that income.

"I hope you've brushed up on your hacking," I say as we land on the hull, Dice using magnets embedded in his hands to attach himself to it while I grab a handle near the airlock. "Because this is far as I can take you. Whatever defenses Harmony's installed on this thing, I'm sure they're way beyond me."

"I have installed several lateral-thinking upgrades," he says. "As well as digesting libraries of recently discovered exploits and back doors. I'm fairly confident in the probability of gaining access."

"Quickly, I hope. We may only have an hour or two."

Dice gets to work. Luckily, ever since the Fall, software vulnerabilities tend to stick around for centuries at a time, if they're ever patched. Most of the companies who made everything are long gone, so everyone's kind of on their own when it comes to security—trapped in an endless, elaborate game of rock-paper-scissors.

It takes Dice less than twenty minutes to gain access, which is the biggest indicator so far that he's now an intellectually superior being. When the ship's airlock opens, I experience yet another moment of doubt about whether I'm doing the right thing in unleashing on the universe a being smarter than any human who's ever lived. True, as long as Dice keeps his current body there's only so much he can do to upgrade his smarts. But what if he hooks himself up to more processing power? How far could this thing go?

I have no idea, is the truth of it. But ultimately, this still feels right.

"God speed, Dice."

"And you. Thank you…Joe."

I nod, and he floats inside the ship, his feet connecting with the deck as the gravity generators draw him downward.

The outer hatch closes, and that's the last I see of him. I push off to float gently backward through the landing bay, and seconds later the ship spins slowly, shedding the magnetic cables tethering it to the bulkhead with an electromagnetic pulse. With its nose pointed toward the massive landing bay airlock, it sails toward it, drifting inside once the first barrier opens.

I raise a hand toward the ship's stern.

Back in my apartment, Cal's still hanging around the living room.

"Make your decision," I tell him. "We're leaving tonight. Either the Broadswords come with us to the Cathedral, or we'll all be taking the long way. There's no way I'm going this alone anymore, Cal. It's suicide."

Cal Pikeman sits on the edge of a purple leather couch and covers his face with his hand. "I'll give you the coords to the Cathedral," he says. "Fount help us all."

ARES

1

At five and a half months, this is one of the longest continuous slipspace voyages I've ever taken. And somehow, despite having another human on board with me, it's also the loneliest.

Harmony's been pissed off at me ever since I let Dice take off in her ship, and we're not on speaking terms. She's especially angry that I forgot to get P3P, the family bot, off of *Europa's Gift* first—meaning he's now wherever Dice ended up. Oops.

It made goodbyes pretty awkward back in Cylinder One, and Maximus Lambton seemed to take a sick pleasure in watching the tension brew between me and Harmony. I won't miss that guy.

After leaving the Lambton Cloud, it took a few trips through slipspace to reach Cal's secret entry coords, the longest leg of the journey no more than a week. Then we reached a star system with barely anything in it: just a gas giant and two small planets. I'm not sure it even had Subverse servers—none of the Troubleshooters knew of any, not even Shimura.

Two days out from that barren system lay Cal's entry coords, and we didn't waste any time transitioning into slipspace the moment we reached them. We can't afford to waste any time.

Lambton stuffed our holds full of supplies, but they won't last much longer than the time it takes to get to the Cathedral. Hopefully whoever we find there are just as well provisioned, and just as willing to share.

It's weird to travel in a space caravan with eight other Broadswords. Before meeting up with Soren, I rarely had cause to travel with other Troubleshooters, or anyone, really. Now there are eight of them with me, closeby in slipspace, but completely inaccessible, even by com. If I tried to contact them, the signal would drop behind the moment it left the ship, never reaching its destination.

During the slipspace voyage, each Troubleshooter has orders to run fighter squadron sims, despite that a Broadsword is more of a cross between a corvette and a fighter. Troubleshooters rarely ever fly together, and I'm hoping that practicing with the sims will help us overcome our inexperience when it comes to coordinating with other ships. If it works, then our Broadswords' agility could grant us an outsized effect on a battlespace—even if we're going up against a warship. That's the hope, anyway.

I gave Harmony my cabin, and she spends most of her time there now, probably running sims on her datasphere. During the first few weeks, it upset me, and I tried to get her talking to me. I knew she'd be pissed at me for clipping her wings, but I had no idea she'd take it this far.

Honestly, though, the longer we're in slipspace, the less I care that we're not talking. I could activate the crew, try to talk to them, but why bother? Marissa's still angry I deleted Moe, Asterisk's just a kid, and I think I'd have a hard time confiding in Belflower now that she's tried to kill me. Hell, I would have had a hard time before that.

But maybe I *should* talk to someone. Ever since the fight with Fairfax's people on Cylinder One, nightmares have fragmented my sleep. That's not unusual, but these are particularly vivid and intense. Sometimes, I wake from them screaming.

One night, I'm wrenched from my sleep, bolting upright in the command seat to hear myself yelling that I'm sorry, over and over. Behind me, the cabin hatch slides open, and I twist around to see Harmony standing in a night gown, eyes wide. "Are you all right?" she says.

"Yeah. Fine."

"Okay." She withdraws into the cabin and closes the hatch.

The nightmares are all set in a graveyard—one made up solely of people I've killed. They drag themselves out of their graves and trudge across freshly turned ground, toward the center, where I sit strapped to a metal chair, my eyelids forced open by a device custom built for the purpose.

They don't say anything—they just stare. My victims don't even seem accusing. Only confused, or curious, or in pain.

Some of them have blurry, indistinct faces, and I know these are people I killed at range, either from my Broadsword or using a scoped laser rifle. There are a few who I blew to bits using plasma grenades. For whatever reason, they don't affect me as much.

It's the ones I killed up-close that really get to me. The ones I knifed in the dark, face to face, or who I took down with a laser pistol or my blaster at point-blank range.

Things were simpler, back when my datasphere told me where to point my weapon, when to pull the trigger. It was so much easier to place my pistol inside that green cone and fire. I could detach myself from my kills, then. But ever since I transcended the datasphere, my kills are my own. They aren't directed by military-grade software, given to me by superiors who will back me fully. *I* committed them. Just me. That means I get all the responsibility, all the guilt that comes with having ended those lives.

Then, the thing I fear most happens. The pirate reappears—the same one who haunted my dreams just before my breakdown, en route to Earth. He walks across the graveyard holding the same photo I found on his corpse, the one of his wife and two children, a son and daughter.

That's the kill that's always haunted me my most, even though my datasphere told me to do it. Because of the picture.

"Why?" he asks as he draws close, deathly pale face inches from mine. "Why did you do it?"

And I wake drenched in cold sweat, the bridge echoing with my screams. I'm going to have another breakdown. Any day, now. I can feel it.

Harmony stops checking on me when I wake up with night terrors, but I catch her shooting me concerned looks. I avoid those looks. During the day, I don't want to talk about what I'm experiencing. I don't want to think about it.

One night, I jerk upright in the command seat to find Cal sitting on the railing of the OPO Station, staring at me, hands clasped between his knees. "Nightmares," he mutters, and gives a muted chuckle.

I say nothing. It's weird when your dad can appear anywhere.

"You've been having a lot of those," he says. "Crying out."

Again, I have nothing to say. None of this is news to me.

"I used to have the same nightmares," he says.

"How could you know what nightmares I'm having?" Dream analysis *is* a datasphere function…could my Fount be giving him access to them?

"I hear what you shout out while you're having them," he says. "It's not hard to piece together."

"Fount. Do you think Harmony knows?"

He just looks at me, face neutral. I sigh, and ask, "You said you used to have them, too. How'd you stop them?"

"Well, do you understand why you're having them? Now?"

I give a slight shrug.

"Now that you've started to take responsibility for your actions —instead of just doing what your datasphere tells you to do— you're also shouldering the consequences. Your kills are coming back to haunt you. And if what they say on Gauntlet is any indication, you have more kills than any Guardsman in recorded history. That's a heavy burden to bear, son. It'll destroy you, if you let it."

My teeth are grinding together in frustration, mostly at the truth in what he's saying. I force them apart. "It never was a burden before. I barely thought about it, though there were dreams…" The nameless pirate who kept his family in his breast pocket, close to his heart. Sometimes his face is marred with my laser shot, sometimes not. "How do I stop them?" I ask again.

"There's no erasing the past, Joe. You can't go back and *un*kill those people."

"Think I don't know that?"

"I think you know it all too well. And it leaves you with just one option: redemption. You must become worthy of your blaster, and kill only when it's the last option. Only when it will unquestionably make the galaxy and the people living in it better off. You must become a Shiva, in the fullest sense. You must embrace the knighthood, own it, become it. More than any Shiva has in the past."

"Is that all?"

A sad smile spreads across Cal's lips. "The transition from Guardsman to Knight means not just knowing who to shoot, but why. It means taking full responsibility for your kills—not just those you will kill, but for everyone you *have* killed. You're the one who pulled the trigger, after all. Even if it felt like your datasphere was choosing who dies, you pulled the trigger."

"I think taking all of that on will tear me apart," I say softly.

"No. *Not* taking it on is tearing you apart. You have to take it on and rationalize it. If you can't redeem yourself *to* yourself—if you can't make those deaths count for something—you'll shatter."

"What can I possibly make them count for?"

The old Shiva drops down from the railing and stands before me, hands dangling at his sides. "You're still here, aren't you?"

"They're not."

"No. They're not. Which means you owe it to them to use your life to do the best thing you possibly can with it."

"Go to the Core. Reset the Subverse."

My father inclines his head. "I think you know the fate of a man like you is to die in battle. Even if every Shiva wasn't destined to perish in the Core, war would take you eventually."

A long silence stretches between us. I'm not sure if Cal's waiting for me to say something, but I'm too busy digesting what he just said.

"You become worthy by turning yourself into the weapon that will save the galaxy. A just weapon. If you embrace the Seven Ideals, if you resolve yourself to dying in order to preserve what peace and stability the galaxy has left, for another cycle's worth of generations…then you will make peace with what you've done. And as you walk down that path, the nightmares will lessen."

At last, I look up to meet my father's eyes. "You're right," I say, and to my horror, there are tears in my eyes. "I'll do it."

2

I pause at the bottom of the narrow stairs leading down to the mess. Harmony looks up from the table, expression blank, then returns her focus to her bowl of milky mush and whatever she's looking at on her datasphere.

You have to give it to her: it's hard to maintain the silent treatment on a Broadsword. Other than the cabin, there are really only two places she can go, and the chances are good I'll be in one of them.

"Hopefully the food isn't too tasteless," I say, glancing at her oatmeal before walking to the counter to start preparing my own from a freeze-dried packet.

She stops eating, peering down into her bowl, shoulders rising and falling. "The stores aboard *Europa's Gift*, weren't much better, to be honest."

Wow. Speech. That seems like progress, even if she is immediately bringing up the reason she's so upset with me.

Her and Belflower have been hanging out with each other—running gaming sims together, bonding over the ones Harmony created herself. They're both tech geniuses, and Belflower always said Harmony reminded her of herself, even before they met. So I guess it makes sense.

"Did you ever enter nanodeath, during your slipspace voyages?" I ask her, waiting for water to boil.

She shakes her head.

"Wow. So you let yourself age all those extra months?"

"Yeah. I didn't see them as wasted, though. I liked the time alone—working on my sims, reading. If I got lonely, I talked to P3P. But I couldn't help noticing you're not in nanodeath, either."

I nod. "I've only entered nanodeath once. Recently." Well, twice, if you count the time I died, back in Arbor. But that wasn't by choice.

"Everyone back in Brinktown always talked about how quickly you age, compared to other Guardsmen. I figured that was why."

A pained expression flits across Harmony's face, then vanishes. It brings home for me how hard it's been for her—not only never having her father there, but having him look older than he should each time he returned. Like losing me in slow motion.

"Harm, I—"

"Why did you give my ship to Dice, Dad? She was mine."

"Well, technically she was your grandfather's."

"And I stole her fair and square. Daniel Sterling's an asshole. You know he deserved it. He *owed* me that ship. At least I got something in return for the shitty childhood you all left me with. And now you just gave it away, without even asking."

"Dice wasn't happy here, Harm. He deserved his freedom."

"*I'm* not happy here. What do I deserve?"

Drawing a deep breath, I try to think of what a Shiva would do in this situation. Cal says I should take responsibility for what I've done—doesn't that include the kind of father I've been?

To buy some time, I pour boiling water from the squat kettle into the oatmeal flakes waiting in my bowl. Then I fish a spoon from the drawer and pause after sticking it into my mushy breakfast. "Look, Harm, I'm sorry. I'm sorry for the awful hand you were dealt, and I accept the blame for it. But there's nothing I can do about it now, except make sure you're safe. With the galaxy falling apart all around us, giving away your ship and taking you aboard the *Ares* was the only way to make sure you weren't in danger. I couldn't very well send you back to Brinktown, and I know you wouldn't want that, even if I could."

"You had no right to give *Europa's Gift* away."

"I know. But if I'd let you take her, your mother would have said I have no right to do that. Look, I'm doing the best I can. I'm going to the Core, and I'm going to stop Fairfax. I plan to make things right in the galaxy again, so that you and your mother have a place where you can be free from danger, and happy."

"I'm not happy right now, Joe. I'm not free from danger, either, and if I actually was I still wouldn't be happy. When I had *Europa's Gift*, I was out there mixing it up, making a difference. Now I'm stuck here with you."

I shake my head. "You were making the wrong sort of difference, working with Fairfax."

"Know what I liked most about being with Fairfax and Eric?" she asks, her voice venomous, now.

I raise my eyebrows, sure I won't like her answer.

"It's the closest I've ever gotten to having a real family. Even Fairfax is less screwed up then you, Joe. At least he's actually there for the people he cares about."

"The only thing he cares about is seizing power."

"Yes, power for his father. And he's grooming Eric to replace him at his father's side, if it ever comes to that. He's lifting others up. All you ever do is tear people down."

That gives me pause, mostly because I can't think of anything to contradict it. "Maybe you're right," I say. "You're definitely right about our family being screwed up—about me being screwed up. But like I said, there's nothing I can do to change the past. It is what it is. I take responsibility for it, and I'm sorry. But I also think it's time you learned to live with it."

Dumping my oatmeal into the waste disposal, I toss my bowl into the sink to deal with later, which isn't like me at all—ever since Basic, I've always washed up after every meal. But I can't look at Harmony right now.

As I trudge up the narrow, metal stairs, I ask myself how else I'm supposed to deal with a conversation like that?

Yes, I've been a terrible father, and I've ended a lot of lives. I'm probably the worst savior the galaxy could have asked for. But I *am* going to save it, Fount damn it. I'm going to hit that reset button, and I can't afford to let anything get in my way. Not even guilt about messing up my daughter.

Saving the galaxy will have to be enough.

3

The next day, Marissa reaches out from the crew sim, asking to speak with me privately. She's been giving me the silent treatment for longer than Harmony—I guess it's easier for her to do that, being able to hide away in the sim—so it's pretty remarkable that she wants to talk.

Still, I can't say I'm thrilled about the prospect. Especially given how it went when Harmony decided to start talking to me.

To get things off on the right foot, I confine Marissa to the OPO Station, refusing to give her access to the rest of the ship. This is how it goes on most Broadswords: crew can do whatever they want while inside the sim, but while on duty they keep to their stations—a firm underscoring of the reason they're here.

"Seriously?" Marissa says. "You're keeping me prisoner in this circle?"

"If your duty is a prison, then yes," I say.

"Oh, wow, Joe. Very philosophical. Fine. I don't want to be out there with you, anyway."

"You said you wanted to talk."

"Where's Harmony right now?"

I tilt my head backward, toward the cabin hatch. "Locked inside her room."

Eyes widening, Marissa says, "You can't keep treating her this way, Joe."

"You did say you wanted to speak in private."

"I'm not talking about that. You've been so cold to her since she came aboard, and I agree with her when she says it isn't fair. You're the one who forced her aboard."

"I would have thought you'd be happy to have her here. Especially considering all the grief you gave me about not doing enough to find her before."

"I am happy. But—"

"What do you know about what Harmony needs, anyway? She talks to Belflower more than she talks to you." That's true, but I doubt it's the sort of thing a Shiva is supposed to point out. Marissa has a knack for getting under my skin.

Right now, she's shaking her head, doing a pretty good job of looking bewildered. Not that I buy it, but she's doing a good job. "You're a real piece of work, you know that, Joe? When was the last time you gave a thought to the needs of others—to anything, other than yourself and this stupid quest?"

"Oh, I don't know. Maybe when I reunited Faelyn Eliot with her parents? Nice to know you think our mission is stupid, OPO."

"Okay, when was the last time you gave a thought to your family's needs? You refused to enter a sim even to embrace me, and then you *deleted* my only companion."

"Yes, because he clearly wasn't concerned for his captain's welfare—wasn't willing to work toward mission success." Suddenly, my vision is starting to blur, and I catch my hands tensing. I'm losing the cool Shiva Knights are supposed to maintain at all times. "You have no reasonable expectation of a *companion,* Chief. No crewmember aboard a Broadsword does. You've gotten way too familiar, and I believe it's endangering the mission. From now on, you're to address me as Captain or Sir. No more one-on-

one sessions unless they're necessary to complete the mission. Am I coming across clearly, Chief Aphrodite?"

Her eyes have grown cold, and I can see that she hates me. Right now, I don't care.

"Clear, *sir.*"

"Good. Deactivate OPO."

Marissa vanishes from the bridge, and I lean back in the command seat, eyes closed, for a long time.

4

We're not even halfway through our five and a half months in slipspace, and I'm actually feeling tempted by the prospect of slipping into nanodeath.

What's happening to me? I've been in slipspace longer than three months before and never felt the urge to sleep through a trip. Maybe it's knowing how much more we have left to go.

Or maybe it's having to contend with my family, seemingly every day now—to confront how badly I failed to keep us all together, to make everyone happy. I'd never accept the blame for that, before. But now that I do, what's really changed? There's still nothing I can do to change the past. Nothing I can do to fix it.

I'm not even sure I can keep them safe.

I keep going back to my time on Gargantua, and the question of who opened that hatch to let the Fallen get at me. Maybe that version of Worldworn really did go rogue, after cutting himself off from all other copies of himself. Or maybe it *was* Belflower, even though it would have run counter to her goal of meeting up with the revolting bots. Or, maybe it was Asterisk, who recently saved my life on Persephone.

The signal came from inside the ship, and Marissa's the one

who brought it to my attention. That would be a pretty good way to cover up the fact she did it, except I refuse to believe it was her. We may hate each other right now—maybe I've hated her ever since she let her father bully her into uploading. But I refuse to believe she'd try to kill me.

The sound of boots on metal drifts up the stairs, reaching me in the command seat. I hear Harmony emerge onto the deck, expecting her to go straight for her cabin, as usual.

Instead, she crosses the deck to stand in front of me.

"Hi," I say.

"Hello," she says, and for the first time in months, she doesn't seem angry. She smiles, and the expression seems to mix a little amusement with a lot of sadness. "I know why you've been acting the way you have."

"What are you talking about?"

"Grandfather came to me, Dad. And he explained everything."

I narrow my eyes. "If Daniel Sterling has somehow stowed away on my ship, tell me where to find him and I'll stuff him into Dice's closet for jettisoning as soon as we get back to realspace."

"You know who I mean."

Studying her face, I realize I do. That puts a feeling of dread in my stomach, like a lead weight. "Cal appeared to you?"

"He did. It's wonderful, isn't it? Why didn't you tell me you were speaking to him?"

"Because I'd sound like a crazy person, for one. Also, my relationship with him is a little complicated, and anyway, I thought he only appeared to prospective proteges."

"Maybe he thinks I'd make a good Shiva Knight."

"That better be a joke."

She chuckles, then her face falls a little. "He told me that, in order to do what you need to in the Core, you'll have to sacrifice yourself. I don't know how that works—he said it involves secrets of the Shiva, some which he hasn't even told you yet—but he said it's true. To stop Fairfax, you have to give up your life. And that's why you're isolating yourself even more from mom and I. Because you expect to die, and you don't want us to get too attached."

My eyes feel so wide I'm worried they'll pop out of my skull. "He told you all that…?" I'm going to have a stern word with Cal Pikeman.

"Dad, it's okay. I can see you're getting angry—please don't. Talking to him helped me realize a few things about myself. I've never really allowed myself to appreciate what you do. And when I was helping with the bot revolution, I even convinced myself that you're part of an organization that's helping keep humanity trapped, enslaved. But grandfather helped me see that what you're doing now transcends all that. Because the alternative would be much worse. Dad, what you've decided to do…it's heroic. I don't want you to go, but I can't help but admire your sacrifice."

I'm nodding slowly, to hide the fact I'm feeling kind of bewildered. "Thanks…I think."

Her smile broadens, and while there's definitely sadness there, it also holds a measure of peace. "No matter what happens, shutting me out has to stop. I think you should consider letting yourself get closer to mom, too. We both almost lost you already, and if these are the last months we get together, shouldn't we spend some time as a family?"

"We're not a family, Harm," I say, and it kills me to see the way her smile falters. But it's true. "I'm not sure we've ever been. I accept the blame for that, but I also accept that it's true. If I didn't, I'm not sure I could go through with this."

Harmony stares hard at the floor, but I can tell she's looking inward, considering what I've said. She's always been thoughtful like that, and if I'm being honest, she's always been beyond her years—in a way that's taken a lot of years off my life all by itself.

At last, she looks up again, meeting my gaze with her jaw set. "You're not shutting me out, Dad. I won't allow it. I'm going to be part of this—a part of what you're doing. A real part of your life.

Look, I want to be TOPO. You need one—you can't just fly the ship yourself all the time."

"Harm, you don't know the first thing about flying a Broadsword. Or being in the military."

"I can learn. We have months left in slipspace, and after we're done at this Cathedral place, we'll have months more. I'll spend that time grinding the sims. And I'll be ready. I want this, Dad. I won't take no for an answer."

"You're going to have to *learn* to take no for an answer," I say, and her lips tighten even more. "If you're going to be a member of my crew, I can't stand for defiance. I can't use an insubordinate TOPO. You need to learn to follow my orders—is that understood?"

Harmony's grin has made its return—beaming brighter than ever. "Yes, sir," she says, throwing up an adorably sloppy salute.

"Welcome aboard, then."

SHIVAN CATHEDRAL

1

We emerge from slipspace to find four of the eight accompanying Broadswords already in-system, arranged in combat-box formation.

I nod approvingly at that, impressed that the Troubleshooters were able to organize themselves so efficiently, despite the nausea-inducing slipspace transition. It seems the hours they've been putting into fighter sims have paid off.

Not only that, but the slipspace transitions have definitely been getting easier, lately. I began to notice they were making me less sick when we first arrived at the Lambton Cloud, but I shrugged it off then, knowing it's impossible.

Impossible or not, it's happening. Could there come a time when I don't vomit at all?

I walk past the TOPO station to toss my reusable barf bag down the laundry chute, to be washed in an enclosed compartment next to the mess before getting vacuumed up to a compartment adjacent to my cabin, where it will be steamed, pressed, folded, and delivered.

On the way back, Harmony gives me a stern nod from inside the station's circular railing, and I nod back. She's all business when she's on duty, and it kind of surprises me how well she's taken to it all. Obedience and conformity never really ran in our family, so I guess she must really want to make this work.

The circular stations were made for uploads, who could simply appear at them. Harmony has to crawl under the railing to access hers. I guess things could be worse for her, considering that she gets to sleep in the captain's cabin. That said, I don't like the idea of getting into an engagement with her just standing there like that. At the earliest opportunity, I'd like to rig up some sort of protective gear to keep her from getting tossed around in battle. Maybe fix it to the overhead.

"Set a course for the outer-system coords you'll find in today's briefing dossier, TOPO," I say. We still don't have a rank for her yet, since I'm pretty sure I don't actually have the authority to enlist her into the Guard. That said, she was right—we *did* need a TOPO. We seem to change them every few months. As for what the brass will have to say about it when I get back…well, it isn't likely I'm coming back, is it?

"Aye, Captain," she says, and gets busy tapping the coords into her console. She still shows signs of hesitation every now and then, hands hovering over the controls as she bites her lip in thought. But like she pointed out, we'll have several more months in slip-space after this, and I'm sure any navigation she'll have to do in this system will be pretty low-stakes.

I sure as hell hope so, anyway. If Fairfax shows up here, I'm positive I'll get the blame for it. Cal probably won't speak to me again.

"Anything I should know about the system's topography, Chief Aphrodite?" I ask, turning toward her. Before I do, I catch the hint of a grin from Harmony—I'll have to speak to her about that. Yes, it feels ridiculous to continue concealing Marissa's identity, given everyone here knows the truth other than Asterisk. But she still doesn't want the truth out, and honestly, I agree with her.

I'd keep her secret for her anyway, despite the current tension between us, but there's also the very real chance that having it out in the open would cause problems on board. Having both a daughter and ex-girlfriend under one's command does kind of scream conflict of interest. But what are you going to do?

"Negative," Marissa says tersely, flicking her hand across her station's surface to send me the sensor data package she's compiled.

"Give me a visual of our destination as soon as you have one." With that, eyes open for anything anomalous, I review the sensor data. The other four Broadswords have arrived and been accounted for. Now, they're all flying in staggered formation around us.

The system features a highly dispersed asteroid ring that sketches a slightly elliptical orbit in between the second and third planets. That may not seem far, but the third planet is a gas dwarf that sits farther from this system's sun than Pluto sat from humanity's native star.

As for the star itself, it's actually pretty similar to Sol. Makes sense, considering this Cathedral is apparently wholly self-sufficient. I guess you'd want to mimic the conditions humanity evolved in as closely as possible, to pull something like that off.

Then again, what the hell do I know.

When we finally get a visual on the Cathedral, it's nothing like I expected. It's a massive asteroid, almost big enough to be called a small moon if it had been orbiting a planetary body. Nothing man-made features on its surface, which looks almost marble-smooth, other than the countless canyons and ravines cutting through it.

The only clue anything lives there? An ethereal sapphire glow that shines up through those ravines.

I will the visual away to find Cal standing beside me. A glance at the crewmembers tells me they can't see him—not even Harmony. As far she'll tell me, he only appeared to her the once, to play family counselor. That may have something to do with the thorough chewing out I gave him after he did it. Mentor or no mentor, he doesn't get to scare the shit out of my daughter like that. Even if he is her grandfather. He hasn't earned the right.

Though I've never tried subvocalizing to him before, I give it a shot now, so the crew don't think I'm here mumbling to myself: "That blue glowing is a strange feature for a place that's trying to stay hidden."

The Shiva sniffs. "Two things keep the Cathedral concealed: general ignorance about its existence, and the fact the slipspace coords for getting here have always been a closely guarded secret." He takes a moment to scowl down at me. "The priests aren't going to appreciate you sharing that secret with so many Guardsmen."

I shrug.

Lips pursed, Cal continues: "As for the glowing, they only activate it when they know friendly ships are approaching. Typically, that's their miner bots."

I frown. "Our sensors haven't picked up any bots."

"Then they likely don't have any deployed."

"You're telling me they turned the lights on for us? That they know we're coming?"

"I consider it a near-certainty."

"How?"

The knight's brow furrows slightly. Probably, he's trying to decide how much to tell me. Finally, he says, "It's likely their Seer informed them."

"Seer? How can they see anything if they're this isolated?"

That draws a sigh. "They do operate a pair of stealth spacescrapers, programmed to run recon in normally trafficked space, to siphon data from other spacescrapers, and to return only when they're sure nothing's watching. But the intelligence they gather is far from the only source of the Seer's predictive power."

"What are the other sources?"

But Cal shakes his head. "I've said enough. If the priests deem you worthy, they'll tell you more."

"You haven't even deemed me worthy."

Now, it's Cal's turn to shrug. "You have your moments."

As we near the asteroid, I take over navigation duties from Harmony, dropping into the direct control sim with its simulated starscape seen through a gridded cockpit that stretches across one hundred and eighty degrees of vision. No such cockpit actually exists, of course, and I can switch views to other exterior sensors with ease if needed. Typically, I won't have to—my datasphere links seamlessly with the ship to warn me about any threats coming from those directions.

I line the *Ares* up with the longest visible canyon, according to Marissa's computer-assisted analysis. That done, I tip the simulated yoke forward, gently nosing down toward the massive gray rock.

"Do you want us to follow you, Commander?" It's Shimura, subvocalizing over a two-way channel.

"Sure, Master Chief," I say. "I doubt there's much chance of hiding the fact I brought you. It'd probably be an insult to try. Keep formation behind me, but try to stay unobtrusive."

"Acknowledged."

I return to focusing on our trajectory. The glowing seems to brighten as we draw nearer—then we're inside the canyon, its towering walls rushing past us several kilometers away on both sides as the asteroid swallows the *Ares*.

It strikes me that by now, I should have seen the source of the blue light. "Where's that glow actually coming from?" I subvocalize to Cal, but he doesn't answer. I open a corner window that shows my view of the bridge, and I see that he isn't there anymore. At least, if he is, I can't see him.

We continue to drop through the canyon, which is beginning to seem bottomless, the blue light shining brightly from all around— above, below, everywhere. The canyon walls look almost white with it, painted as they are with the strange light.

Then, abruptly, the walls fall away, and we're inside an immense underground cavern filled with row after row of thick pillars that stretch endlessly into the blue-lit murk. The light's much less intense, here, though a brilliant white beacon shines up ahead, as though beckoning. I make for it, unsure where else to go.

As we draw closer, the beacon resolves into a massive crystal resting atop a spire of rock—the only actual light source I've seen. Standing in a semi-circle in front of it, directly facing the *Ares*, a group of seven robed figures in scarlet and white await. I see nothing that marks out a designated LZ, so I fly toward them, setting my ship down a few meters away.

"This feels…weird," Marissa says, which is about as vocal as she gets with me, these days.

Harmony, left with nothing to do, is standing at her station with her arms crossed. "How are they able to stand out here without suits on? We haven't passed through any sort of airlock."

"I can shoot them if you want," Asterisk offers. "They're easy targets."

I give him a look, which he returns blankly, the chains extending from his ears to the corners of his mouth hanging perfectly still. Then, I shake my head. "Great to learn that's an option, Ensign," I say with some sarcasm. "I'll let you know if I decide to vaporize our hosts."

"Any time," he says, giving no indication he realizes I was being ironic.

I turn to Marissa. "Chief, run a chemical scan to figure out the air composition—or, uh, lack thereof." The figures are still standing there, seeming almost to stare past my ship, looking solemn.

Asterisk must be looking at them, too. "You *sure* you don't want me to shoot them, Captain?"

"I'm sure. Chief, run the scan."

"Already done," Marissa says. "The results are saying there's air, and it's breathable, sir."

"Send me them."

My daughter's mother gives me a sour look, which draws

Asterisk's curious gaze. The indiscretion makes me want to roll my eyes, hard, but I keep my composure and she flicks the report over to me.

She's right, it seems—seventy-eight percent nitrogen, twenty-one percent oxygen, with a little argon and carbon dioxide thrown in for flavor. Basically ideal for human respiration.

"How is that possible?" I mutter.

"Why don't you go out and ask them?" Harmony says, then adds: "Sir?"

That almost makes me chuckle. It's funny how from her, a lack of decorum is amusing, whereas from Marissa it's just irritating. I guess the novelty hasn't worn off having my daughter back, despite that our relationship's been a bit rocky. Give us another half-year cooped up together in the *Ares*, and it might well be another story.

"All right," I say, getting up from the command seat and making for the airlock, willing the hatch to open. It closes behind me once I'm inside, and I let it go through its full cycle, just as I intend to on the way back in. No need to risk bringing contaminants in with me, unless I'm being chased by someone with enough firepower to end me.

Walking around the *Ares* toward the figures in blood-red robes, I glance backward at the lights of the other eight Broadswords, which have landed in formation a few dozen meters behind my ship. I'm still impressed by how organized they are, but then, it's important not to forget that Shimura is one of them. Getting Troubleshooters into proper formation might be like herding cats, but walking in on Shimura drilling cats probably wouldn't surprise me.

"You brought outsiders," says the robed figures' leader as I draw near. At least, I'm guessing he's the leader, given he occupies the point of the V-shape they've arranged themselves in. My datasphere analyzes his garb and confirms it: apparently his longer sash, which has golden fringes, makes him a bishop.

I'm also guessing these are the priests Cal was talking about.

They look like Church of the Fount priests I remember from the various Brinktowns I've visited, except these are more ceremonial-looking, if that makes sense. Each wears a white sash over his left shoulder with an ornate design marching down one side. The sashes are worn over flowing red robes that expose the right shoulder, and six of the priests have a flame shape tattooed on their foreheads, extending between their eyes to point at their noses. The leader has a white fork tattooed in the same spot, the bottom of which runs halfway down his nose, with a thin red line bisecting the fork.

"I'm an outsider, too," I say, trying not to sound impatient. A big part of me thinks we should have just flown right past the Cathedral to the next slipspace coords, to make sure we get ahead of Fairfax, but Cal refuses to give me the coords until I visit with these people. "How is it that we're able to breathe the air?" I ask. "I didn't see an airlock."

"*You* are said to be He Who Is the Fount Embodied in Flesh. If that's true, you aren't an outsider, in any sense. But we have difficulty believing the *true* Fount Embodied would bring such outsiders here."

"Who's saying I'm that guy?" I ask, genuinely curious. "Was it this Seer person I've heard so much about?"

The bishop's eyes widen. "Who told you of this?" he asks, his voice harsh.

Fount. These priests are a lot less friendly than the ones back home, who mostly tried to convert you so they could start vacuuming tokens from your bank account every week. "A friend. A Shiva, actually. Didn't you expect I'd have one palling around the galaxy with me? Isn't that how this is supposed to work?"

"It seems Cal Pikeman has been *most liberal* with the information he's given his son."

I chuckle. "Yeah. Well, where I was trained, we were taught that better recon means likelier mission success."

"*Mission* success?" The bishop's eyes narrow. "You see this as a mere military operation?"

"Oh, come on." Just how far up their own asses have these guys crawled, anyway? "Are we really going to bicker over terminology?"

In response, the bishop lifts a finger to point, blood-red robes drooping toward the ground. I follow the gesture, which leads to the *Ares*, along with the cluster of Guard ships parked behind mine. "I sense that a great evil has followed you. How can the Fount Embodied have brought such an entity here, to the Cathedral?"

I consider asking how this guy thinks he can "sense evil," but I decide I don't care. Sure, Cal's always talking about listening to my emotions, since they make up the interface each Shiva uses to tap into the Fount. But "sensing evil" seems a bit much.

"Look," I say, and seven pairs of eyes snap toward me, as though I've offended them with just my tone. "There are two possibilities, as I see them." I extend my right pointer finger. "One, everything you believe is wrong." Seven sharp gasps sound out in unison. "I'm not finished. Two, I really am the Fount Embodied or whatever, and you don't understand as much as you think you do about the Fount. If I'm the one it's chosen to do this thing in the galaxy's Core, where I'll face more than any Shiva before me, then there's a good chance I'll act in ways you don't expect. If you can't accept that, then I don't see how we're going to move forward."

The priests stare at me, bafflement warring with outrage in each of their expressions. Do they share the same emotions, or what?

Finally, the bishop manages to school his face, his brow smoothing.

"Follow," he says curtly, and all seven priests turn as one, walking briskly around the crystal-bearing pillar.

On the other side, a narrow staircase cut directly into the rock awaits, and the priests begin filing down it, one by one.

2

Each step leading down into the asteroid seems to form a perfect right angle, and gleams like polished granite. Weird details to notice, but it's throwing me for a loop a little bit. I would have expected a cathedral built into an asteroid to have more of a rough-hewn look, but these angles look perfect.

"The Shivan Cathedral was carved out by bots, a little over a century after the Fall," the bishop says, as if he can read my mind. "We still have most of those ancient bots, kept in good repair, although they are quite ancient by now. If you are here, you must know that the Fall happened millennia ago, not centuries. Regardless, the bots are barely used. His Holiness likes for the priests to do most of the manual labor, now. It keeps us in touch with the realities of the flesh. And gives us something to do."

I grunt, saying nothing. That is, until we reach the bottom of the stairs, which deposit us into a hallway big enough for all eight of us to walk along with room to spare. The ceiling hangs at least a dozen meters overhead. A simple orange carpet runs down its length, and modest alcoves dot the walls, each with a torch-filled sconce projecting from the center. The flames look real, and a datasphere query tells me they *are* real—not a digital projection. No wonder it's so toasty down here.

"Just how many priests live in this thing, anyway?" I ask, marveling that there's not a single torch that's sputtered out, not a single speck of dust or dirt on the carpet and rock floor…

"Two hundred and seventy-nine," the bishop answers, "hailing from all over the galaxy."

I eye the priest walking beside me, who pointedly avoids my gaze. He towers at least a foot over me—he may be the tallest person I've ever seen in the real. "Where are you from?" I ask.

"He's taken a vow of silence," the bishop snaps. "But if you must know, he's from the Desolate Sector."

"Doesn't look like it," I say. "It looks to me like he's from the Extremely Well Nourished Sector."

The giant peers down at me impassively, and we walk on.

The hallway lets out into a vast warehouse filled with white, brown and green—a hydroponic farm, with row after leafy row of crops marching away in both directions. Downscaled versions of Cylinder One's sun tube line the ceiling above, shining down on at least a dozen bare-chested acolytes wandering rows nearby, some harvesting, some planting.

"As I said, we're kept very busy," the bishop goes on. "The Cathedral can accommodate up to a thousand. One of its original purposes was to act as a sanctuary in the event of galaxy-wide chaos. It's why we will be able to restock your ship fully before you leave, provided you are indeed found to be the Fount Embodied."

"Who'll be determining that?"

"His Holiness."

"I see," I say, returning the curious gaze of an acolyte whose scarlet sash is drawn so tightly around his waste I wonder how he can breathe. "You said there are almost three hundred of you here…but priests are celibate, right? How do you make new priests?"

"We travel the galaxy, seeking the worthy from among Church followers," the bishop answers, without a trace of amusement in his voice. "Not those priests who pervert our doctrine to line their own pockets. I'm sure you've encountered those. I mean true believers: not only the priests who practice because of the beauty and simplicity of the Way, but also members of their flocks, who live in humility and virtue." With that last, he casts an accusing eye over me. Looks like he's been talking to Cal. "Before new acolytes are brought here, they are made to understand they can never leave. Ever arriving, never departing—this is the Way. As the Embodied, you are exempt, but you have brought non-believers. They may be made to stay."

"You really think you're going to prevent eight Guardsmen from following their duty?"

"We will see."

After that, the priests lead me through the Cathedral in silence as we pass through great dining halls with soaring ceilings, broad, echoing passages, and places of worship with varying shapes. One church, lit by lights hidden behind massive stained-glass windows, is shaped like a five-pointed star. Another, with sun tubes criss-crossing the ceiling, is a triangle. Presumably, the shape means something, but I have too much else on my mind to ask.

"Where are you taking me?"

"The Hall of Weights and Measures. Where his Holiness awaits."

"Is that where he normally hangs out?"

"Only when someone arrives claiming to be our savior."

"Hey, I didn't claim anything. The Church put that title on me."

"Yet you answered our call. That in itself constitutes a claim."

Narrowing my eyes, I consider arguing the point, but screw it. I didn't get any "calls" from anyone, but I guess I did hear about them proclaiming me the one who would renew galactic symmetry. And then I came here.

As our path starts trending downward through the asteroid—

along ramps and staircases that spiral and bend—I consider how crazy it is that they have a room that will only ever be used once. But then, it's a pretty big asteroid.

There's also the possibility that I really am a fake, and the real Fount Embodied will be along a little later. Then the room will get used twice.

The torch-lined corridor we're walking through begins to narrow and round at the corners. In a few dozen meters, it become a perfect circle, so that we're forced to walk single-file. The bishop gestures for me to take the lead, and I do.

There are no torches or other light sources in the circular tunnel, and it grows dimmer and dimmer until finally we're walking in total darkness, my boots clicking against the rock as the priests' sandals shuffle across it.

Then the tunnel begins to brighten, with a pinprick of light beckoning us at the end, steadily getting stronger. At last, we emerge into a room with what must be a thousand candles— hanging from the ceiling, sitting in holders sticking out from the walls, forming a path to a golden throne at the far end of the room, where sits a bearded man wearing a towering orange hat and red robes that flow over the floor with a length that seems impractical. A scarlet stole is draped across his shoulders, hanging down in broad bands to cascade into his lap and over his knees.

I don't know about Weights and Measures, but entering this place is like walking into an oven. I will my shipsuit to start lowering my body temperature while resisting the urge to wipe my brow.

The bishop who brought me here steps forward. "Your Holiness. The Candidate is here, but…he brought others, I regret to say. Interlopers."

"I know," says the man on the throne, stroking his midnight beard pensively.

"You…know?"

"Of course. And I'm glad of it. I believe it's the most important part! His friends are being brought here as we speak. It is vital that they're here to witness what will happen next." The holy leader's eyes drift to me. "Commander Pikeman, I know that you have Subverse uploads on your ship as well. I would ask you to grant them the permission to come here, so that we all can see them. We in the Cathedral never upload—to do so would risk its location getting out. But your friends are here already, and we welcome them."

"Holiness," the bishop says, his voice strained. "Can we afford to allow these people to leave the Cathedral? Perhaps this man, if he is truly the Embodied, can be trusted, but these others…"

"It may be that our time here is drawing to an end, Alfonsus," the holy leader says, and all seven men who accompanied me here gasp—even the ones under vows of silence. "What?" the man says. "Didn't you expect the arrival of the Fount Embodied would bring radical change? Or did you think we would simply continue business as usual?"

I take a step toward the throne and onto the path marked out by the twin seas of candles. "You're the leader of the Church, then?" I ask.

"No more than you are," he answers. "My name is Cardinal Hansh, and I serve as a sort of focal point for the Cathedral, just as the Fount Embodied becomes a focal point for all our destinies. But the Church of the Fount has no true leader, just as the Fount's essence is dispersed, with no centralized infrastructure. We recognize that all who have allowed the Fount inside of them are holy, though most of those don't follow the Way."

"Okay," I say, shaking my head slightly and feeling sorry I asked.

Footsteps echo behind me, and I turn to see the shadowy profile of a man who I'm sure is Shimura. As he approaches, glimpses of others flash behind him, which is consistent with the number of footfalls I can hear.

Then, they start filing in: Shimura, Harmony, and the other

seven Troubleshooters, plus their bots. That surprises me, and so does the fact they all still have their laser pistols.

"The rest of your crew, Commander?" the cardinal says.

"Right," I mutter, linking my datasphere to the *Ares'* computer to route their consciousnesses to here. I do this reluctantly, for some reason. Something's tugging at the back of my mind, and I find myself wondering why I let Cal talk me into coming here. Where is he, anyway? Doesn't he want to meet up with his Church of the Fount pals?

After the Troubleshooters and bots finish filing in, the flood of people doesn't stop—acolytes, priests, and bishops continue to flow in, taking up positions standing in the back of the room, clutching their robes to keep them away from the candle flames. They make room at the front for the Guardsmen and Harmony, even giving the digital beings their space.

"Welcome, all," Cardinal Hansh says, speaking now in ringing tones that echo through the candlelit room, "to the Hall of Weights and Measures. We gather here to take the measure of one Commander Joseph Pikeman. What sort of man is he? You are here to listen to my testimony, which is truly the testimony of the Fount.

"The commander was trained by the Galactic Guard to become a Troubleshooter—a member of their most elite fighting force. One who is here, Shimura, was an instructor who played a central role in that training. Shimura and his fellow instructors succeeded. They forged their charge into a weapon that would strike out in lethal fashion, in whatever direction they aimed him—or rather, in whatever direction his *datasphere* aimed him. But the datasphere they gave him served their ends, followed their orders. For Commander Pikeman, it allowed him to redirect responsibility for his kills to his superiors. As for those superiors, with the datasphere they could 'set it and forget it,' as the ancient expression goes. It was this technology, then, that became the storehouse of the guilt they would otherwise have felt for erasing from existence other human lives.

"Throughout his career, Commander Pikeman has distinguished himself as one of the most effective wielders of a military-grade datasphere who ever lived. It's quite possible he is the best. He's killed more foes than anyone else on record, and his success is such that he began to scare even his superiors. They would deploy him when they needed him, but otherwise they preferred to keep him out of the way. They cringed every time he had leave to visit his family back in Brinktown—cringed at the idea of exposing him to polite society, and they did everything they could to diminish that leave."

When I turn to meet Shimura's eyes, he winces, lowering his gaze to the ground. So I turn back to the cardinal.

"Commander Joseph Pikeman proved to be a one-man war machine. And yet, he was also a babe in arms—with just as much agency, just as much control, just as much responsibility for his actions. His training taught him only to follow his datasphere's instructions. Nothing else. And when his own daughter stole his laser pistol, and he was forced to resort to a weapon so ancient it was incapable of linking with his datasphere, the inadequacy of his training was revealed."

Cardinal Hansh pauses to shift in his chair, rearranging his stole over his legs. His face is a mask of calm, though his lips twitch as he continues with—was that distaste?

"Few are privy to the Seven Ideals of the Shiva Knighthood, but I share them with all of you now."

The gathered priests begin to murmur—the ones who haven't taken vows of silence, I assume—and Cardinal Hansh lifts a hand. "Yes, children. I break the Covenant of Silence, as I have been instructed to do. Let it be a symbol of the tide of change that crashes over us as we speak. Now, then. The Seven Ideals. Hear them, and consider: Courage. Respect. Loyalty. Service. Restraint. Humility.

Honor. They have no order, because without any one of them, an individual cannot be admitted into the knighthood. Now, return your attention to the commander. Can he truly be said to embody these qualities? Could he really be the Fount Embodied, when he may not be worthy even to join the holy ranks of the Shiva?"

"If you don't actually think I'm the Fount Embodied," I cut in, "then you've wasted time we don't have."

The cardinal raises a single finger. "You are not invited to comment on the process of taking your measure." His voice is as calm as ever. I force myself to unravel my hands, which have curled into tight fists. "Joseph Pikeman is a man of many faults," he continues. "He is a loner—a lone wolf. Isolating himself whenever he can, taking the road less traveled and allowing himself to age faster than his contemporaries, he seems determined to burn out just as quickly as the candles in this room. He is temperamental, quick to lash out at perceived slights or injustices. He is prejudiced, seeing sentient cybernetic beings as less-than. He is dependent on his tech. He kills without appropriate forethought. He has failed to take responsibility for his family. And his goals do not extend beyond himself. They will not help his family, his community, or his galaxy to prosper."

"You're wrong," I say.

Cardinal Hansh quirks an eyebrow. "How?"

"You're describing the old me. I've changed."

A slow smile spreads across the holy man's face. "Yes, I am describing him. And I'm not finished. Joseph Pikeman the Troubleshooter…is a man of contradictions. A loner, but fiercely loyal. Temperamental, yet honest to a fault. Dependent on tech, yet more competent in its use than any other. Prejudiced, yet perceptive. Irresponsible, yet passionate. Lacking in proper goals, yet diligent. Murderous, yet sentimental."

My eyes are glued to the cardinal's face. I'm not sure where he's going with this.

"I say to you, Commander, and all who are gathered here, that you have become less reliant on your technology for killing. You have learned to kill with your own hand, your own mind, your own heart. No longer do you slaughter indiscriminately. Now, you are as a surgeon, excising malignant masses threatening to destroy the whole. It isn't pleasant work that you do, but it is necessary. And you have found the courage to do it.

"You have never struggled with loyalty, and now that you have aligned yourself with the proper causes, you are providing service —not just to those around you, but to the entire galaxy. You carry an immense burden, and there is honor in that.

"You are learning restraint—when to end a life, and when to spare it. As for respect and humility…well, you struggle with those still. But I believe you are getting there."

Raising his hands into the air, smile widening, the cardinal says, "Friends, I say to you that Commander Joseph Pikeman walks the path. He has found the Way. Whether he is truly worthy —truly the Fount Embodied—is not for me to say. But I *can* tell you that I believe he's earned the right to meet the Seer."

A stillness follows the cardinal's words, as if every priest and acolyte in the room is holding his breath. I turn and exchange perplexed looks with Harmony.

When I face Cardinal Hansh again, he has stood from the throne. "Come, Commander. Walk with me around my seat and enter the chamber beyond. It is time you beheld the Source."

3

Maybe it was a trick of the candlelight, but I'd assumed the cardinal's throne was flush with the wall behind. But as I approach the rear, I see there's actually a fair bit of space, with an opening cut into the wall that looks matched in size with the throne's back.

The cardinal beams at me from the other side of the throne, hands buried in his sleeves.

"After you, Commander," he says.

"All right," I say, taking the first step down the cramped hall.

Just like the circular tunnel that brought me to the Hall of Weights and Measures, this rectangular one also descends into total darkness for a time. Finally, a light appears ahead, though not nearly as bright as the congregation of candles we left behind.

The tunnel ends, letting into a chamber whose ceiling isn't much higher than the hall's. The walls are close, too—if I reached out with both arms, I'd be able to touch both walls simultaneously.

But it's the far wall that makes the room remarkable. I can tell it's a digital display, and it seems to provide the room's only light. Except, something seems very off about it.

For one, it shows a blasted, windswept hellscape; the view

glitching and twitching before my eyes, with pixels jumping several feet before snapping back into place. Reds and browns dominate the vista, with great wind-driven whorls of dust flowing over a cracked and sere land. For flavor, skeletons dot the plateau the strange window looks out on, and the plains below look just as desolate.

There's something else, though. Something not quite right with the display.

Watching my face, Cardinal Hansh steps forward and swipes a hand through the wall. The view explodes into thousands of ripples, as though he'd wrenched his fingers across the surface of a pond. As I watch, the disturbance continues, with ripples flowing back from the walls to meet those headed outward.

"The Source," Cardinal Hansh says, speaking in the same unpretentious tone he used out in the Hall.

"What is it?"

"It's the closest thing we have to the Fount Incarnate. It shows us images of things to come."

"Okay, but…what *is* it?"

Hansh's grin widens, as though we're sharing a private joke. "Lately? Just violence and chaos. It doesn't always show us this sad, lonely place, though this is the most common image. Sometimes it shows other planets—images of the future. Occasionally, it will show us a video of something yet to happen. But like I said, of late, it's all scenes of pain, sorrow, and destruction."

I frown. "A bit of a pessimist, then. You still haven't answered my question."

"No. I've carefully avoided answering it, because the truth is, I don't know what it is. That is a secret the Cathedral's original builders chose to keep from even us, their successors. Some say it wasn't created, but found once the bots tunneled here. I think that's a load of crap, personally. Others say it's a physical gateway to this system's Subverse, which was corrupted shortly after the Fall, with everyone living inside it turned to twisted demons of one sort or another. To me, that seems more believable, though the idea of physically entering the Subverse does stretch the imagination."

I've done it a few times, but I decide not to mention that right now. "Have you entered it?"

Hansh shakes his head. "No, but I will when I die. In his final days, every priest enters the Source."

"I thought you said the priests here don't upload to the Subverse."

"Ha! I think we both know that isn't what happens when they enter. Regardless, though, no one has ever returned after entering. You can probably see where I'm going with this—can you?"

"I can guess."

"Why don't you guess?" Hansh says, chuckling.

"The Fount Embodied is supposed to be able to enter and return."

Hansh nods, his head bobbing low. "Unharmed. The first and the last to do so. Prophesy says the Fount Embodied *must* meet the Seer. That will also be a first. The Seer speaks to us through the images it shows, but no one has ever seen it."

"And this is how you'll know whether I really am the chosen one, or whatever."

"It's one way."

"Has it occurred to you that all of this might be bullshit? Maybe it's true that I am capable of stopping Fairfax from resurrecting the Allfather—but maybe it's just as true that there is no Fount Embodied, and by sending me into this thing you're sending me to my death and dooming the galaxy."

"Of course!" Hansh says right away, and I blink. "There can be no faith without doubt, child. But I *do* believe in the Fount Embodied, and I also believe he *must* meet with the Seer to renew galactic symmetry. And so I must insist."

"What if I refuse?"

Hansh shrugs. "Then we were wrong. You aren't the chosen

one after all. The Fount Incarnate would not refuse. So we will await the true one."

I nod, take a deep breath, then step through the Source, where ripples still run gently back and forth across the surface.

Darkness envelops me, and I pitch forward into nothingness, hands groping for purchase. They find nothing, and I'm falling, falling, falling.

4

I tumble endlessly through a formless void, numbed by the thought of what awaits me at the bottom—probably a bone-crunching impact, and then death.

That doesn't happen. Instead, the world lights up again, and I find myself on the same wind-blasted hellscape I saw through the Source. One second I'm falling, the next I'm standing there on the deserted plateau. I stagger a little, instinctively bracing for the impact that already should have happened, then straighten up, feeling foolish.

There's no sign of a gateway or entrance of any kind behind me, and I wonder whether Cardinal Hansh can see me looking out at him, blinking in bewilderment.

To my right, out of view from the chamber where I stood before, the plateau is littered with men wearing the white and red of a priest, and several with the more ornate garb of bishops. Their bodies lie on the ground, twitching periodically, hands occasionally spasming together into gnarled claws.

They all have their eyes open, staring at nothing, and their mouths hang open, drool sliding down chin and cheeks. A few have thick cables of slobber connecting their jaws to the ground, and for a moment I'm reminded of Maneater, for some reason.

All these holy men—thousands of them—dotting the land before me, apparently still alive on some level. Staring in horror. A plain of twitching, inert corpses.

Distractedly, I wonder if Cardinal Hansh can see me gaping in horror.

A patch of nearby land glitches, disappearing altogether, leaving a black-streaked void of white in its place. When it reappears, the two bodies it held are no longer there.

Creepy.

Another plateau rears over this plain of bodies, with several other plateaus surrounding it. They seem to form a staggered path to the base of a mountain nearby, and at the top of that mountain sits a foreboding fortress cast all in shadow by thunderheads that linger above it, sprouting lightning and rumbling with thunder.

An idea occurs to me then, and on a whim I haul up my datasphere's menu. The interface looks exactly as it did whenever I entered a Subverse conflict zone. Hansh hinted that the Source might just be a corrupted Subverse. If that's true, then somehow it got a hold of my account stats.

According to the readout, I'm now a level twelve Space Marine with an assortment of decent spells. I'm wearing magic-enhancing gloves, and I have a kinetic assault rifle in my inventory, which drops into my hands out of nowhere when I will it to.

"Wait," I mutter.

Every other time I've entered the Subverse after falling unconscious, the other Joe has taken over—the one Marissa had her dad copy for her, so that she wouldn't be lonely. Why isn't that happening now?

"I'm here," the other Joe says, using my mouth. "I guess we're working together. Neither one of us is at the helm."

Fount, but that's weird—feeling my lips move with something I'm not actually saying. "*I'm* at the helm," I say. "Got that?

I'm the one with the training and the experience. If you have ideas, I'll hear them, but you'll run them past me before execution."

"When did I become such a control freak?"

"This is *my* body. I don't plan to stop being a control freak about it anytime soon."

"Technically, it's a digital construct. But fine. Take the reins, hotshot. Just remember, I'm the one who got us all the sweet spells and gear."

"Noted."

With that, I start making my way against the wind through the priest-littered terrain, toward the plateaus towering above this one in the distance. It's kind of weird to be heading toward the base of a mountain, considering we're already at least a couple kilometers above the deserted-looking plains below. But that's clearly my destination. There are no foothills, no slopes leading from that mountain down to the plains. It simply begins up here, on a plateau larger than the rest.

As I near the edge of this one, I begin to realize something: none of these plateaus are actually connected to anything. They're all floating in midair, which leads me to infer that the one I'm walking across is, too. Not the most comforting thought.

The ground continues to glitch, sometimes shifting a few meters over to cover a nearby patch of ground, other times vanishing altogether. I arrive at the edge to find there's no path connecting this plateau to the next. The next land mass just floats there, out of reach. If I jump for it, I'll fall short, especially with the wind buffeting me.

Without warning, the ground below me glitches and I glitch with it. It shifts up and over, onto the middle of the next plateau, and it drops me there, along with a layer of dirt and rocks, sending dust drifting up into the dry air.

How convenient.

There are more twitching priests lying around up here, but

fewer than the first plateau. I guess they're the beneficiaries of the glitching ground too.

Nearby, a patch of dirt glitches every few seconds, changing from a black-striped void to regular ground and back again.

Timing my jump, I land on it when it's ground, and then it transports me to another plateau. I leap off it before it vanishes again.

I'm pretty sure that just brought me two plateaus up—I skipped one. There's only one priest lying up here. The farthest any of them ever got toward that mountaintop fortress. Toward the Seer, presumably.

I continue wandering the plateaus, waiting for the ground to glitch and transport me to another. There's not much point in actually heading toward the fortress—the glitching seems pretty random, and I figure I'm better off exploring each plateau and observing its surface, waiting for a patch to glitch out.

It doesn't take long for the dirt I'm standing on to transport me three meters off the side of a plateau that's pretty near the fortress. I let out an involuntary grunt at the vertigo-inducing drop on all sides.

Without thinking, I back up and sprint across the rough square of disembodied ground, leaping a second before the patch glitches back. I hit the side of the cliff, and my breath gushes out of my lungs, but I manage to haul myself onto it and lie there gasping for a minute, staring up into the blighted sky.

I need to get clear of this place before I plummet to my death—digital or otherwise. All it takes is for a patch to take me two or three meters farther out, and I'm finished.

The next glitch transports me back several plateaus, and the next takes me to the one at the very beginning. Then I find a patch that transports me almost to the far side of the land masses. And so on.

When I reach the third-last plateau, I see that I was wrong about that solitary priest being the one who made it the farthest:

somehow, three of the twitching, stationary bodies made it here, their eyes staring in horror at the restless sky, their fingers spasming together.

"Worst traveling companions ever," I mutter.

"I know, right?" the other Joe says, and I resist the urge to tell him to shut up. Finally, a glitching patch takes me to the mountain's base, and I take a moment to breathe. Chances are, I'm not out of the woods yet where the teleporting terrain is concerned— no doubt any path up the mountain will behave similarly. But if I go slowly, I should be able to chart a safe course by observing each stretch of ground for a while before walking over it. That said, a few of the patches seem to have pretty long periods between glitches. If I happen to choose the wrong time to walk over one that only glitches every hour, I'll probably be screwed.

A small, cubic stone structure lies ahead, just a few dozen meters up the path. From here, its walls look seamless, but I can tell the stones were brought down from the mountain and stacked together, pretty skillfully judging from the fact it's standing. Otherwise, the wind would have begun the deconstruction process. Not to mention the glitches.

Maybe the fact it's still standing is a glitch.

I become aware my thoughts are wandering at the same time a Kitane lopes around the stone structure, lips drawn back in a silent rictus. It pads toward me. Unlike the Kitane I faced in Cylinder One, this one's regular-sized, so probably an easier fight. Then again, I don't have my blaster—just a bunch of imaginary spells.

A jaguar-like howl draws my attention up the slope to my right, where two more Kitane are standing, antennae rigid, feline faces contorted. Their scale-covered 'fur' has taken the color of the sere mountain, all red and brown.

The one who appeared from around the structure is joined by another, and they both start running toward me. The first one glitches forward, gaining several meters in an instant.

"Oh, shit," I say, readying Blue Fire.

5

Eyeing the drop to my left, I decide my best option is to charge the two Kitane ahead.

As I do, hurling fireball after white-blue fireball, the pair of cats on the slope pounce, landing where I was just standing. I'm surrounded, but at least I'm not hurtling to my doom.

The oncoming Kitane glitch around my spellfire—apparently they've learned to harness the glitching to their advantage. Just as they're about to reach me, I crouch low, striking out with a blast of Telekinesis. Both cats go flying, hurtling over my head to land scrabbling on my other side.

There. Now my enemies are all gathered together, at least.

Spitting Blue Fire from my fingertips, I inch backward, wondering what to do next. The Kitane continue to teleport out of the way, so I deactivate the spell and call up the assault rifle instead, spraying burst after burst across the chests of the four aliens.

The Kitane's senses are honed, and their reflexes are as quick as you'd expect, almost as though they have dataspheres to warn them of the trajectory of shooting that's about to happen. Even so, the path is narrow, and as they try to dodge my firem they bump into each other to avoid falling off to their left. Round after round bites into their scaly, red-brown hides, and they roar in protest.

Still, they're tough, and the damage I'm inflicting only seems to enrage them more, moving them to advance faster.

Then, I remember the new spell the other Joe acquired during the battle for Persephone: Fire Wave. It would be perfect here. Willing the rifle back into my inventory, I thrust my spellcasting gloves forward.

A cylinder of flame appears, spinning down the path with a lopsided 'gait,' its speed alarming. The conflagration crashes into the Kitane, making them howl and flinch backward.

Good.

I use the bought time to run for the stone hovel. Maybe it'll provide shelter against the aliens. Then again, maybe it's a terrible idea to trap myself inside.

When I round the corner, the question is answered for me: there's a wooden slab that looks like it should be a door, but lacks any way to open it.

"Damn it." Desperate for something to use to my advantage, I continue around to find the mountain slope begins just a foot away from the structure's closest wall, and the incline is pretty steep from there.

I charge at it, using my momentum to run up the slope, then I twist around, leaping. My fingers close around the lip of the structure's roof, and I haul myself up as the Kitane skitter around the hovel in pursuit.

The roof is a rough wooden slab, but there are no gaps big enough for me to slip inside the hovel. I gain my feet and turn in time to watch the first Kitane bound up the slope and leap, clearing the roof. Yelling, I drop, kicking up with my legs and connecting with the thing's stomach, which brings a tortured scream. Paws flailing at empty air, it flies over the structure and onto the path below.

Without thinking, I activate Blue Fire again and start blasting it with fireballs, which provide enough momentum to send the Kitane careening over the mountain's edge. It glitches upward, but the distance isn't enough to save it. One down.

Whirling, I bring my hands up in time to hit the next Kitane with Blue Fire point-blank in the face. It rears back, and I aim a kick at its face, but it shakes off the blow then lunges, claws raking across my torso. Pain explodes in my chest, and I gasp.

A Telekinesis strike throws the beast back, and it careens into the next Kitane trying to make its way onto the roof. They both fall back, buying me time to pepper them with a few more fireballs as they tumble off. The spell hits cooldown, meaning I have to wait for it to recharge. Fire Wave is still on cooldown, too—not sure how well it would do up here, anyway. So I let my assault rifle drop into my hands and continue hitting them with round after round, kneeling on the edge of the roof to pelt the Kitane fighting to disentangle themselves from each other.

They take a couple swipes at each other, which can only help my cause. Then one of them explodes into a cloud of pixels under my fire, and the other staggers back, snarling.

Resisting the urge to celebrate, I focus on the remaining Kitane while wondering where the fourth one went.

I have my answer when it leaps from the ground to my left, making it to the roof without the aid of the mountain slope and crashing into me. I stagger sideways, dropping my assault rifle as I lose my footing, managing to twist around to land on my back, the Kitane coming down on top of me.

It sinks its teeth into my bicep, ripping through muscle and sinew. I scream, and my datasphere lets me know I'm losing health points at a critical rate. Razor-sharp claws find my face, biting into flesh and skull and tearing downward. A curtain of blood hides the world.

"YOU ARE ABOUT TO DIE," my datasphere informs me.

My weapon is gone, but I decide to try something. Forcing my uninjured arm under the Kitane, I will the rifle to drop into my grasp.

It does, and I squeeze the trigger, muzzle hard against the alien's underbelly.

Rounds rip through flesh, organ, and bone, and the Kitane screams, rearing back. I swipe a hand across my eyes to clear away the blood, then I kick the beast in the face. This time, the move is more effective, and it flinches back. Another kick sends it off the roof, and I send a stream of rounds after it. As it hits the ground it converts into pixels, dissipating.

The remaining Kitane waits for me on the edge of the roof, crouched, ready to pounce. I didn't hear it come up here, but it seems to be hesitating—maybe the death of its friends has given it a healthy fear of me.

I whip the assault rifle around one-handed, my other arm dangling uselessly at my side. "You dinner?" I ask it, and it twitches, half-turning as if to flee.

"Screw that," I snarl, depressing the trigger and sending a burst of rounds into its face. The beast has taken all it can, it seems, and it becomes a puff of pixels.

Not a moment too soon. My health is dangerously low, and blood continues to stream into my eyes, obscuring my vision. I'm in no shape to do any more fighting.

I sit on the edge of the roof and awkwardly try to lower myself with one hand without jarring my injured bicep too much. My left boot comes down on the steeply slanted terrain, and I stumble back against the stone, sending spasms of pain emanating from my arm, which aggravates my chest wound.

"Fount," I mutter. "I'm a mess."

When I round to the front of the structure, I find the mountain path filled with an ethereal host—what I take to be the ghosts of the holy men whose bodies litter the plateaus below. Except, when I look down there, those bodies are all gone.

A solitary figure steps out from the crowd, holding his right hand up, fingers tight together in a gesture of peace.

"Thank you, warrior," he says. "You have brought us peace by slaying the fell beasts who took us, one by one."

Despite my agony, his words kind of make me want to laugh. The Kitane are just animals, really—no more "fell" than any other evolution has produced. But I guess when you're a priest, you have to inject everything with ceremony and mysticism.

"No problem," I say instead.

The priest inclines his head, then vanishes along with the rest of the otherworldly horde.

"QUEST COMPLETE," my datasphere displays in fanciful golden text.

This place is weird.

I turn to contemplate the wooden slab of a door, wondering how I'm supposed to open the damned thing. "Oh," I mutter as the answer hits me. "Fount. I'm dumb." Raising my hand, I hit the thing with Blue Fire, and when that doesn't work I hit it again, and again.

The third fireball catches, burning away the wood in a much shorter time period than seems realistic, but then again this is essentially a video game. The roof catches too, also burning away to nothing in a few seconds and letting the sickly light of this world stream inside.

That light gleams off a full suit of frankly badass-looking armor. The vambraces, rerebraces, and greaves are all made from a dark metal that reminds me of Dice, except thin blue lights run up these in parallel. The rest of the suit is a dully gleaming dark blue, except for the gorget, which is blood-red. The helm and visor are dark gray, and the single eye slit glows with blue light as well.

On the floor beside the armor is a chest, which opens with a kick in a pretty satisfying way. Inside sit two full-health potions. I toss one in my inventory and slurp down the other.

My chest, face, and arm all itch fiercely for a minute as the muscle and tendons knit themselves back together. Then, I'm good as new, and ready to mess up whatever waits for me at that fortress.

Especially with this new set of armor. Luckily, like burning down the door, donning the armor isn't nearly as time-consuming as it ought to be. By touching it, I both claim ownership and unlock the ability to put it on. When I exercise that ability, the armor vanishes from the stand and appears on my body.

Immediately, my datasphere displays a level-up alert: "YOU HAVE REACHED LEVEL THIRTEEN," it tells me. I guess just putting the suit on gave me experience points.

"Nice." Already, I feel more powerful, like the suit's lending strength to my movements. I need something like this in real life.

Poking around my datasphere's in-game interface for a few seconds, it doesn't take long to find the option to view myself from a third-person POV. I hit it, and admire myself standing there in front of the burnt-out hovel, looking very ready for action with my hands held out to the sides.

Softly glowing blue lights wreathe my arms, legs, and chest, and my visor glows with light as well. My gripped boots are planted firmly on the ground. I get into a fighting stance, bobbing slightly with my breath, and a thrill runs through me. Hell yeah.

Wait—am I actually getting into a sim? Fount.

I exit third-person perspective and re-enter my own head. Nah, it's nothing to do with the sim. I just want this armor in the real. That's all.

Before leaving, I give the hovel one last once-over. That's when my eyes fall on the weapon hanging from the wall near the door, which I somehow missed the first time.

It's a two-handed broadsword, steel-edged with gold-colored metal running up through its center in segmented chunks. The hilt resembles the innards of a clock, with gears and spokes sticking in all directions, and the long handle is ridged. The edge of the blade itself glows with a blue that matches the armor.

I remove it from its stand, holding it aloft in the diseased light, which nevertheless gleams along its length.

All right, then. My life is complete, I guess.

Stowing the broadsword in my inventory, I start running up the mountain path, armored boots pounding the red-brown dirt and sending up little puffs of dust. As I go, I check over the stats boost each piece of armor has conferred. Looks like the gauntlets don't boost magic like my spellcasting gloves, so my magic power is down a bit. Still, there's no way I'm wearing the worn-looking brown gloves with this futuristic space knight suit. It would look goofy.

Jogging up the mountain is pretty uneventful. Sometimes the path ends in a wall, which I'm forced to scale, but that's not hard with a little patience. The armor seems to improve my grip strength, so even the more challenging surfaces don't give me much trouble. Other than that, the path just winds around and around, up and up, and the fortress gets bigger and bigger, though sometimes the mountain blocks it from view.

If this is supposed to be a video game, this part is pretty boring. I'd probably stop playing.

As I near it, I'm beginning to realize that the fortress isn't actually a fortress at all. Its black, foreboding look was due to the shadows cast by the roiling storm clouds suspended above it. But as I draw closer, I'm realizing the massive structure is actually white.

Judging from its architecture, I'm pretty sure it's actually a cathedral. As in, a traditional cathedral, the kind the Christians built over timespans of centuries back on Earth, with spires and triangular shapes all pointing heavenward. It has big, rounded doorways, and intricate designs and images painted on the exterior.

At last, I reach the final approach, and I come to a stop as something near the great structure's main entrance catches my eye.

There's an armored figure up there, too. He looks kind of

diminutive, but he's adopted a powerful pose, hands on hips as he peers down at me. Waiting for me.

Is that the Seer, or the enemy I have to kill to get to the Seer? Or both?

Only one way to find out. I march up the sloping path, my stride measured, steady. When I reach the halfway point, the figure starts dancing around, seeming to touch points in the air with his gauntleted fingers. In turn, the air responds by shimmering, then fracturing into a grid, as though revealing some invisible barrier.

What's he up to? Is he laying traps of some kind for me? I'll need to be careful. It's probably stupid for me to go up and confront him on the battlefield of his choosing—a place he probably knows well, and has had time to prepare to his advantage. But what else can I do? I'd feel stupid just having a staring contest with him from here.

At last, I reach the end of the path, pulling myself onto the broad plateau that holds the cathedral. The little knight is standing with his hands on his hips again, and when I come to a stop twenty meters away or so, he raises a hand.

At first, it looks like he's going to salute me, but then he flips up his visor to show his face.

Uh…her face. It's Harmony. The person wearing the armor, the person I'm sure I'm supposed to fight, is my daughter.

"Hey, Dad," she says. "Ready to rock?"

6

Stunned, I just stand there, weapons still stowed in my inventory. She holds out her hand, and a ridiculously long blade falls into it, which she shifts in front of her, gripping it with both hands and holding it toward me.

"Where's yours?" she calls, her tone challenging.

Hers is a long sword, though it's like nothing I've seen or read about in any of the media I've consumed. It's a Frankenstein mashup up of computer components—old-school vacuum tubes sticking out from the hilt, digital displays running up and down the blade with readouts flashing streams of data faster than it's possible to comprehend. Transistors and chips line the sword's edge.

"I'm not waiting!" she yells, then slams her visor down, charging at me.

A thrill shoots through me, and I stagger back, summoning my new broadsword and getting it up just in time to block an arcing overhead blow.

The two blades meet, and Harmony's tech sword seems to emit an energy blast that casts mine back, inching it toward my helm.

With a grunt, I throw her weapon off, sidestepping and holding mine out in a defensive stance.

"You're not fooling around, are you, sweetheart?" I say. She just hacked at my head like she wants to cleave it in two.

She chuckles. "I'm not even your daughter. You know that, right?" With that, she rushes at me, thrusting, and when I try to parry, her sword jolts forward as though propelled by rocket fuel, jetting past mine and scoring my armor on the shoulder. The tip of the long sword works its way into the seam where my gorget attaches to the breast plate, and she wrenches, trying to pop it off. I whirl away before she can, finally manging to knock her blade aside before dancing back.

"Strike at me, *Father!*" Harmony yells, still chuckling. "You can't do it, can you?"

She leaps, blade sweeping in from the left, and I bring mine up to block it. With a deft motion, she reverses momentum, bringing the tech sword around to crash into my right rerebrace. Her sword rockets inward, cutting through my armor and sending blood spraying. I jerk back before she can sever the arm, knocking the flat of her blade away with my left gauntlet.

Harmony's cackling madly, now. "Pathetic. Do you really understand what saving the galaxy means, Father? Do you know where it's likely to leave me in real life? Once you abandon me?"

Staggering back, I set off one of the traps she was setting as I made my way up the path. The air itself seems to explode, tossing me forward in Harmony's direction. She dodges neatly, allowing me to land face-first in the dirt.

The tech sword grinds into the ground inches away from my face, and I realize she's toying with me—she could have killed me, then, or at least done massive damage.

I start to stand, but a booted foot slams into my back, forcing me back down. "Let's review," she says. "I'm not actually your daughter, and you know that. I've had time to prepare our battleground, and you're in danger for your life. But even so, you can't bring yourself to strike at me, because I wear your daughter's face. You're useless, Joe!"

My adversary steps off, letting me rise to my feet. "Come on!" she yells, mirth gone now, replaced with anger. "Show the galaxy you're worth something. *Strike me down!*"

I lunge, broadsword swinging down on the diagonal, but she deflects it almost contemptuously before launching into a counter-attack, raining blow after blow toward my head and neck. I manage to deflect each one, but I'm wearying, and she's forcing me backward toward a cliff.

"You call that an attack? Your heart's not in this, Joe. Ignore that I have Harmony's voice. Forget that you saw her face. And strike down the one you know to be your enemy!"

But I can't. I can't. The illusion's too convincing, and I know that striking down my daughter, even my daughter's evil doppelgänger, would haunt my dreams till the day I die.

My arms fall to my sides, and Harmony pushes up her visor to look at me with an expression of disgust.

Her leg raises, and she plants her foot in the center of my chest, thrusting forward. I tumble backward off the cliff, blade vanishing from beside me seconds before I hit the ground. All goes black.

7

I'm sitting on a cool, seamless surface that feels like marble. I can't see a thing, but somehow the mind can always summon an image of a place, can't it? Whether it's right or not. The impression I'm getting is that this place is so vast and dark and cold it might as well be the darkness between stars.

Is this where Subverse combatants go when they die in the Great Game? Somehow, I doubt it's that simple. Even though this corrupted Subverse node—or bizarro otherworld, or whatever the hell this thing is—somehow managed to port some data over from the regular Subverse, I doubt the similarities between the two go very far.

Then come the low groans and rumbles, echoing off distant walls. It's possible I've been hearing it since I got here but only just noticed it.

"What is that?" I find myself asking a small figure, a child, who sits with his bare back to me a few meters off. I could get up and approach him, but I won't. Maybe that's how this place keeps you where it wants you: by sapping your will.

"Pak t'em ahbrüla lahm-gard," the boy whispers.

"Come again?" I say, matching his voice in volume.

The boy turns without moving. Rather, he merely resolves into a position that faces me, and when he does, I see that it's a younger version of myself, his bloody birthmark much redder and fresher than mine—not faded by the onset of decades. His pants are the beige corduroy pair I wore running with the urchins in Brinktown's streets.

His gaze is accusing. "I said, call it the architecture of the universe. Grinding under the pressure being put on it." Though he still whispers, his voice is growing harsher. A shout-whisper.

"What do you know about architecture?" I say, meaning it. "I remember how much you know. "Just—"

"Fighting, petty vandalism, testing the law bots daily. Wondering whether I could fool them today, like I did two months ago."

"Exactly," I say, haltingly. That *was* all I knew, but I wouldn't have been so articulate about it.

"Did you know that's the first filter the Guard uses for its recruitment?" he says. "The boys who fight a lot. The ones comfortable with violence are the ones most likely to bring themselves to pull the trigger when the time comes."

"I didn't get in meaningless fights. I fought when I saw someone who needed protecting."

"Someone you *thought* needed protecting. You maintained your own breed of justice. But…are you sure it wasn't just an excuse to fight?"

I fall silent, lacking an answer for that.

"It's ironic," the boy says, a slow smile stretching the birthmark out. "The Guard taught you to kill without remorse. And then the Shiva taught you restraint. Now, you have too much of it. You just lost your first fight, Joe. Ever."

"It was against my own daughter. Of course I did."

"It wasn't, though. You fought an enemy who wore your daughter's face. And because you couldn't summon your old ruthlessness, you lost."

"I would never have harmed my daughter. Even the old Joe wouldn't have."

"Not directly."

My eyes widen, and my fists clench in my lap, but I say nothing. Neither does the boy—I get the impression he's willing to wait an eternity for me to speak next.

I give him ten minutes, and he still doesn't speak. His gaze remains unwavering on my face. His expression solemn.

"So, am I trapped here now?" I say at last. "Like the priests? Because I died, like they did?"

"No," the younger me says, chuckling. "Not you, Joe. No such luck for you. You would have been free to go whether you won or lost."

"What was the point of that, then?"

"The fight outside the cathedral was a test, and now that I have the results I feel ready to prophecy."

"Wait, what? Prophecy?"

More laughter. "For the most effective Shiva who ever lived, you're certainly dense sometimes, aren't you? Haven't you realized yet who you're speaking to?"

"You're the Seer," I say, saying it as I realize it.

"That's right."

"What's your prophecy, then?"

"Simple. You'll make it to the Core, and you'll fail. The Allfather will escape into the world. Chaos will follow."

I'm shaking my head, vigorously. "No. You're wrong."

The boy shrugs. "Prove it."

With that, the room melts away, and I wake on a bed of corpses.

8

It's like someone dumped a cargo hold full of rotten eggs down a chute, then tossed me on top of it. The stench is unbearable—it invades my nostrils, fills up my lungs, where I'm irrationally afraid it will leave its residue.

I retch violently, puking on the bodies, the walls, on myself. I vomit until nothing is left in my stomach, and then I dry-heave. I've been around corpses before, and always prided myself on having a settled stomach. Not today. Not lying on all this.

Light filters down from somewhere above—enough to see that the bodies are in varying states of decay. Some are mere skeletons, either picked clean or with bits of blackened, dessicated flesh clinging to them, where the maggots haven't quite finished their meal.

Did I mention the maggots? The place is lousy with them, and they're covering me. In my ears, dotting my face, squirming, writhing. I emit a loud curse, and for a moment I wonder whether I'm about to go insane.

Deep breaths. Deep breaths. Have I been lying here this entire time? Oh, Fount.

I will night vision to come on, and it self-calibrates based on the weak light coming from above. Four walls jump into visibility: four sweating walls, each crisscrossed with cracks and fissures. Were those caused by the moisture, freezing and thawing? Judging by the color of the rock, this hellish pit was cut right from the asteroid.

There's no getting a proper foothold on the slimy, shifting mound of corpses, so I work my fingers into the nearest crack, then find another for my left hand. With that, I pull myself up out of the bodies with a titanic effort of will. And I begin my ascent.

The walls are moist, and some of the more intrepid maggots have taken it upon themselves to worm their way up it, for whatever reason. A few meters above the corpses, and I'm past the maggots, but the walls are still moist. I don't want to think about why, but it sure makes maintaining handholds and footholds a challenge.

About halfway up to the light source above, I get stuck, unable to see the next handhold and losing my grip.

"No," I grunt, horrified by the idea of slipping to fall back into the corpse pile with a wet splat. At last, I spot a crevice big enough to work a couple fingers into, and I do, roaring with the effort it takes to propel myself upward. My foot finds a better resting place, and I pause to take a breather.

Do the priests have any idea what happens to them when they walk through the Source? Do they know how they're treating their dead?

For that matter, who began this tradition? Who built this place to be like this? Why?

And why doesn't the smell reach the tiny chamber above?

Maybe the Fount that comprises that display filters out the stench, somehow. As for why anyone would start something like this…maybe they figured the mysticism would ensure that generations to come kept this place a secret. Imbue death with mystery, make it appear like you're becoming one with the Source, which these people seem to worship…apparently, it's been enough to keep the Cathedral hidden all these years. While they remain ignorant of the humility and defilement their priests face at the bottom of this pit.

At last, I reach the top, and of course the light was coming from the back of the Source all along, showing a dim mirror image of the brighter display that can be seen from the chamber beyond. I heave myself through it, my hair matted with the fluids I encountered below, my clothes and skin still dotted with maggots.

Stumbling onto solid ground, I bring myself to a halt. The tiny room is packed full of holy men, and more are crammed into the cramped hallway beyond. Each holds a candle, lighting the room almost as brightly as the Hall of Weights and Measures.

How must I look—how must I *smell* to them. Indeed, they're all gaping at me with wide eyes, with what I can only assume is horror.

But no. Perhaps they will feel horror, when they realize what my appearance, my smell must mean. But for now, they're awestruck, and one by one they fall to their knees.

"Chosen one!" the bishop who escorted me here cries, falling, knees hitting the stone with a thud.

"It is the Fount Embodied, come among us," Cardinal Hansh says, a twinkle in his eyes as he smiles proudly and lets himself fall.

"Fount Embodied!"

"Fount Incarnate, at last!"

I stare around the room, slowly shaking my head, at a complete loss for what to say to these people. Can't they see me? Can't they see what I just went through?

And how do I tell them that their precious Seer told me their entire cause is doomed?

"Dwell intently on what you saw and heard while in the Source," Hansh intones. "Whatever it was, it will ultimately facilitate your quest, whether it seems that way at present or not."

"Yeah," I croak at last, then clear my throat. "Thanks for all your help. We're leaving."

With that, I push through the priests and bishops, the corpse fluid wiping off onto their white and red robes.

Out. I need out. Now.

ARES

1

I spend a long time wandering the asteroid they call the Shivan Cathedral. Word must spread fast around here, because every time an acolyte sees me, he drops to his knees, gibbering wildly about the chosen one.

Part of me can understand their enthusiasm. They've built their entire lives around this moment, after all. But what I just experienced was too messed up. I'm in no mood to stick around and make chitchat about destiny and divinity. I want to lead them to their screwed-up existence and get on with proving the Seer wrong. With stopping Fairfax.

"Fount Embodied," one acolyte says from a kneeling position, clutching at my death-stained uniform. "I'm not worthy to share the same air as you. Please—since I was a small boy, I sensed that the entire universe had a divine purpose, every molecule, and now I finally have the chance to—"

"Landing bay," I growl.

"Pardon?"

"That giant cavern where we landed. Where is it, and are my people there?"

"Oh. Um—yes. Your fellow Troubleshooters have returned to

their ships, and so has your daughter. As for the way…just ahead, a spiral staircase will be on your right. Take it up two levels, then turn left down the corridor, and again down the next. From there, you—"

"Thanks," I say, marching off in the direction he indicated. I'm too frazzled to hold any more directions in my head than that, so I'll just have to extract the next leg of the journey from another breathless acolyte.

When I finally make it back to the narrow staircase that leads up to the vast space where we landed our ships, I find the *Ares* surrounded with bags and crates filled with food and supplies. Harmony's there with Shimura, his bot, and another Troubleshooter named Halsey plus his bot. They're all working together to load the supplies into my ship's open hold.

Shimura stops working when he sees me approach, and he snaps off a salute. I come to attention, returning it. He runs an eye over my uniform, no doubt taking in its general state of dishevelment. Most of the maggots have fallen off, and the suit isn't damp —it's designed to repel moisture. But the stink is still on my face and hands.

"Did they replenish the other ships' stores as well, Master Chief?" I ask Shimura.

"They did. Most generous of them, considering we were unwelcome guests. The other ships are already loaded."

I narrow my eyes, considering this. For Shimura and the others to have had time to load so many supplies aboard their Broadswords, I must have been in that pit for a while. Another thing: the priests didn't decide I'm really the Fount Embodied until I returned from their Source. So, why restock our ships?

Probably, they wanted us gone either way.

"What's next, Commander?" Shimura asks, face as composed as ever.

"We leave at once. At least, that's the plan." With that, I turn to my ship and will the airlock open. Its cycle takes longer than usual, and it spends a particularly long time on the part where it sprays me down with hot, soapy water, then makes me deposit my uniform in a chute for decontamination. I walk onto the bridge naked, check the computer to make sure my crew returned here, then go to the cabin for a fresh shipsuit.

After I went to the Source, the crew could have lingered among the priests, if they were inclined to. I hadn't expressly sent them back to the ship, so it would have been their prerogative, technically. That said, I'm glad they came back. I like it when my subordinates assume they don't have permission to do a thing unless I've expressly given it.

"Cal," I say into the empty air, emerging onto the bridge wearing new clothes. "I need you."

"Present," my father says behind me, and I turn to find him standing between the command seat and the stairway leading down to the mess.

"Why do you always appear at my back?" I ask him.

He shrugs. "Manifesting from the ether is a very personal experience. I don't like to do it while others are watching."

I sniff, deciding not to mention that I could have easily watched through my uniform's back sensors. "I need the coords out of this place. I assume you kept an eye on what happened here? Do you have access to what happened inside the Source?"

"No," he says, adding nothing else.

"You're not going to ask?"

"I do as is required of me by the collective wisdom of the Fount. It is not my place to seek to know every detail of the outcome. For me, the only relevant detail was that I made sure you come here, and I did."

"Right. Will you give me the coords, then?"

"Yes. And Joe—you should know that Fairfax seeks the Cadogan Sphere."

"The Cadogan Sphere..." I mutter. "I take it that's where the Cadogans hang out?"

"Indeed."

"Okay. Why does Fairfax want to find it?"

"The Cadogans are unlike the other families. They've had a lot more children, for one, and they have many aunts, uncles, and third- and fourth-cousins who live with them there as equals, not to mention thousands of employees, including a security force. The family has maintained an ongoing interest in the real, and if they upload to the Subverse, they do so only when they are about to die."

The Shiva still hasn't come anywhere close to answering my question, but I'm used to that by now. I wait.

"The Cadogans haven't rested on their laurels since creating the Fount. They've continued their scientific pursuits, and Fairfax knows if he can enlist them—or coerce them into helping—it will speed him toward his goals."

"What about Ludmilla Cadogan? Hasn't she been helping him?"

"She hasn't proven as cooperative as Fairfax hoped, or as susceptible to intimidation, though he's making progress on that front. Remember that she supported more people moving *into* the Subverse, not leaving it."

"Right. How do you know Fairfax is looking for the Cadogans, or about how his research is going? The same way you were able to hop back to Gauntlet to warn the brass about the attack on Cylinder One, way faster than even slipspace travel allows? Using your 'entangled particles' trick?"

Cal doesn't answer, and I shake my head. "Why haven't the Shiva ever shared that ability with the Guard? If we could communicate instantly, it would have given us an incredible edge. Changed the game in our favor. Made galactic stability a cakewalk."

"We kept it a secret for the same reason I didn't trust you with the information until recently, Joe. To risk the technology getting out would be to risk the enemy harnessing it. Fairfax would become unstoppable if he could coordinate instantly with all his people, no matter where they were in the galaxy. The fact that his operation is so slow and difficult to steer…that's what makes it possible for us to oppose him at all."

"How big is his operation, Cal?"

But my father's lips press together, his jaw tightening. "I'll send the slip coords to your datasphere. Distribute them to the others. We're nearly out of time."

2

We have four months in slipspace, and I refuse to let them go to waste.

The first thing I do is dig around in the cargo hold until I find a webbed harness, which I install over the TOPO station, so that it hangs down into it. When Harmony straps into it, it'll allow her to reach her console while protecting her from being thrown against the circular railing if the ship gets hit with anything, or if we have to make sudden course adjustments.

Once I'm finished with that, I throw myself into my training like I never have before. Even Cal starts to dole out rare praise, which I take to mean I'm making unbelievable progress.

Two weeks in, he hits me with a bombshell. "I didn't expect myself to be saying this so soon, but there's a way you can accelerate your preparedness to face Fairfax." He's actually smiling, and it might be the first time I've ever seen his lips arranged in that configuration.

"How?"

"You're not going to like this. But it ties into that humility thing we've been talking so much about."

I study his face, and I can see he's waiting for me to guess.

But it's barely a guess. "Sims. You want me to start using sims to train."

Cal nods. "A few parameter tweaks, and they'll allow you to experience overclocking without the tax on your physiology. You can practice experiencing time at that frame rate—at having that much strength, that much dexterity. It's also probably the only way to familiarize yourself enough with the muscle convulsion technique to replicate it reliably in battle."

I'm sitting on the armrest of the command seat, and I take a few moments to stare down at my hands, which dangle between my legs. When I turn them upward, I notice one of my calluses has split open. That's going to hurt next time I train with the grav-bar.

Ultimately, I don't have a choice here. I'm going to need everything Cal can teach me—I need to squeeze his training for every drop. The muscle convulsion technique seems like the best way to level up. It involves using the Fount to tense entire muscle groups in concert, in the same way all the muscles in your body convulse when you get a powerful electric shock, and you fly back from its source. According to Cal, knights have mostly used the technique to increase jump speed and distance, but I plan to try using it to make each blow I land pack more power.

"Fine," I say, looking up at him. "Let's do it."

And so we begin. I give Cal access to the ship's computer, and he cooks up a number of scenarios, typically involving an enemy that drastically outnumbers me, or one powerful enough that I wouldn't have a chance of defeating him in my normal state.

Sometimes, though, he introduces feats of physical strength and speed—like the simulation where I have to escape from a self-destructing space station, which involves lifting fallen debris out of the way, leaping over large gaps, and expelling the air from my lungs before I leap through airless, depressurized compartments.

They're not all scenarios he invents, though. He also has me redo a lot of the engagements I've participated in since this entire escapade began on Earth.

Overclocked facing the pirate impersonating Corporal Maynard? It's barely worth mentioning. The pirate doesn't have a prayer, and neither does the dog. I kill the pirate and wrestle Maneater into submission without Dice's help.

Makes me miss Maneater, though. Quite a bit.

On Tunis, I'm not able to defeat Fairfax, but I do manage to force him to flee without taking Faelyn. Of course, if that had happened in real life, I would have had no reason to go after the pirates and find out what they were up to.

Running from Fallen on Gargantua is a cinch—I easily outstrip them, and any that catch up to me I dispatch without remorse, remembering what Asterisk said about the symptoms they exhibited, of kuru, which comes from eating human brains. Cal didn't skip that detail, in the sim. The sores are there, all over their faces, necks, and arms, and their coordination leaves something to be desired. Overclocking to beat them is definitely overkill.

You'd think reliving all these kills would cause the nightmares to get worse, but the opposite is happening. Even in my conversations with Cal, I'm doing everything I can to embody the Seven Ideals. I know I have a long way to go, but I'm making progress with it, and more importantly, I'm starting to believe that I actually can live my life according to them. That alone is helping to convince myself of exactly what Cal said. That those kills are justified, now, because I'm going to do something that will affect everyone in the galaxy positively. I'm resting easier, not just because of the idea that I'm becoming worthy of the title "Shiva," but also because of what I plan to do: stop the galaxy and save humanity from being enslaved by the Allfather.

Of course, it isn't easy, and the pirate still visits me at night, whose family photo I found while searching his corpse.

"Do you think they made it?" he asks me in my dreams,

holding out the images of his wife and kids. "Without me, I mean. Were they able to provide for themselves? Or are they dead, now? Fount knows they couldn't afford to upload to the Subverse, so if they're dead, they're dead." The pirate doesn't sound angry, just sad. Solemn.

I've stopped screaming as I wake from the nightmares, but they still leave me in a cold sweat, and feeling terrible.

I'm trying to approach my relationship with Marissa and Harmony like a Shiva would, too. That isn't going quite as well as the training.

With Marissa, the most important Ideals to apply are definitely humility and respect. Restraint shouldn't hurt, either—and even a little service.

Except, whenever I try to talk to her, she ends up yelling at me.

"Stop being so fake!" she says. "You're being condescending, up on your high horse, and you don't even realize it. Can you be real for one second? Can you be the old Joe?"

I stare at her, blinking and feeling baffled. The old Joe is the one she had all the problems with. "I'm trying to fix things between us, Marissa. For Harm."

"Turning into a Fount-damned bot isn't the way to go about it. Please, can you just give me some space?" With that, she deactivates herself and returns to the crew sim, which she can do unless she's needed to perform one of her duties.

Talking to Harmony is worse, in a way. She just cracks up whenever I open my mouth.

"Listen," I tell her, half-confused, half-annoyed. "You can't just stand there laughing at me all the time. Do that in front of the crew and we're going to start having some serious discipline issues."

"I won't do it in front of the crew," she says, still giggling, "because you don't act like this in front of the crew. It's only when you're trying to be the model Shivan dad or something that you get like this—so stiff and proper, like you're some reincarnated saint brought back to teach us all table manners. It's actually hilarious."

At that, I bite off the retort I want to deliver and turn, leaving the cabin with as much composure as I can muster. A restrained Shiva knight wouldn't rise to his daughter's bait like I was just about to, so I won't either.

CADOGAN SPHERE

1

After we exit slipspace, hunting down the Cadogan Sphere seems to take almost as long, and I'm getting restless, peering out hull sensors at the stars, wondering where Fairfax is now.

Cal says Fairfax is putting together the last pieces for the Armageddon he wants to visit on the galaxy, and once he has the Cadogans locked down he'll basically be there.

No sign of Fairfax presents itself during the excruciatingly dull hours I spend scanning the cosmos as our nine Broadswords cross system after system, making short slipspace hops on our way to the Sphere. But one thing does show itself, big and orange against the interstellar medium: the gas cloud where Cal says the Cadogans are hiding out.

"It's unusually large," Marissa muses as Belflower runs system checks for the next slipspace jump. "And unusually dense."

Asterisk leans on his station railing, blowing idly at a lock of his own hair. The motion causes his face chains to shake. He's facing pointedly away from Harmony—two jumps ago, I snapped that if I have to tell him to keep his eyes on his station once more, he's deleted. The kid has done a lot to impress me lately, but if he starts behaving inappropriately toward Harmony I won't hesitate to snuff out his life like a candle.

Marissa's right about the gas cloud. There aren't many astronomers around anymore—the spacescrapers do some low-level observation of the cosmos, to avoid any big navigational hazards, but they don't share that data with anyone. Bottom line being that my ship's computer has no information on this cloud: not where it's been, how long it's been in the area, or when it might have formed. My datasphere suggests the gas cloud G2 as a possible ancestor of this one, but if that's the case G2's been beefing up, and might have combined with another cloud somewhere along the way.

That's all basically academic, though, and if it were the whole picture then wasted time would be the only hazard this cloud poses us. But no: the cloud happens to occupy a part of the galaxy known to house dozens of mini black holes, ranging in size from a token to a trampoline to a few city blocks. Any one of them would spell my ship's doom, and they're all hidden from view. Great for the Cadogans, whose black hole-littered hiding place should repel anyone who's not insane. Not so great for me, who's a little lacking in the sanity department lately.

"Ever feel like the universe is against you?" Belflower muses as she runs diagnostics on the *Ares'* Becker drive. "Here we are, trying to save the galaxy, and that gas cloud just happens to occupy one of its most treacherous regions—if not *the* most."

"I used to think that way," I answer, without really thinking about it. "Now that sort of thinking just feels useless."

I blink, surprised at my answer, but knowing even so that it came from a place of truth.

A few days later, on the edge of the cloud, we get a lucky break —a Cadogan scout ship, mostly drone but with a human occupant to act as an emissary, contacts us, sending a blanket transmission request to all nine Broadswords. Marissa accepts it, patching it through to me.

"You're Commander Joseph Pikeman?" the emissary says, youthful voice speaking straight into my thoughts.

"I am," I say, a little puzzled.

"I'm Dale Cadogan. Your father paid us a visit—a man we have a great amount of respect for. When he told us his son was searching for our home, I was dispatched right away to guide you in through the Moor."

Wow. They sent an actual Cadogan to greet me. Yes, I know Cadogans are way more numerous in the real than the other Five Families, but still.

"The Moor?"

"That's what we call this big gas cloud."

"It's been around long enough for you to name?"

"Yep. Unusually long, actually. That's one of the reasons we were so keen to come here—to study the Moor's properties. Try to figure out why it's sticking around so long."

"Right. Well, lead the way, Dale," I say, ending the transmission.

"Looks like your optimism paid off, Captain," Belflower said. The crew all had access to the conversation. I tend to let them listen in on exchanges with unidentified ships, so that I don't have to explain anything if things turn violent.

Once we enter the cloud, visual sensors show nothing but an orange miasma all around us, and radar's just as blinded by the gas, plasma and dust. We navigate by the Cadogan craft's intensely bright taillights, which cut through the cloud and appear on visual like a flashlight that's running out of energy. To achieve even that effect, Cadogan has to remain just a few dozen kilometers ahead—pretty close when you're talking about astrogation, but he stays to the right a few kilometers to reduce the chance of collision. The eight other Broadswords need to stay even closer to maintain sight of the *Ares'* lights, so I make sure they maintain a properly staggered formation.

And when I say Dale guides us through the cloud, I mean his

ship does. He's not the pilot, but a passenger. My initial read of the craft was correct: the ship's a drone operating under preprogrammed parameters—not quite a bot, but one with a comprehensive set of orders and predetermined responses to a number of situations. The fact the Cadogans bothered with any of it shows they're taking my visit seriously, which is encouraging.

"We're here," Dale Cadogan declares abruptly, sounding overenthusiastic. I doubt that's just his youth: I'd get restless too, stuck in a ship I have no control over. "Can you spot the Sphere?"

I give the whole crew access to visual sensor data, and we all pour over the images, scrutinizing the surrounding cloud for anomalies.

"There," Harmony says, isolating a section of cloud and flinging it toward me so it hits my datasphere. "See it?"

"No," I say, squinting.

"There's a circle where the cloud is slightly closer than it should be. It's showing a projection of the cloud beyond it, except the edges are edited to blend seamlessly with the gas around it."

That gives me pause. "That entire thing is a display? How big is it?"

"Big, Captain," Harm says.

"There," I say to Dale, transmitting an image with the Sphere highlighted.

"You got it," he says, and I can hear the smile in his voice.

"How do you guys hide it like that?"

Dale chuckles. "You're looking at the station's exterior layer, which is comprised wholly of tightly integrated, self-replicating Fount to form a giant, three-hundred-sixty degree display. Fount engineering has been the secret to most of our breakthroughs since the Fall."

"What breakthroughs?"

"Ah, well, I'm not sure what I'm authorized to say. But you'll see at least a few of them. Just follow the light, Commander."

With that, his drone ship swoops in from the right, sailing

toward a spot near the bottom of the sphere—the bottom, at least, from our orientation. Probably the bottom in truth. No reason not to approach it that way. Makes it easier for newcomers like us.

Harmony takes manual control of the *Ares* and keeps her glued to Dale's taillight. She was as good as her word when it came to immersing herself in astrogation sims while in slipspace, and now she flies like she was born doing it. That's my girl.

As we approach a part of the sphere that looks no different from any other, without any discernible opening for us to enter through, something occurs to me and I contact Dale. "Hold on—is this thing slipspace capable?"

"Sure is, Commander," he answers, as chipper as ever.

"How is that possible? Your *home* is almost as big as the largest station I've seen."

"Like I said, Commander. We've learned a thing or two."

That gives me something to chew on. Fount engineering is the Cadogans' specialty, and as many uses as the nanobots have, starship propulsion isn't one of them. Seems the Cadogans have been branching out into other fields.

It turns out the Sphere has airlock technology similar to what the priests were rocking back on their asteroid. That is to say, there is no airlock—instead, there's a layer of Fount that "unzips" as a ship passes through, then closes back up again to maintain a perfect seal. Without having to be asked, Harmony points the *Ares* at the spot where Dale's light disappeared, and we pass through seamlessly, the Fount opening and closing around us.

It occurs to me what a good defensive measure this is. Any invading ships would have no idea where they're supposed to enter through, and chances are they'd end up crashing into the station's side. Probably not great for the station itself, but I'm sure the Cadogans have implemented provisions against that too.

Sure enough, we find ourselves in a narrow tunnel just big enough for us to navigate comfortably. Probably they have other entrances elsewhere, to accommodate bigger ships if needed. After a few minutes, the choke point of the tunnel opens up into a larger landing bay—much larger. The word cavernous would do it injustice. It's like someone hollowed out the bottom section of a moon and decided to park some ships there.

All this has me wondering whether the Cadogans have the ability to order the Fount to "harden" into a shell, maybe weaving together to form a solid barrier. It wouldn't have to be all that solid, actually: just durable enough to rough up a ship, surprise its systems, maybe throw off its navigation and send it into one of the tunnel's sturdy-looking walls.

For a hybrid starship-station occupying one of the best hiding places in the galaxy, the Cadogan Sphere certainly gets a lot of traffic. Drones swarm in and out, spewing out of the variously sized tunnels in single file before forming up to drop off cargo inside rectangular pits, turn around, and exit just as quickly, presumably to go out and harvest more materials.

Dale Cadogan must have the ability to read minds, since he seems to sense my curiosity about the drone fleet. "We're actually on the extreme outskirts of a mineral-rich star system," he says. We don't get the opportunity to go on these mining expeditions often, so when we do, we like to load up as much as possible."

Trailed by the eight other Broadswords, the *Ares* sails after Dale's ship, toward the forest of impossibly high transparent tubes that dominate the landing bay's center. Most of them terminate in one of the great pits; two for each one, an up and a down. Freight elevators zip upward, stuffed to bursting with mined ore, and empty elevators descend to pick up more.

The scale of the operation is staggering. What are the Cadogans using all these resources for?

Dale leads us to what seems to be the perfect center of the landing bay, though that's hard to judge with the Sphere's inner walls so distant. Finally, I'm stepping out of the *Ares* airlock and walking toward Dale's drone ship to meet him in person. It feels amazing to be out of the ship and breathing—well, not *fresh* air, but the Cadogans seem to have their filtration systems pretty much perfected. Hell, the fact they cart around this much atmosphere, even gallivanting around slipspace with it, boggles the mind.

Dale's grip is firmer than I expect, though he stares at our hands as we shake, not making eye contact. "It's a true honor to meet you, Commander Pikeman. We have great respect for everything the Guard's done, but it's the fact we have another Shiva at large in the galaxy that really has us excited. Of all the things to come out of the Fount, the Knighthood is the one that humbles us the most."

I give a thin smile. Honestly, it's hard not to like the Cadogans —as recklessly as they handed over their most famous invention to Jeremy Fairfax, who unleashed it on the galaxy, leading directly to the Fall…as many risks as they seem willing to take with their research…they're a plucky bunch, damn it, and a lot humbler than you'd expect.

Dale starts off toward a cluster of elevator tubes—a ring comprised of six smaller rings, each featuring six tubes—and I follow behind. I've decided to visit with the Cadogans alone, leaving the other Guardsmen here. One armed Troubleshooter tends to make most people nervous, so I doubt showing up with eight more of them would get things off to a good start.

My guess is including so many passenger elevators was a safety measure, in the event the Sphere had to be evacuated on short notice. Right now, not one of them appears to be in use.

The speed of the trip up manages to surprise me again. Even after watching the freight elevators flit up their tubes stuffed with heavy ore, the trip goes by faster than expected, despite the awkward silence as Dale stares at me wearing a fawning expression.

The elevator takes us past the landing bay's ceiling, and I stare through the fiber-reinforced plastic sides, blinking as I try to reorient myself. Dale's still staring at me, grinning now, clearly having anticipated this reaction.

We appear to be zooming through—well, sky. Even though I know we just passed through the landing bay ceiling, I look down into endless blue. Above, there's a layer of wispy clouds, through which I can glimpse what looks like the highly developed surface of a planet, stretching in all directions until it hits the Sphere's inner walls.

Then, with very little warning except for the glimpse of something that doesn't look right in the upper edge of my vision, the elevator hits a curve in the tube, flipping upside down and then *dropping* us toward the ground. My thoughts are screaming at me that I should have slammed into the elevator's ceiling, but of course I don't.

"Welcome to the Sphere, Commander," Dale says, and I don't humor him by answering. Kid could have given me some warning.

Looking down on the sprawling town the Cadogans have built for themselves in the center of their sphere, I'm reminded of Cylinder One, except with more green spaces.

But there's more to it than that. Where the Lambton station has factories, depots, and admin buildings, the Sphere boasts structures whose architects placed aesthetics way over function. There are ivory towers topped by delicate, lacy crowns that stretch impossibly high, bridges spanning broad rivers with so little support they look like they're liable to crash into the water at any minute, sprawling public malls overshadowed by buildings with brash horizontal protrusions.

All throughout the town, the freight elevator tubes stab down into the only industrial buildings I can discern: massive refineries that shoulder toward the sky, the least elegant structures in sight, through still beautiful.

The passenger elevator tubes all terminate in the middle of the largest open space, but thankfully there are no buildings nearby that look like they're about to topple over onto us. Instead, massive, identical redwoods stand trunk to trunk, forming a wall of almost solid bark to enclose the area in a broad ring.

The elevator slides open to let us out onto the cobble, and I step off, grateful to be clear of it for the time being.

"Just this way, Commander," Dale says, already striding toward a break in the ring of trees. "The welcoming committee will already be assembled. They'll be waiting for you."

As we emerge from the elevator landing area and onto a street beyond, I pause, and I catch my hand wandering toward my blaster.

Dale stops, looking back at me quizzically. "Is something wrong?"

I cock my head and stand perfectly still. Yep, there's definitely a rhythmic tremor running through the ground below my feet. The same kind of tremor that reminds me of facing down the giant Kitane back in Cylinder One.

Unclasping the holster, I turn, and in less than a second the blaster's in my hand, my left hand coming up to steady it.

Trotting down the street toward us, still distant but closing in steadily, is a giant fox. It's around half the size of the construct Electra Fairfax inhabited, but still big enough to make a snack of anything human-sized.

2

"Commander, no!"

I pause as my finger begins to depress the blaster's trigger—just as I'm about to start spamming white bolts into the oncoming beast's hide. Glancing back at Dale, I snarl, "What?"

"That's one of our citizens you're aiming your weapon at. Please, don't shoot!"

I look between the young Cadogan and the oncoming construct, the rumbling in the ground increasing with its approach. An elderly couple strolling past nearby, hand-in-hand, are studying me quizzically, and none of the other pedestrians seem bothered by the beast.

Haltingly, I lower my blaster. "What's going on, here, Dale?" I ask.

Scarlet flushes his face as he casts his eyes downward. "It's one of the advances I mentioned."

"You're putting people's minds into these things?" I growl, turning more fully toward him, blaster still in hand but pointing toward the ground.

"Y-yes, Commander. It's something we've been working on for a l-long time. I know you're distrustful of the Subverse, of humanity's decision to upload into it almost wholesale, and we've always felt the loss of the real was a significant one too."

"You've been working with Fairfax. Haven't you?" I replace the blaster in its holster and snap it into place. The tremor in the ground increases, and I glance behind me with gritted teeth.

"Not anymore," Dale says in a rush. "We've followed his doings, and he's taken research paths we don't condone."

"Like abducting children, for instance?"

"Y-yes. Like that."

"But it was your contribution that allowed him to explore those 'paths' in the first place."

Dale's face sags even further. "Yes."

"Take me to your welcoming committee," I snap, despite trying to moderate my tone, like a Shiva would. Arguing with a brain-washed youngster in the street doesn't seem productive. I want to be taken to the source of all this madness.

We continue down the boulevard, where the traffic seems to be exclusively pedestrian—if you can count giant four-legged monstrosities as pedestrians. No vehicles, which probably keeps the population fit. Not a bad approach for living in the real, minus the unleashing of abominations.

"Not everyone wanted to work with Fairfax, even when we thoughts his intentions were pure," Dale says, his voice pitched higher than before. "A lot of people warned about the risks."

"What type of leadership do you have here, Dale?"

"Leadership, sir?"

"Yeah. Mayor? President? Prime minister? Intergalactic overlord?"

"Oh. Um, we don't really have any 'leaders,' per se."

That explains a lot. "What sort of government do you have, *per se*, Dale?"

"Anarcho-syndicalism."

"The hell is that?"

"Uh, basically the workers control everything? It's a system based on meeting human needs, so that's good, and no one gets paid—"

"No one gets *paid?*"

"Yeah."

"What's the incentive to work?"

"Well, we have an algorithm for measuring productive output, and the most productive people get the biggest say in governance, so that's the incentive."

"What about people who have no interest in governing? What's their incentive?"

"Well, no one *has* to work, Commander. Everyone's needs are provided for."

"What do most people do?"

Dale stays quiet for a while. "We've had a lot of people uploading to the Subverse, lately," he admits at last.

"Uh huh. The Subverse." The ultimate anarchic-whatever-the-hell.

After that, I decide Dale's kind of a smart ass and I don't pursue the conversation any more. He leads me to one of the biggest buildings in town, a clamshell-shaped structure sitting on the edge of a convincing-looking artificial wave pool.

We enter through the middle of the clam's mouth—kind of looks like the clam's missing its front teeth, if clams had teeth.

Beyond the glass doors, there's no lobby or anything else to get visitors used to the idea that they're about to speak to a group of powerful people. We're just right in the thick of things, with more Cadogans than I expected seated in ascending rows before me, each one behind a desk. Or, wait, are all these Cadogans?

"Are all these people Cadogans, Dale?" I ask as we approach the lowest point in the building—a shallow bowl with a micro-phone attached to a black rod sticking out of the floor.

"No, Commander. We search the galaxy for anyone with an interest in science and invite them to live in the Sphere with us."

"Right."

The upper rows are reserved for just a few, and the highest seat holds a bearded old man. The desks get larger as the rows go up. "What do you know," I mutter. "There's even a pecking order under mob rule."

I walk to the center of the room, and the microphone ascends to just below my mouth, depriving me of the opportunity to yank it up like I wanted. "Hi," I say, hands at my sides. "Commander Joe Pikeman. Can you tell me what made you think unleashing monsters on the galaxy was a good idea?"

An uneasy silence settles over the clamshell. Before, I'm sure the silence as we crossed the floor was meant to unsettle me; to impress me with the majesty of the building and maybe a sense of the soaring productivity represented by the gathered coalition of workers. Now, there's some uneasy shifting in the ascending rows, mostly but not entirely concealed by the desks between me and them.

"Uh, welcome to the Sphere, Commander," wheezes the wizened man sitting at the greatest height. He's dressed in what they would have called business casual, before the Fall: a partially unbuttoned dress shirt rolled up past liver-spotted elbows, slacks neatly pressed with a crease. "I am Brendan Cadogan, and as current Prime Producer, It's a pleasure and an *honor* to—"

"Yeah, it was nice to visit until I saw a giant fox wandering the streets. Young Dale here was pretty vocal about how you helped Fairfax get his galactic conquest thing off the ground. Tell me about that."

Cadogan clears his throat, and the nervous shifting throughout the room increases. "Well, Commander, I believe we have much in common with you on this front. We share your sadness for humanity's loss of the real. Perhaps for different reasons—our pursuit of the sciences has little application in the Subverse—but our interests *do* align. A revival of the real is something we've pursued for a long time, and initially, Fairfax's interest in our work seemed very promising. As I'm sure you're aware, the Fairfaxes have a long history of financing Cadogan research."

"Yeah, and look how well that's gone for everyone."

"Human longevity has been extended beyond historical precedent," Cadogan says after a pause.

"Which would be great, if there were any actual humans left to take advantage of that fact."

That brings a collective rumbling rising from the assembled politicians, or Supreme Workers, or whatever they are. "Order, order," Cadogan says, leaning forward, the tip of his beard brushing against the desk. "Commander, I'm afraid I can't condone any statement to the effect that uploads somehow aren't full humans, nor can I allow it to be uttered again in this chamber."

"Humans have human nature, which comes from our evolution. Uploads have abandoned the bodies nature gave them. They've become something else. Posthuman, if you like."

The tumult of voices increases in volume, and I shout over it. "Fine! Listen, I won't say it. This isn't the important thing. What matters is that Fairfax is seeking out this place right now, and since you stopped cooperating with him, he's probably not planning on paying a standard house call."

A woman with graying hair stands from the exclusive second row that sits just below Brendan Cadogan, glancing back at him. The old man nods.

"Commander," she says, her voice echoing through the clamshell's hollow, "Harriet Cadogan here. I think we'd be remiss if we didn't inform you of the full range of public opinion on this subject, both inside this assembly and without. A sizable minority *does* support helping Fairfax to realize his goals. I count myself among their number."

I stare up at her, blinking, mouth slightly open. "Wait," I say finally. "You all know about the abducting children thing, right?"

"We are aware," Harriet says. "And it is deeply regrettable. However, the inclusion of such malleable young minds *did* contribute greatly to solving the problem of transferring conscious-nesses that have achieved incredible complexity while in the Subverse. That was a hurdle we were never able to solve, bound as we are by much tighter, um, ethical restraints. And while Fairfax's actions did cause some limited suffering, it's likely his advance will be of great benefit to humanity, for centuries to come."

Oh, great. So they've justified sacrificing children, too. I decide to try another tack: "Why don't you tell me, then, how Fairfax's plan lines up with the way you've arranged your society, here? If this is the best way to govern yourself, how can you be okay with Fairfax's aim of liberating all his rich friends from the Subverse first?"

Harriet nods, not missing a beat. "We share your concerns, Commander. We do. Our biggest problem is with the corrupting influence of tokens, and while that is a problem, tokens *do* act as a rough proxy for how much value—how much *output*—someone has contributed to galactic society. With many notable exceptions, of course. But Fairfax's decision to bequeath the first constructs to Five Families members actually does roughly line up with how we choose to reward members of our society. Our hope is that we can work with him to build a new society in the real, a society that is a true worker's paradise, where someone's output and not their net worth determines the say they have and where all needs are provided for from the fruit of that output."

I stare up at Harriet Cadogan, shaking my head slowly. When it comes to debating politics, I'm woefully outgunned, but even I can tell what she's proposing here is screwed up.

My jaw tenses, and I realize I'm grinding my teeth as I try to put together a counterargument that will help these people under-stand just how insane these ideas sound to someone with more than a drop of common sense.

But I've got nothing, and I'm almost relieved when the entire structure suddenly shakes with an ominous creaking, and everyone looks instinctively up at the ceiling.

The trembling ends in total silence, which lets me hear one of the doors creaking open behind me, followed by footsteps pounding across the floor.

A young man who's balding before his time runs up, taking over the mic and breathing heavily into it. "It's the *Ekhidnades*," he pants. "Fairfax. He found us, and he's hitting us with everything he's got."

The Sphere shakes again, this time more violently than the last, and I have to throw out my hands to maintain balance.

"Fount damn it," I mutter as the tremors subside, then I sprint toward the entrance.

3

The *Ares* screams out of the same narrow port we entered through, and I use my datasphere to call up a 3D model of the surrounding battlespace, suspended in a black void.

"So the Cadogans aren't totally toothless," I mutter.

A fleet of fifty-three fighter drones swarms Fairfax's destroyer, using kinetic weapons to engage the beastly ship. They aren't doing a great job of it, and the *Ekhidnades'* point defense systems alone are keeping them at bay, without the need of Fairfax actively firing on them. But between the drones and the Sphere's own point defense, the destroyer has its hands full, meaning we probably have a window to inflict some real damage, maybe even push the warship back and give the Sphere time to flee.

The gas cloud is still playing havoc with our sensors, but Marissa's able to tap into the drones' data feeds, which keeps the 3D tactical display dynamic and up to date.

Waving away the display, I glance at her. "Chief, tell Shimura to choose three Broadswords to adopt a finger-four formation with —they'll be Delta Flight—and start running laser alpha strikes on areas where the destroyer's hardest pressed. Then tell whatever ships he doesn't choose for Delta to form up with us and do the same. We'll be Epsilon Flight."

"Aye," Marissa says, the tension in her voice palpable.

"Keep a cool head, all of you." That draws a sharp glance from Marissa, but I really do mean the remark for all of them. "We're starting with Fairfax on the back heel already. I think he's realizing he bit off more than he can chew. If we stay frosty, we can make him pay for that."

I call up the 3D tactical display again, shrinking it down to rest in the middle of the bridge between the four crew stations, nestled in a gray rectangle included for the purpose.

Good—Shimura and his pilots have already formed up. Delta Flight pounces, using macros to fire from every laser turret facing the *Ekhidnades*. The great warship responds in kind, and the four Broadswords accelerate on an angle that edges them left, until they're flying perpendicular to the target.

"Epsilon, advance," I bark over a channel that includes the four Broadswords formed up with the *Ares*. As one, we fly forward, adding our laserfire to the attack. A few point defense turrets refocus on us, taking their attention away from the fighter drones and Delta Flight.

"Focus fire on those point defense turrets targeting us," I order over the wide channel, and we do, popping them one by one. More turrets start firing at the Epsilon Broadswords, but by now we're getting close—almost close enough for me to deliver my sucker punch. "Keep up the pressure, Troubleshooters."

The lead Broadsword loses a laser turret, and the second ship loses their primary. That makes me wince, but we're so close…

There. "Epsilon Flight, accelerate beyond the *Ares*, clearing a firing lane on the primary laser battery I'm marking out for you now." A section of the destroyer's hull blinks red on the synced tactical display, and the other Broadswords speed ahead.

"Asterisk, fire!" I had the WSO prepare two missiles even

before I boarded the *Ares* in the massive bay—I sent the order ahead by datasphere.

But now he grips his station, staring down at it in consternation. "S-sir, something's wrong. The starboard Javelin launcher isn't responding…"

Belflower shoots a sharp glance at the ensign, but my attention's mostly on the tactical display as Asterisk punches frantically at his console, his face chains shaking. Our window of opportunity is closing.

"What about the other launcher?" I bark.

Asterisk punches a few commands into his station.

"Anything?"

He shakes his head.

"Fount damn it," I mutter, dropping into a direct control sim for the weapon systems. For a moment, I blink at the digital interface in confusion. Both missile tubes are painted green. I select the one best angled to target the destroyer's laser battery, double check the nav-macro installed in the Javelin, then fire.

The missile screams across space, traveling the short distance to the *Ekhidnades*. Multiple point defense turrets redirect their fire toward the missile, but its speed combined with the random guns-D movement programmed in is enough to see it to its target. An explosion blooms where the laser battery was, tossing shrapnel into the void.

"Ensign, there was nothing wrong with those launchers," I say, glaring at him.

"I'm sorry, Captain. I don't know what happened. Could be my station's misreporting diagnostics."

"Belflower, check his system. In the meantime, Ensign, I need you to get yourself together. Malfunction aside, I can tell you're not operating at full capacity."

"Aye, Captain."

All this time, Harmony's been taking us away from the *Ekhidnades*, introducing her own evasive maneuvers into our flight pattern, keeping the laserfire off us. That's an easier job, now that we've neutralized a main bank of weapons, and the gas cloud's obstruction probably doesn't hurt. Fairfax doesn't have the luxury of dozens of drones flying through the battlespace, acting as his eyes and ears.

That said, there's a good chance he's deployed sensor drones, and we just haven't spotted them in the murk.

Either way…Fount, but it feels good to finally be doing real damage to Fairfax. Is it possible we could stop him today, just as he's trying to assemble the final piece he needs to resurrect the Allfather?

"Sir, the Cadogans are down fourteen fighter drones, for a total of thirty-nine remaining," Marissa says. "The relayed sensor data's getting more limited. Fairfax is slowly blinding us."

Gritting my teeth, I force myself to nod, chastising myself for celebrating our victory well before we've achieved it. "Get in touch with the drones' controller aboard the Sphere. Suggest that they pull half the drones back for now, in a loose net surrounding the *Ekhidnades*. That will keep them safe while giving us the best possible information on its movement through the cloud."

"Aye," Marissa says, bending over her station.

"Also tell them to let us know if they encounter any drones that don't belong to them. I'd predict Fairfax has put out a sensor net of his own—if that's the case, we'll want to start picking it apart."

As Marissa sends the message, I continue to monitor the battle-space, watching as Delta Flight goes in for another alpha strike on the area we've already weakened. Having apparently learned to fear the Broadswords, the enemy destroyer fires on them preemptively while turning the vulnerable section of hull away. Delta Flight lays on more speed, doggedly moving in on the target area.

"Let's pitch in, Epsilon Flight," I say over the wide channel. "This isn't over, but if we can keep up the pressure there's a chance we can win this thing right here, today. If—"

"Sir?" Marissa says.

I get the urge to glare at her, but something in her voice stops me. When I turn, her expression is distraught, and her avatar's face is drained of color.

"What is it?" I say, forgetting to deactivate the wide channel.

"The Cadogans took our advice to peel back half the drones, and well—they found something."

"Found what?"

"At least four more warships are closing in on the Sphere."

A silence settles over the bridge as I stare at Marissa, struggling to process what she just told me. "Define 'warships.'"

"From what I'm seeing…one is big enough to be another destroyer. There's also a cruiser and two frigates. They'll be in firing range within minutes."

4

"There's something else," Marissa says, squinting at her data. "Another Broadsword, flying in formation with the incoming warships. Captain, I…I think it's the *Hermes*."

Soren. No longer trying to hide his allegiance with Fairfax, apparently, but then why would he? He spent the element of surprise on trying to finish me on Persephone, and it didn't work. No need to skulk in the shadows any longer.

"There's no way Fairfax just gained four warships that second," I say, barely aware I'm speaking out loud. "He's been keeping his strength in reserve. Why?"

Belflower's face is a grim mask. "Maybe he didn't want to tip the Guard off. Looks like his military buildup has happened quicker than anyone could have anticipated. If he has much more than this, then he's poised to start taking over as soon as the Allfather's free."

With a sinking feeling, I realize she's right. If the Guard had known how powerful Fairfax was becoming, they might have finally called back all their Troubleshooters to face him down. Now, it's probably too late.

The four newcomer ships are marching across the tactical

display, moving to join the *Ekhidnades* and back her up against the Broadswords.

Without warning, neon-blue laserfire lances out from all four warships, flickering across the hulls of Delta Flight as they return from their latest strike. Most of the beams focus fire on one ship—Captain Halsey's—and after a few seconds, his hull can take no more. The Broadsword explodes.

"Pull back!" I yell over the wide channel. "All Broadswords, withdraw and form up with the *Ares*, staggered formation!"

As soon as the Broadswords back off, ports begin opening on the *Ekhidnades'* hull, launching spike-shaped vessels toward the Sphere.

"What the hell are those things?" I say, and Marissa has an answer.

"I believe they're boarding craft, sir."

Fists clenched, I watch as the spikes sail toward the top and bottom of the Cadogan Sphere. That confirms my suspicion that the *Ekhidnades* distributed a net of sensor drones before the battle: they must have watched us exit from those areas of the Sphere. Probably some of the spikes will end up embedded uselessly in solid parts anyway, but others will find their way into the tunnels meant for incoming craft, and there'll be nothing to stop them from getting in.

For our part, there's nothing we can do. The newly arrived warships are keeping us busy with a torrent of laserfire. Then, as I watch, each warship looses two missiles each at the cluster of Broadswords.

"All ships, focus on shooting down those missiles before they reach us!"

Broadswords weren't built to take any kind of sustained missile fire. In the current desolate state of the galaxy, coming under that kind of attack is supposed to be so rare it almost never happens. Pirates typically can't get it together enough to pool their resources to purchase even a single missile, and when they do, it usually has something debilitatingly wrong with it, making it easy to shoot down well before it reaches you.

The missiles crossing the battlespace now fly straight and true —and fast. As we reverse thrust in formation, the last thing I want to do is expend our own limited supply of missiles to stop the oncoming ones, but it's looking like that's the only way to ensure no more Broadswords go down.

Our laserfire takes down one missile, then another. On the 3D display, the remaining six birds inch ever closer. A third goes down.

"Captain, the first enemy dropships are reaching the Sphere. A few have embedded themselves in its hull, but most have made it past the Fount layer."

Another missile falls to our combined laserfire. But we're not neutralizing them fast enough. "*Medusa* and *Gorgon*, ready a Javelin each and prepare to target down the last two missiles on my command," I say over the wide channel.

It seems to take an eternity to destroy the next two missiles, and for a panicked second it looks like I'll have to queue up a third missile with almost no time to do so. Then missiles five and six explode in quick succession. "Fire missiles!"

The Javelins scream out of the designated ships, slamming into their targets, which try and fail to evade.

"Now what, Captain?" Harmony asks from the TOPO station.

For a moment, total silence pervades aboard the *Ares*, and it's deafening.

Then I shake myself out of the trance threatening to descend. "We can't beat five fully operational warships with just eight Broadswords," I say. "Not even with the help of the drones and the Sphere's point defense. That said, we can assume Fairfax doesn't want to destroy the Cadogan's home—he needs them, and he needs their technology."

I spend another second mulling over what I'm about to say, then nod to myself. "If I know that bastard, he probably went aboard the Sphere on one of those dropships. Our only chance now is to board the Sphere again ourselves and take the fight to him there. If we can find him and stop him—kill him, ideally—then we can work on getting the Cadogans to start fleeing from the warships." The only question is why they didn't do that the moment the other four warships showed up.

I get back on the wide channel to my seven remaining Broadswords. "All Troubleshooters, back to base. We're taking the fight straight to Fairfax, in the streets of the Sphere if need be. Take your bots with you, and order your WSOs to shoot anything that tries to get near our ships." Closing the channel, I turn to Harmony. "Set a course for the part of the Sphere we exited from, and share it with the others TOPOs."

Our staggered formation turns, all thrusting toward the Cadogan Sphere. Not as fast as I'd like, though. The more we accelerate toward the Sphere, the longer and harder we'll have to decelerate, making it trickier to thread our ships through the invisible tunnel we came out of.

Noting our retreat, the four warships send another eight-missile volley to help us on our way. The rockets close just as quickly as the first barrage, but I instruct the Troubleshooters to ignore them. If the drones and the Sphere's point defense can't handle it, then the station itself will just have to absorb it.

Three of the birds go down, but the rest are catching up alarmingly fast, and for a moment I worry whether I'll get all of my Broadswords into the tunnel before they arrive. The other seven successfully find the entrance, darting through, and it's just us left.

Harmony revs up the counter-thrust needed to propel us toward our target, and I open my mouth to tell her she's going too fast. Then I shut it again, eyeing the five missiles still bearing down on us. The station turrets take down one, then another. Three left…

The *Ares* dives through the layer of Fount covering the Cadogan Sphere, and we miss careening into the side of the tunnel by a matter of inches. As Harmony levels us out, the station rumbles with the sound of three missiles impacting its side, with one of them making it into the tunnel to collide with the bulkhead a few meters in.

Flame roars forward to lick at the *Ares'* stern, but we outpace it.

Back in the landing bay, nothing looks different—it's as though the Sphere isn't being invaded by several dropships' worth of pirates-turned-soldiers.

That is, until Marissa spots a spike-shaped ship that's skidded to a stop half a kilometer away from the passenger elevators. Black-helmeted soldiers are pouring out of it, their uniforms black as well, other than the gold trim. Blue lights evocative of Fairfax's eyes shine out of their helmets.

"Asterisk, hit them with a Javelin. Now."

The ensign jerks at his station, glances back at me wearing a look of uncertainty, then turns back to his console. What's going on with him?

"Ensign?" I say a few seconds later, when he's failed to acknowledge my order, or to act on it. Though he doesn't know it, I'm monitoring his progress using my datasphere, and he's made no step toward initiating the missile-loading sequence.

"Y-yes, Captain, I—"

Shaking my head, I queue up the missile myself and fire it. The Javelin sails across the landing bay, whistling with speed, and the spike-ship blossoms in flame, tossing shrapnel in every direction. Twenty-three of the enemy soldiers escape the explosion, but shrapnel takes down five more.

"Ensign, take out the rest of those men, or spend the rest of this engagement in the crew sim."

"Yes, sir," Asterisk says, loading macros into the laser turrets and taking direct control of the primary. As we close with the ring of elevators leading up to the city, he fires on the fleeing soldiers. They don't stand much of a chance against the *Ares'* weapons, which are designed to take out starships. Killing them doesn't take long.

Shimura has led the Troubleshooters to the center of the forma-tion of elevator tubes—a smart move. From there, we can exercise control over who enters or leaves the city.

From this end of the Sphere, anyway. More dropships headed for its northern end, where they'll have free reign, unless the Cado-gans put up a much stiffer defense there than they have here.

It occurs to me that Fairfax may already know the Sphere's layout well. Brendan Cadogan mentioned they once worked closely with the Fairfaxes to progress the program for recolonizing the real. It makes sense that that would entail multiple visits to the research facilities aboard the Sphere.

"We have eight Guardsmen and seven bots," I tell the other Troubleshooters once we're all out of our ships and gathered between the defensive ring we've formed with them. "Each of you take your bot and head up one of the six elevator clusters—two clusters will have two pairs of bots and Guardsmen. Be ready to back each other up once we get to the city, flanking any threats waiting for us. During the trip, I'll send you datasphere footage of the terrain I encountered there. Familiarize yourselves with it as fast as you can."

We each get in our respective elevators, and as the others study the images of the town above, I peer out over the sprawling landing bay below. The higher we climb, the more enemy units I can see advancing on the elevators. Depending on the kind of fire-power they're packing, there's a chance they could blow these tubes apart while we're in them.

And if they did, there's not much we could do to stop them.

5

Luckily, the enemy soldiers leave the tubes alone—maybe because they know they'd be messing with their own way in. We keep climbing.

The elevators take us through the landing bay ceiling, then zooming through the sky above the city. When we reach the part where the elevator loops back, turning us upside down, I realize I forgot to warn the others about it, just like Dale forgot to warn me.

Signs of the battle can be seen even through the wispy cloud layer below, with explosions dotting the landscape, and smoke pillaring up through the Sphere. Looks like Fairfax and his people are making short work of everything the Cadogans have built.

At last, we near the ground to find the ring of trees surrounding the elevators breached on the side opposite the original exit. The redwoods there are battered in, bent toward the ground like splintered fingers.

The street in front of the landing area is hotly contested, with Fairfax's fighters warring with what must be Cadogan security forces, clad in green and blue. Inside the ring, the fox construct from before is doing battle with one based on a weird alien crab species I've never seen before. Its black eyes bulge at the end of thick eye stalks, which bob over a maw containing row after row of serrated teeth. Its shell looks more like a tortoise's than a crab's, and though it moves slower than its opponent, if it manages to grip the fox's leg I'm sure it will snap in two.

Who would want to live their lives in control of such a beast? Exactly what market are the Cadogans catering to with such a 'product?'

The fox darts behind the massive crustacean, putting its shoulder against the thing's rear then throwing its weight forward. Flailing, the crab tumbles—straight toward the ring of elevators I'm descending. Its claw finds two of the tubes, gripping them for purchase, and then the great pincers close, shearing the elevators at least a dozen meters above the ground. Although, it's hard to judge the exact distance from my position hundreds of feet up.

The important thing is that one of the elevators it destroyed is the one I'm descending.

"Commander," Shimura says, no doubt having seen the fate that awaits me. "Are you—"

"I'll be fine. Get clear of those constructs the moment you touch down, and *do not engage them*, whatever you do. Hustle over to where the redwoods were snapped off and climb out of this area."

I get chorus of acknowledgments in return, spoken with varying degrees of uncertainty.

I'm speeding toward a drop several stories high, but for me, everything's slowing down. Focusing on my breathing, I let my emotions flow through me, letting them become an interface for reality instead of letting them rule me.

There is anger. But I am not the anger. I simply observe it.

There is excitement. But I am not the excitement. I simply use it.

There is fear. But I am not the fear. I simply wield it.

I overclock.

Using my datasphere to access the elevator's interface, I smack the EMERGENCY OPEN button, but nothing happens. The ground rushes closer, and I work at the gap between the doors with my fingers, trying to pry them open. A trimmed nail cracks off, and the pain is sharp and sudden, but I don't let it stop me.

With seconds to spare, I back up, unholstering my blaster and pulling the trigger once, twice. A melted section of hardened plastic glows before me, just big enough for me to cannonball through—which I do, leaping, bringing my legs up to my chest and holding them there by the ankles.

I pass through the smoldering hole just as the capsule leaves the torn tube to shoot toward the ground. For a moment, it feels like I'm flying, suspended at the peak of my parabola.

Then, I'm hurtling toward the ground, every muscle relaxed.

When I hit, everything contracts in sequence: first my calves, then my knees, then my thighs and hamstrings, followed by my abs and chest and arms, all acting in concert to absorb the impact of hitting the ground. A slow-motion symphony that I control utterly.

I'm coming in at a slight angle, and I use my momentum to throw myself forward, channeling the impact into a roll. As I exit into a run, my neck and back and shoulders sing in pain. But I'm up and ready for action. That's a small miracle in itself.

The tangle of fallen redwoods presents little challenge to me, and I hurl myself over, foot glancing off a trunk to propel myself up and over the jagged barrier.

Immediately, I stop overclocking. Through the shattered trunks, I can see the other Troubleshooters and their bots sprinting from the elevators toward me. The battling constructs ignore them, and soon, my men are climbing up and over the mess of trees to form up nearby.

I chose to exit on this side because of the relative lack of hostiles, which affords us a moment to regroup. Yes, the crackle of laserfire reaches us from every direction, but here it's relatively quiet.

"You should not have survived that fall intact," Shimura says, his face grave.

"Not with just Guardsman training," I say, nodding. "Shiva training's a bit different."

Immediately, I wish I hadn't said it. A couple of the other men are looking at me with awe, and I need their minds on the fight.

"We're Troubleshooters," I tell them, my voice low but emphatic, "and normally it takes just one of us to turn the tide of a fight. Right now, there are eight of us. Stick with me, follow my orders without hesitation, and we'll hit these bastards hard enough to make them question everything.

"Our first objective is to head for the place where I spoke to their leaders, to see if any of them have stuck around to govern during the crisis." I know the Cadogans don't actually have 'leaders' or whatever, but it's just easier to say right now. "Bounding overwatch, people. I know we're used to operating alone, but you've all run the drills. Reach back into your training and work together to keep each other alive. Divide yourselves into our squadrons from outside the Sphere—Kincaid, you go with Shimura's squad to replace Halsey. My squad moves first. Shimura, yours will provide suppressing fire, then leapfrog."

On the way down, I put together a dynamic map of the battlefield, figuring out where the most contested areas were from above and using my datasphere's predictive software to model where units would likely end up over the next twenty minutes.

Using it, I now plot a course through the town to the clamshell building where I had my friendly little meeting with the Cadogans.

The software isn't perfect. We get into firefights twice, with the leapfrogging team running for cover while the other suppresses enemy fire. Both times, the leapfrogging team—first it's mine, then it's Shimura's—is able to find a decent angle, forcing the enemy back enough to allow the rear team to move forward.

Our opposition quickly falls apart. I'd love to stay and put paid to more of Fairfax's soldiers, but we need to stay focused. Enlisting the aid of the Cadogan government will hopefully prove to be a force multiplier in this fight. Barring that, I'll just kill Fairfax himself.

The constructs are the biggest unknown. It's impossible to tell which ones are on our side, or if the ones who are would even recognize us as friendlies. They move fast, preceded only by a rumble which can be hard to notice in the heat of combat. When they appear, they move quickly, and whenever we see one I tell the men to hold their fire unless one of them is clearly about to engage us.

But they don't engage. The constructs seem to be seeking each other out. Is this really a civil war between the Cadogans who want to help Fairfax and those who don't? Or has he found a way to control some of the beats?

At last, we reach the clamshell, which seems to have been spared from the fighting. We sweep inside with blaster and laser pistols raised, getting the drop on a squad's worth of security forces near the center of the vast chamber, where I spoke to the assembled Cadogan government earlier.

They start to raise their weapons, but I bark the order for my Troubleshooters to lower theirs. "We're friends," I yell, and a few of the guards glance toward the small group huddled beyond them, near the bottom row of the desks.

"Commander Pikeman," Brendan Cadogan calls across the room, and that seems to make the guards relax. They reholster their weapons, though we keep ours out, in case someone less friendly comes in behind us.

I motion for two Troubleshooters to stay at the door and watch for such an outcome. That done, I continue across the clamshell.

"Why are there constructs fighting constructs out there?" I ask as we near the Cadogan Prime Producer, who's sitting with his legs dangling from the first raised platform, surrounded by much younger attendants. His dress shirt is untucked, now, spilling over his thighs. "Are those all of Cadogan make?"

The Prime Producer's eyes fall to the floor. "It seems…." He coughs, eyes darting.

"We don't have much time," I urge.

"You're right," he says, gaze finally rising to meet mine. "We don't. It seems the debate over whether to join with Fairfax was much less academic than I assumed. It's all very un-Cadogan like, but after you left to confront Fairfax, Harriet, my own cousin, declared my government illegitimate. She accused me of using my position to artificially inflate my level of output just to hold power. Then she declared that she and her supporters would aid Fairfax in overthrowing my government."

I refrain from asking if he really did rig things in his favor, since the answer will probably be "no," whether that's true or not. "Let me guess. Plenty of the constructs supported her?"

"Of course. I was blind not to see it before, but…of *course* they would support an initiative to revitalize the real, especially one that looks so promising."

"You would call what Fairfax is doing *promising?*" Shimura interjects, and I glance at him.

"Misguided, but…well, promising is one word. There's no doubt he's poised to usher in a new era, one focused on the real instead of the Subverse. But of course he's going about it in entirely the wrong way."

I nod. "Which is why we need to stop wasting time talking and focus on stopping him."

"Most of my forces are concentrated on doing exactly that," Brendan Cadogan says. "But according to the most recent reports, I fear they won't be able to pull it off. As we speak, Fairfax presses closer and closer to the station's master control room. Once he's taken that, he'll have the Sphere, and we'll all be at his mercy."

"Not if I can help it. Where's the master control?"

Cadogan's gaze had fallen to the floor again, but now he looks up, casting his eyes across the assembled Troubleshooters as if seeing us for the first time. With that, he rises, adjusting his dress shirt around his waist.

"Follow me."

6

I call for the Troubleshooters guarding the door to join us, on the double.

"You there," I say to the security guards lingering nearby. "Set up a watch near the entrance, for Fount's sake. You're asking to get mowed down."

A few sullen looks greet my advice, but their leader taps a couple of them on the shoulder, and the pair sprints across the clamshell toward the doors.

Cadogan's already underway, heading toward the side of the building, and I motion for the Troubleshooters and their bots to follow, the latter's feet clanking softly across the marble floor.

The Prime Producer leads us to an unremarkable doorway off to the right, artfully concealed behind the rows of desks. It slides upward into the wall, and we continue through into a square room whose only feature is a large circle cut into the floor.

"What's this?" I ask.

"A gateway," Cadogan says. "One of many leading to the Sphere's R&D Hemisphere. That's where the master control room is located. I'll feed that hemisphere's architectural blueprint to you now."

The package hits my datasphere, and I open it to find a breathtakingly large facility represented in a 3D blue-and-white diagram. Our point of ingress flashes green.

"The control room resides at the highest point. There are a series of lifts that will take you there, but that route poses a risk. Should Fairfax gain the master control room while you're using them to ascend, you will be at his mercy."

Closing out the blueprint, I say, "I assume we stand on the circle?"

"Yes. Do you intend to take the lifts?"

"Mark them out on the map for me. Sorry, but I don't have time to discuss my intentions with you, and I don't really have a reason to fully trust you. Either way, thanks for your help."

Brendan Cadogan bows his head and says nothing else. Once the Troubleshooters and their bots are all gathered onto the circle, Cadogan raises his hand, then the floor *flips*.

Apparently, the Cadogans' mastery over gravity is leagues beyond the rest of the galaxy. The platform continues to attract us to it, even after it rotates upside-down. Even more startling, the massive, white-and-gray facility that rears above us is oriented in the opposite direction from the city below. That isn't supposed to be possible—gravity generators are supposed to exert an equal force downward, which structures are normally designed to absorb. According to everything I know about gravity generation, this facility should be repelled from the surface it rests on, to tear through the Sphere's shell and launch into space. But it seems sturdy enough to me, and we aren't repelled, either.

A series of ramps, platforms and buildings make up the facility, in a rough pyramid shape. The Sphere's architects had just as much space to work with in this hemisphere as on the city-side, but instead of filling the upper portion with an artificial sky, they used nearly every available inch for labs and supply sheds and cafeterias and admin buildings and so on. They're all neatly labeled on the blueprint, and at the top sits the master control room, a sturdy block sitting precariously on stilts, with multiple ramps leading up to it. An elevator projects from the control room's roof, just as several other tubes rise up from various parts of the facility, some stretching to the ceiling kilometers overhead, others connecting to various parts of the structure.

"Master Chief, take your squad up the lifts—I'll forward you the blueprint Cadogan sent me. My squad will take the long way, up stairs, ramps, and ladders. Neither approach is very attractive, but I don't think the Cadogans designed this thing with tactical considerations in mind."

After a brief study of the blueprint, Shimura nods. "We'll be up well before you, Commander. Should we attempt to take the control room once we get there?"

"I'll make that call when the time comes. Before I can say, I need to know what the conditions are like up there."

Shimura nods again. "Remember your training, Guardsman. Shiva. Visit defeat on our enemies."

"I'm not a Shiva yet. But thanks. You too."

With that, Shimura jogs off with his squad, weapons raised and at the ready. I motion for my squad to follow, and we head up the first ramp.

The facility's sheer verticality, plus the way it winds back on itself, makes bounding overwatch so limited a tactic as to be basically useless. To compensate, I keep a close eye on our route upward, looking for places where enemies might lie in wait, hoping to ambush us.

For the first twenty minutes of the journey, things are unsettlingly quiet. The only challenge to our ascent is the ascent itself. Troubleshooters pride themselves on maintaining rigorous exercise regimens, but even I'm starting to breathe heavier after hauling myself up so many ramps and staircases. Too often, the quickest route is up a ladder, so there's been a few of those too, some of them stretching multiple stories. I have the boys climb up them two at a time, with the others ready to lay down suppressing fire from the bottom of the ladder, and then from the top the second we get some guys there. The ladders make us pretty vulnerable, but usually the alternative involves venturing too far out of our way across horizontal boardwalks packed with research buildings.

I'm ascending a ramp leading to a platform halfway between one level and the next when I get a weird spike of anxiety that makes me want to turn around. Then my datasphere lights up black near the top of my vision, and laserfire crackles. I throw myself sideways, and two of our bots step up, laser pistols already snapped into place to return fire.

"Let's go," I subvocalize to the others, pushing up the ramp as the bots continue laying down suppressing fire.

Our assailants occupy the roof of a supply shed on the next level, which offers them a commanding view of the ramp. One Troubleshooter stays behind with his combat bot, waiting to see if our ambushers will pop up again, while I lead the other two and their bots up to the next level.

"Circle around the shed and see if you can find a way onto the roof," I say, hauling myself onto a metal crate that sits near the top of the ramp. Crouching on top of it, I rise to my full height, leading with my blaster—to come face to face with a surprised soldier crouching on the roof near my side, his laser pistol pointing in the direction of the ramp.

He begins to swing it toward me, and I put a blaster bolt into his throat, flinging him back, where he slides off the shed and falls toward the bots below.

The men and bots I sent around make it onto the roof, and they clean up whoever's left up there with laserfire.

"Clear," a voice subvocalizes into my ear.

"Affirmative," I say.

It's not often I get to work with men who have the hair-trigger responses Guardsman training drills into you. That training truly is for life. If someone fires on you, you get to safety and shoot back, without thinking about it. Barring that, you shoot back right away. More often than not, your adversary will be taken off by your quick response. That unthinking reaction that was drilled into our brains with sim after sim.

Something odd happened as I was going up that ramp, though —a spike of anxiety that was almost directional. It came right before my datasphere warned me off the soldiers about to shoot at me. Cal once said that eventually, I'd get to the point where I wouldn't need my datasphere to warn me of impending attacks. Is this the beginning of that?

"We're in position," Shimura's voice says suddenly into my ear.

"Give me a sitrep, Master Chief."

"Fairfax is on the master control's doorstep, pushing hard. The security detail inside is holding fast for now, but I get the sense they're about to crumble. Orders?"

I narrow my eyes in thought. "How many soldiers does he have with him?"

"Too many for us to engage alone. But I think if we're stealthy, we can work our way around and join the guards inside the control room. Help them shore up their defenses, hopefully keep Fairfax at bay till you get here."

"Do it. And give that bastard my regards." I switch off the channel. Come on," I say to the others as they gather at the top of the ramp. "Fairfax is almost inside the Sphere's control room. We need to move fast so we can back up Shimura."

"But we just started encountering resistance," says Baker, a Troubleshooter who's also a commander. "This is the worst time to start pushing hard. We'll get taken apart."

I stare Baker in his eyes, and he holds his ground. "What did I say about following my orders unquestioningly?"

"Funny thing for you to say, Pikeman," he says, with a hint of a sneer on his lips.

Great. Insubordination, now. At this stage of the game.

"Tell you what, Baker. If your balls have shrunk back into your stomach, I'll take the lead. If I get 'taken apart,' then you run back down the facility crying. Sound good?"

Baker says nothing, his jaw tight, but no one else complains.

"Let's go," I bark, consciously deepening my breath.

7

There is fatigue. But I am not the fatigue. Instead, I overcome it.

There is irritation. But I am not the irritation. Instead, I arm myself with it.

There is determination. But I am not the determination. Instead, I cloak myself with it.

Overclocked, my vision sharpens—the ramps, platforms, and stairways of the facility jumping into sharp relief. My mind didn't feel foggy before, but now it feels clear as a summer's day. My brain's ability to analyze the blueprint jumps, and I immediately identify a nearby stairway that climbs the side of the facility, offering poor positioning to anyone lurking above. Any soldiers below might shoot at us, but we'd also have the height advantage on them.

I lead us up two more levels without encountering any more resistance.

Then, ascending a long, gentle ramp up to the next level, I experience another anxiety spike. A heartbeat later, three dark spots appear on my datasphere. Without hesitation, I throw myself forward, laserfire crackling behind me. Whirling, I raise my blaster, loosing three pure-white bolts in quick succession.

Three soldiers are thrown back with holes seared into their faces and necks. A fourth soldier is fiddling with his weapon—clearly, he wasn't ready for us to appear. Stricken, he drops the weapon and raises his hands.

My finger tightens on the trigger, then loosens.

Restraint.

"Hold your fire," I subvocalize to the Troubleshooter behind me, who's coming up the ramp after me with laser rifle raised.

The soldier starts to tremble as I approach him, his blue-lit helmet suddenly not so menacing. I snatch up his weapon, safety it, and eject the charge pack before flinging the rifle off the platform to spin through hundreds of feet to one of the bottom levels.

"Give me your other charge packs," I bark, and the soldier unclips them from his belt, handing them over. They look compatible with the weaponry the three Troubleshooters with me are carrying, so I distribute them. "Now go get your rifle." He hesitates, and I yell: "Run!"

He runs, sprinting down the ramp, almost tumbling over the side in his haste.

"Wouldn't it be easier to just shoot him?" Baker says.

I frown. "Not for me. Not anymore."

We press onward, with me on point, disabling most of our attackers before they can do any damage. These regular grunts don't pose much of a threat to me anymore. At least, not when I'm overclocked—which poses its own threat. I can almost feel it wearing out my body, my energy reserves stretched out like jam spread too thin. But we're tearing through the enemy resistance, getting ever closer to the top, and that's what matters right now.

At last, we arrive, topping the final ramp leading to the platform that sits just below the master control. My breathing is ragged, and my pulse pounds through my head. It's almost like the tail end of a caffeine spike, when your body begins to feel hollow and shaky, except it's like I drank a few gallons of coffee all at once.

Fairfax is ahead, standing arrogantly out in the open while his men crouch at the bottom of the ramp that leads up to the control room. They're firing up at the people inside.

Meanwhile, the half-bot, half-man is facing us, hands spread. That he knew we were coming is no surprise—he's probably linked to the dataspheres of his men distributed throughout the facility.

"Pikeman," he calls, hand resting on the pommel of his scabbarded sword. "I've already killed you once. Do I have to do it again?"

"I'm standing here, aren't I?"

"Very well. I know why you've come. You believe that if you kill me, you'll have lopped the head off of the snake that is my operation. And maybe that's true. But there's no need to turn this platform into a shooting gallery—that wouldn't end well for your men, anyway, given how many soldiers I have inside the Sphere to call on. Let's face each other in single combat, and decide the outcome that way."

"Fine. A shootout?"

"I was thinking fisticuffs."

Removing my gun belt, I hand it off to Baker, who's wearing an incredulous expression. Fairfax removes the strap both his blaster and scabbard hang from. And we approach each other across the metal plateau.

"This reminds me of old times," Fairfax says.

"Me too. I remember you winning our last match by using your sword. Looks like you won't be able to cheat, this time."

"Oh, I always find a way to cheat." We're circling each other, fists raised to just below our chins, Fairfax's blue eyes blazing above his.

Suddenly, those eyes turn white, flashing brilliantly. Starbursts blossom in my vision, and Fairfax charges across the metal toward me.

I sidestep at the last minute, throwing a clumsy elbow him. He grabs it, using it to heave me toward the side of the platform. I stagger toward it, managing to keep my feet while trying desperately to blink away the light.

"Bastard," I spit, turning, trying to triangulate his position by the sound of his boots scuffing across the metal.

"Don't get too upset," Fairfax says, laughing. "You can't be blamed for an overreliance on vision, and it's far from the only failing of the human body."

My sight is starting to return, and I'm able to pivot away as Fairfax rushes in, sending a fist toward my side. It glances off my ribcage, and I stumble backward, but I keep my footing. Then a boot flashes out, taking me in the stomach, and the wind rushes out of my lungs. I double over, clutching my abdomen.

"The nice thing is, I can take all the time I need to make this point," Fairfax says. "The Sphere is all but mine. Both landing bays are shut down, and I've already taken the city. You and your men inside that control room are all that stands between me and freeing the Allfather. Once you've been dealt with, the new era will begin."

Fairfax steps forward to sidekick me, but I step into it, gripping his leg and barreling forward, throwing him off-balance. He falls backward, hands shooting back to catch himself before he wrenches his leg away. I step in farther, chopping at his throat, but he rises, deflecting the blow with his shoulder.

We circle each other once again. "The time of the mere human is over," Fairfax says. "The beings that will rise up next to rule over the galaxy will *transcend* humanity. They'll have none of the human limitations of intellect or physical ability. They will be immortal."

"Immortality's been your problem all along," I say, chuckling.

The levity seems to get to Fairfax more than the words do, and his eyes glow more fiercely. They flash white again, and I throw a hand before my eyes, reeling.

Taking the opportunity, Fairfax charges.

I duck low, tackling his legs and letting his momentum carry him over my back, sending him to the floor in a heap. Turning, I stomp on his fleshy arm, his only human part visible. Fairfax grunts, pulling away, and I aim a savage kick into his side to help him along.

"How many times do you think a cheap trick like that's going to work, Rod?" I say, sneering. It was an easy thing to set my data-sphere to briefly darken my vision at the onset of abnormally bright light.

Ignoring the strung-out feeling of overclocking for too long, I gather my will, then rush my adversary, raining a series of lighting blows on his head, throat, and torso. Fairfax's hands flicker with movement almost as fast, but I'm getting through—with knuckles to the throat, a jab to his sternum, a slap to the side of his head that seems to disorient him.

I end with a boot planted in his stomach that sends him staggering backward.

"Commander!" It's Baker, yelling from the edge of the platform.

"What?" I snap, eyeing Fairfax to watch for any sudden movements.

"He was baiting you, to buy time. His men are rushing up through the facility toward us. We're going to be overrun within a couple minutes."

I glare at Fairfax. "Why'd you take off your sword? Why challenge me to fight one-on-one?"

"Because I knew you were stupid enough to agree. With your men flanking me from inside the control room *and* from the ramp, you might have actually gotten something done. Now, you're about to be crushed under the boots of my army. I told you. I *always* find a way to cheat."

"Commander Pikeman." It's Shimura's voice, dropping right into my thoughts.

"Speak to me, Master Chief," I subvocalize back.

"The Cadogan security guards in here with us can see all the men pouring up through the facility. It's only a matter of time before they overrun the control room, and once they do, they'll lock down the Sphere. There'll be no escape."

"Your point?"

"You have to escape, Joe. You need to leave, now. Get away from here, and find some other way to stop Fairfax."

"What about you?"

"The men are ready to stay and hold the control room, to buy you time to get out."

"No. Unacceptable."

"It's the only option, Joe. The alternative is all of us dying. Now are you going to stay here and argue with me—dishonor us, by squandering the gift we're willing to die in order to give you? To give to the galaxy?"

I grit my teeth, and my eyes start to sting. "Shimura…thank you. Thank you for everything. I'll never forget your sacrifice, and I'll make sure the galaxy doesn't forget, either."

"I know it. Now, go. There's an elevator leading to the upper landing bay on the other side of the master control room."

Fairfax chooses that moment to rush at me, and I meet him with a knee that rockets into the groin, every muscle in my leg and stomach contracting to send him staggering backward.

That done, I turn and hold up my hands. *"Toss me my blaster,"* I subvocalize, and Baker heaves the gun belt through the air. I catch it by the holster, thumb already on the clasp, which I flick open and wrench out the weapon. "Open fire on the man-bot!" I yell, not bothering to subvocalize now.

As the Troubleshooters focus fire on Fairfax, I spam bolts at the backs of his men beyond, each shot precision-targeted. A couple of them manage to get out of the way, alerted by my order, but eight of them fall. For his part, Fairfax is stumbling backward, his skin and circuitry pockmarked and twisted by laserfire.

"To me!" I scream. "*Move!*"

With that, I stop overclocking, and the weight of the accumulated stress and strain I've placed on my body comes crashing down. Almost, it knocks me to the metal, but that isn't an option. It can't be. Not after the sacrifice Shimura just put on the table.

I force myself to get moving, and then we're all sprinting around the platform, toward the side with the elevator. I subvocalize orders to Harmony to get the *Ares* and the other Broadswords out of the southern landing bay and straight to the northern one as fast as they can.

On the next plateau down, soldiers are rushing toward the stairs and ramps, and I slap in a fresh charge pack to unleash a storm of blaster fire on their heads. Behind me, the remaining four Troubleshooters and their bots are running and gunning as well as they can.

We reach the elevator, whose doors open at my command. Then we pour in, packing tightly into the round passenger compartment. I will it to shoot upward, and it does, the facility dropping away below us.

It's a much shorter trip from the top of the facility to the ceiling than it was from the city to the Sphere's southern landing bay. We jet through the barrier, the elevator rotating upside-down just past it to orient us with the landing bay's gravity.

The bay is swarming with Fairfax's men—more than I would have thought possible. Those other warships must have been carrying troops and dropships too, for this many soldiers to be here.

Rockets start to sail toward the tube we're in, two of them screaming past us as we descend. One of them misses by what seems like inches. But we're completely helpless in here. Even if I thought I could overclock right now, I wouldn't be able to survive a drop like this, and my brothers certainly wouldn't either.

Wow. That's the first time I thought about the Troubleshooters around me as my brothers. But it's true, I realize, of every one of them. Even Baker.

A third rocket streams up from one of the platoons below, and this time it seems certain to hit—whether above or below our capsule, I don't know. Either way, it's sure to be catastrophic, since I'm pretty sure these things operate using vacuums. Pierce the vacuum, and we become sitting ducks.

But then, blue laser light flickers out of nowhere, detonating the rocket before it hits us. Looking up, I see the *Ares* charging toward us, at the head of five other Broadswords.

"Harm! How'd you get here so fast?"

"You kidding? We've been out of the other landing bay for fifteen minutes, now. Place became way too hot to hang around in. Besides, Brendan Cadogan told us what you were doing, so we figured you'd probably need us up here anyway."

"Thank Fount someone kept you updated." I've never been great at keeping my crew abreast of things, which could have spelled disaster here.

The Broadswords' laser turrets hammer the forces below, sending them into disarray. Rockets stream toward the ships on intercept courses, but Harmony and the uploads piloting the other ships make dodging them look like child's play.

By the time the elevator reaches the base, the Broadswords have cleared a wide swath around it of hostiles, and we rush out toward our respective ships. Baker's ship was destroyed, so he takes Shimura's—a grim necessity, and not one we have time to debate.

"You lost two more ships, then?" I ask Harmony as soon as the inner airlock hatch hisses open, and I jog to the command seat.

"Yeah. I see you're down some people, too."

"Half our number," I say, my voice tight. "But we'll repay Fairfax a thousandfold. For now, just get us out of here."

8

As one, six Broadswords speed out of a tunnel leading from the Cadogan Sphere's northern landing bay.

The moment we do, Fairfax's battle group starts hammering us.

"They've completely mopped up the Sphere's fighter drone fleet," Marissa says, bent over the OPO station. "Neutralized a lot of the point defense turrets, too. They can focus entirely on us, now."

"What do we do, Captain?" Harmony asks, not looking at me as she takes the *Ares* through a series of tight evasive maneuvers.

"How are the enemy ships arranged?"

"Mostly on the same side of the Sphere where we left them. The *Ekhidnades* is just sitting there, but the other four warships are converging on us."

"All right. Take us around the Sphere to buy time. Asterisk, prepare missile countermeasures. Standby to deploy decoy drones."

"Aye."

The decoys don't do much in battle, since they don't have the same mobility as a Broadsword, and so they're quickly found out in combat situations. But with their Broadsword-like EM signatures, when retreating they can throw off pursuers, at least for a time.

Except, I'm not sure retreat is the right move. Well…I *am* sure we can't hang around here, but where are we supposed to go? If we leave the gas cloud, Fairfax's warships will track us easily. But if we head deeper into it, we'll be flying completely blind, with no way to navigate to slip coords that lead deeper into the galaxy.

"All warships except the *Ekhidnades* are orbiting the sphere," Marissa says. "Ten missiles inbound."

That makes up my mind. If we don't leave now, we'll end up running headlong into one of the warships—probably Fairfax's. "Acknowledged. TOPO, take us deeper into the Moor. Ensign, deploy decoy drones now, and Chief Aphrodite, tell the other crews to follow closely, standing by to do the same on my mark."

All three crewmembers give some variation of "Yes, sir," then they get to work.

On the 3D tactical display, I watch the decoy drones leave their bays from under the Broadswords—three from each, making eighteen. The drones absorb all but two of the missiles, which slip past them, and I get on a squadron-wide channel, there being no time to relay the next order through Marissa.

"All ships focus laserfire on the lead missile."

Light flickers through the gas and debris, exploding the first rocket.

"Now the next."

The six Broadswords work in tandem to perform the feat.

With that, Harmony thrusts laterally, hard, putting the *Ares* on a course perpendicular to her prior orbit, hugging the Cadogan Sphere. I can see what she's up to: she's hoping to bypass the pursuing warships and slip into the cloud unnoticed while the decoys distract them.

No such luck. The warships must have anticipated the maneuver—two of them are coming around the sphere the wrong way. And Fairfax's destroyer approaches from the opposite direction, threatening to pincer us.

"Ten more missiles inbound, Captain," Marissa says, sounding strained.

"Punch it, Harmony. Marissa, tell the Broadsword crew that lacks a Troubleshooter to expend their missile stores on absorbing the enemy fire."

"A-aye," Marissa says uncertainly, looking at me with eyes widened in surprise and hurt.

What is she—? Oh, shit. I said her real name, didn't I? Fount damn it. The strain is getting to me. Well, there's no going back now. A glance at Asterisk tells me that maybe he didn't hear.

The empty Broadsword's crew of uploads manages to take down four of the incoming missiles before absorbing the next rocket with its hull. The explosion cripples her main engine, and the next bird slams into her stern, turning the ship into a ball of flame.

Four more rockets still on our tail. The more agile Broadswords are outstripping the bulkier warships, now, and I doubt their even their sensor drones can see us through the murk. But their missiles are still locked on.

"All ships, focus fire on the missile I'm designating."

The other ships comply, and we take it down. The next goes down just as easily.

The last two rockets connect with Baker's Broadsword, neutralizing it.

"*Damn it!*" I yell, and Belflower shoots me a concerned look. I never let my emotions run me, but—Fount, how did this happen? I was on the verge of *defeating* Fairfax. Of ending all this. But he outsmarted me, and killed most of my men. Now we're on the run with no clue what to do next.

"I think we lost them, sir," Marissa says, still sounding sullen from my slip-up with her name. That almost makes me want to laugh in her face. We have *much* bigger problems right now.

"Great," I mutter, and the word comes out flat, emotionless. I can see my crew's morale is about as poor as mine is: the way their shoulders slump almost imperceptibly, their hands moving sluggishly across their consoles.

Fount. What a mess.

ARES

1

I'm sitting on my bunk, head in hands, trying not to think about how badly I've screwed up this mission—this quest, though somehow it seems absurd to call it that now.

"Stupid," I mutter.

Cal hasn't appeared to me since before I arrived at the Sphere, which seems ominous all by itself. After all the training we put in, he was probably banking on my next encounter with Fairfax to be the big one. The one where I put an end to all this. Not so much.

I've been awake since before we arrived at the Cadogan Sphere, but I'm afraid to go to sleep, because I expect the nightmares to be worse than ever. Losing Shimura and the other Troubleshooters just so I could escape eats at me like nothing has before. Taking them with me into the Core was supposed to give me an edge, but Fairfax made short work of them. Worse: I feel like if I'd handled things differently, they'd still be alive.

A message alert pops into my vision. It's from Marissa. No doubt she wants to berate me for slipping up and saying her real name in front of the crew.

But you know what? It's nothing more than I deserve, so I open the message.

"Hey," it reads. "Can I come in?"

She wants me to give her access to my cabin? That's sure to raise eyebrows with the crew. Well, with Asterisk, anyway. He's the only one who might still be in the dark about who Marissa is.

Nevertheless, I grant her the necessary permission, and she appears a few seconds later, standing near the bolted-down desk.

"I'm sorry," I tell her, staring at the floor, resisting the urge to plant my face in my hands again. "I screwed up, and I don't know how to make it right."

"What are you talking about?"

"Using your real name in front of the crew. The pressure of trying to escape got to me, and—"

I look up. Marissa's shaking her head, smiling wanly. But that's not why my heart catches in my throat.

Her avatar…it's not the curvy blond of Aphrodite. Instead, it's how she used to look—pale and lithe, with cascading midnight hair and deep brown eyes. I'm speechless as memories come flooding back, of times spent wrapped in each other's arms back in Brinktown, hiding away in our warehouse loft from the world.

"Don't worry about the name, Joe. I'd forgotten about it."

"Uh…seriously?"

"Sure. We have way bigger things to worry about, right? At this point, who cares if my father finds out I joined the Guard?"

"Yeah. That's kind of what I was thinking, actually."

"Besides, I'm not sure Asterisk even heard you say it, or if he would know who 'Marissa' is, even if he did. He hasn't brought it up, so…"

"Good," I say, nodding. "Wait. Why are you here, then?"

She shrugs. "I was having an encrypted text conversation with Harmony, to keep it from the others. We're worried about you, Joe. Now isn't the time for you to hold yourself apart from us, you know. Even if you think you're headed toward your death…that's all the more reason to pull together, actually."

She crosses the room to sit on the bunk beside me. It's weird not to feel her weight there. Yes, there are datasphere mods I can install to enhance the "physicality" of uploads I interact with, but I've never had much desire to use them. I'm against anything that masks or disrupts my experience of the real.

"I'm not sure there's much for us to talk about," I say. "I mean, it is what it is. Stopping Fairfax will involve dying. Just like every Shiva that's come before me."

"Well, that's funny. When I first came in here, you looked totally defeated. But according to what I'm hearing, you believe you still have a chance of stopping him."

"Well, I have no idea how. I just know I have no plans of giving up."

"That's a start," Marissa says, her smile spreading across her cheeks. Despite their paleness, rosy redness dots each of them. That's not artifice—she had that natural blush even in her biological form. "But haven't you picked up on any signs that there might be something different about you? About the way you interact with the Fount, the way you wield it?"

"I guess. But I don't think it's in line with the Seven Ideals to consider I might succeed where other Shiva haven't."

"You might, though. It's very possible you could defeat Fairfax without dying yourself. And then you'll have the rest of your life to lead." Marissa slides her hand across the bed until it rests on mine. I can't feel her touch, but knowing it's there is something.

"What if he manages to bring the Allfather into the real?" I say. "I'm not sure I'd be able to defeat the Allfather. Even if I overclock for so long that it kills me."

"Then I guess you have no option but to stop Fairfax from doing that," Marissa murmurs.

She's so beautiful. Naturally so. As striking as her Aphrodite avatar is, she's like a perfectly sculpted stature—to be admired from afar, but I can't imagine actually holding her. As for Marissa, I have plenty of memories testifying just how sweet it is to hold her. To be with her.

For a moment, I want nothing more than to kiss her. I can't, of course. She's an upload. She isn't actually real. I could jump into a sim and delude myself about that, but it would be the most foolish thing I could do.

I pull my hand away. "I need to sleep. I can't think about what we're supposed to do next until I do. My head's all muddled."

"All right," she says, her smile replaced by a creased brow. "Just think on what I said, Joe. Okay?"

"Yeah. Sure."

With that, she vanishes from my cabin, and I lie back on my pillow. Mourning the real Marissa.

SINGULARITY MOOR

1

Traveling through Singularity Moor offers a strange experience. Few things in my Troubleshooting career have brought me such a sustained, consistent level of creeping dread.

The fear that we'll be lost in here forever…the fear that we'll stumble into a black hole. We'll know if that happens right away, because each black hole sucks in the cloud around it. But encountering a patch of clear space will offer no warning. It will only mean we've crossed the singularity's event horizon. We'd be doomed.

At least the Moor should thwart Fairfax as much as it does us. Not that it matters. I don't see us making it to the Core through here, and if we do, it will almost certainly be too late. From the Cadogan Sphere, Fairfax will be able to escape the cloud easily, but we're flying blind. Deeper and deeper into the Moor.

"We could reverse course," Harmony muses. She's sitting in the command seat, and I'm leaning against her TOPO station. "Use the *Ares'* accelerometer memory to calculate each turn's degree. It would get us back to the Sphere, at least, and from there we should be able to find our way out."

"Fairfax will know that's a possibility for us," I say. "And he'll have something waiting for us at that location, for a long time. The chances of him doing otherwise are zero, if you ask me."

"I know. But it's a thought."

It is. And I'm still mulling it over. "I guess we could follow our trajectory back until we're almost at the Sphere, then deviate from it. Aim to come out of the cloud well away from where Fairfax could detect us."

Harmony's nodding. "To be sure we avoid him, it would take a lot longer. But it could be done. And from there, we could head for the next slip coords into the Core."

"The alternative is to wander inside the Moor for years, potentially."

"Well, we could reach the closest star system in a couple weeks, if we knew what direction to go in. But I know what you mean."

I push myself off from the railing of Harmony's station. "All right. You'd better climb in there and strap in. Let's activate the crew and get started."

But when Marissa appears at the OPO station, she's frowning. "Joe. I was about to contact you. I just received a brainprint."

That gives me pause. I narrow my eyes. "Out *here?* From who?"

"It's from Soren."

I feel my body tense involuntarily in the command seat. Soren. If he's close enough to send a brainprint, it means Fairfax is probably near, too. But how? On our way from the Sphere, we made sure to randomize our course enough that the chances of successful pursuit were so close to zero it should have made no difference.

"Do you want to take the brainprint now?" Marissa asks.

"No. Try never. I have nothing to say to Soren Garrett." The fact of the brainprint's arrival has sent me for a loop, though, that's for sure. I shake my head a little, to clear it, then turn to Harmony. "All we can do is assume their finding us is a massive fluke and continue to randomize our course. Let's lay on some more speed, too. It should be impossible for them to get within firing range, but I'm not taking any chances."

Sitting with the mystery a few seconds more, it occurs to me that Fairfax may have deployed dozens of sensor drones throughout the gas cloud, in dozens of random directions, all carrying a copy of Soren's brainprint. No doubt it's a ploy to use our years of friendship to somehow win my trust enough to stop and meet with him, after which Fairfax and his goons would appear and vaporize my ship. Seems kind of stupid, since after Persephone there's no way I'm trusting that asshole, but it's also the only thing that makes sense.

"OPO, check with the other Broadswords to see whether they've received any transmissions." The four remaining Guard ships are flying in tight formation, to make sure we can keep in close contact and avoid losing each other in the cloud.

Marissa's shaking her head. "Nothing, sir. It's just us. It —oh, Fount."

"What? What is it?" This whole experience has me twitchier than I've been since a boy on the streets of Brinktown.

It turns out I'm right to be worried.

"Incoming missiles, Captain," Marissa says. "Four of them."

2

"Harmony, tax the Becker drive as much as she'll handle," I bark. "Max acceleration."

"Aye." She punches a sequence into her console, and in less than a second the acceleration presses me into my seat. Harmony stumbles back from the railing, but the webbing catches her.

Moving this fast through the Moor is pretty close to the stupidest thing we could do, but it's not *the* stupidest—that would be slowing down.

"All Broadswords, focus fire on the lead missile," I say over a wide channel to the other three remaining Troubleshooters.

Together, we manage to explode the first bird within seconds, but the second takes longer, and then I'm forced to have one of the other Broadswords spend two missiles neutralizing the last two incoming rockets before they reach our hull.

"Four more rockets inbound," Marissa says, the words jumbling together in her haste to get them out.

This time, we're only able to remove the first rocket from the board before being forced to expend more missiles to defend our ships. The problem is that out here, deep in the Moor, our visibility is severely limited. Incoming missiles show up on our sensors shortly before they'll impact us, and so we're burning through our missile stores at an unacceptable rate.

But our assailant—who I have to assume is Fairfax—seems to know exactly where we are. Every last missile volley flies true, despite that neither his warships nor his sensor drones are showing up on visual or radar. Are his sensors just better than ours? Or is there something else going on?

The four-missile salvos continue to arrive with merciless regularity, and it's all we can do to keep them off our hulls while fleeing at top speed.

Then, Marissa delivers the news that seems to spell the end: "The *Ekhidnades* just showed up on visual and radar, Captain."

I grit my teeth, saying nothing, knowing what that means: they're gaining on us. The smaller Broadswords are more agile, meaning we can change trajectory much faster, flitting around a warship and dodging its ordnance. But in a long-distance chase like this, the destroyer's more powerful engines are prevailing.

"Another destroyer just appeared," Marissa says, her tone flat, dejected. "And there's the cruiser...and the two frigates. Fairfax brought his entire battle group."

For a moment, I just sit there in shocked silence. I guess I still haven't fully processed the reality that Fairfax is apparently able to track us through the Moor. It still seems like an impossibility to me, but clearly that's not the reality I'm living in. If it were impossible, it would have made sense for Fairfax to remain at the Sphere and consolidate his control over it. To begin his final preparations for going to the Core and bringing the Allfather into physical being.

But considering he clearly *can* track us, of course he'd want to come and deal with us once and for all. Like he said back in the Sphere—once I'm out of the picture, he can complete his objective at his leisure. There's no one else with the slimmest hope of stopping him.

"Four more missiles incoming, sir."

"Acknowledged, Chief."

The birds seem to flash across the ever-shrinking distance between the pursuing warships and our fleeing Broadswords. One goes down to laserfire, and then we spend three more missiles to defend ourselves.

We need to try something else. "All Troubleshooters, launch a pair of missiles each at the *Ekhidnades*."

Seconds later, eight Javelins fly from our ships, heading straight for the destroyer leading the pack.

But neon-blue laserfire flashes out from the surrounding warships. Between that and the destroyer's point defense system, they make depressingly short work of the attack. The warships didn't even decrease their speed, mopping up the volley without slowing down.

It seems this is it. Our missile stores are nearing depletion, and the chasing warships are getting closer and closer. Even staring the end in the face, I can't help but think I've missed something. Something that, if I'd picked up on, would have allowed me to avoid this outcome.

"Four missiles inbound," Marissa says.

I nod. It's like they're toying with us. It would be more efficient to overwhelm us with a barrage we'd have no hope of repelling, but it's as though Fairfax is obsessed with demonstrating his might before grinding me into dust.

We neutralize the current volley, but the next comes too quickly, and two missiles slam into the trailing Broadsword in quick succession. I stare numbly at the blossoming flame, which quickly falls behind as we speed on.

The next barrage takes out a second Broadsword. Now it's just the *Ares* and a Guard ship called the *Ganges*, piloted by Captain Amery.

"It's been a pleasure serving with you all," I say to my crew. "You've served honorably and competently. Harmony, I love you."

"It's not over yet, Dad," she says, but we both know it is.

For a brief moment, Marissa's eyes are on mine, and I see a strange mix of emotions there. Longing, regret, sadness. But no hope.

Slowly, she turns back to her console. "Four missiles inbound," she says, her voice low and barely audible.

I lower my head, eyes closed, waiting for the impact.

"Wait," Marissa says, and my eyes open. "Something else just left the *Ekhidnades*, out of the same landing bay airlock we used during our visit. It's…it's a Broadsword, Captain. The *Hermes*."

"Soren," I snarl. Just had to get in some hits, I guess, before the chance is taken from him forever.

"Sir, he's engaging the approaching missiles from behind!"

I call up the 3D tactical display, unable to accept Marissa's words at face value. But it's true: between our lasers and Soren's, we're eating through the approaching missile volley. Two go down…but they catch up to the *Ganges* before we can take them out. She doesn't explode, but her engines falter, and she starts to fall behind. Lasers spray out from the nearest warship to finish her off.

Every Troubleshooter who accompanied me into the Core has now died on my watch. From Shimura's sacrifice, to the ones who fell as we fled the Sphere…all for what?

But now, Soren's Broadsword blazes with light, laserfire spitting from almost every turret. He also seems to be sending every missile he has on board at the warships, and at the close range, many of the rockets are landing.

At last, the warships are slowing, regrouping to face a threat they clearly didn't expect. They turn their lasers on the *Hermes*, loosing a stream of missiles to end him.

A transmission request flashes on my datasphere—it's from Soren. I accept it.

"Soren, what are you—"

"There's no time for that. I can buy you the room you need to escape, but you need to leave now. You haven't opened my brain-print yet, have you?"

"Uh, no."

"Go, and open it as soon as you can. Deactivate your crew first."

"Why did—"

"Joe, you need to leave now!"

I turn toward the TOPO station. "Harmony, get us out of here. Re-initiate course randomization."

"Aye, Captain," she says, bending over her station's controls.

But my focus is on the visual sensors, and the brilliant display as Soren takes on five warships at once.

His Broadsword exploding is the last thing I see through the gloom of the Moor.

3

"Deactivate crew," I say, and Belflower, Asterisk, and Marissa vanish from their stations.

Harmony glances over her shoulder. "I assume you don't mean me—right? I mean, do I need to go into the cabin or something?"

I shake my head. "Continue randomizing our course while I take this brainprint."

Soren appears in the area between the four stations, where I'd normally position the 3D tactical display. I deny Harmony access to the conversation—not because I don't trust her with its content, but because I need her whole focus on continuing evasive maneuvers. It's bad enough Marissa isn't at her station right now. Fairfax's battle group could reappear through the cloud at any second, and until I have my OPO back, I have no way of knowing. Not without operating the sensors myself.

"Hi," I say, not able to help myself from sounding venomous. The fact Soren just allowed us to escape counts for something, but not much. He still tried to kill me on Persephone Station.

"Joe. Before I say anything else—disable your ship's ability to broadcast. Do it now."

"Why would I want to do that?"

"Because if you don't, Fairfax will be able to track you through the gas cloud. One of your crew is transmitting your location on an encrypted channel. If you disable broadcasting, the signal won't go out."

Eyes widening, I open my mouth to reactivate Marissa, but then I hesitate. What if she's the one transmitting? I should ask Soren which one is actually responsible, first.

But no. I won't believe it's Marissa. I can't.

"Reactivate OPO," I say, and Marissa reappears, blinking at me. "Chief, disable the *Ares'* ability to broadcast." She furrows her brow, and I snap, "Do it now. No questions!"

She turns, punching a few commands into her station's console. "It's done," she says flatly, probably sore that I snapped at her.

"Thanks. Deactivate OPO." I turn to Harmony. "If this asshole's telling the truth, then we should be able to actually escape the *Ekhidnades*, now. Continue evasive maneuvers. Step them up, if you can, Harm."

"Will do," she says, eyebrows slightly raised.

"Wait," Soren says. "Why am I getting the impression that Fairfax has already tracked you through the gas cloud?"

"Because he has."

Soren's face darkens. "So you didn't open my brainprint as soon as you got it. If you had, you would have shut off broadcasting in time to lose him before he caught up to you."

A ringing starts up in my ears, and my vision blurs. Is he really suggesting *I'm* responsible for losing the final three Troubleshooters? Of course, he has no way of knowing they fell. Still...

"I didn't open it right away because I have no reason to trust you, you backstabbing son of a bitch."

My old bunkmate puts up his hands, palms facing me. "Hey, look, Joe. I understand. Trust me. Ever since..." His voice hitches, and he pauses, shaking his head and swallowing. I narrow my eyes. Is he actually on the verge of breaking into tears?

"Ever since what I did to you on Persephone, I haven't been

able to live with myself," he goes on. "I kept telling myself that it was for my family. That Fairfax is going to rise to power, no matter what, so I had to make sure my loved ones have a place in the world that follows. But the more I told myself that, the less I believed it. The fact is, I've always been jealous of you, Joe. Since the day I met you. And the bitterness that jealousy gave birth to has grown and grown, until I struck out at you in the most vicious way I knew how, using the flimsiest excuse. I'm sorry, Joe. You've been nothing but a friend to me, and you're right—I'm nothing but a backstabbing scumbag."

Well, no disagreements there. Except… "What the hell did I ever have that made you jealous, Soren? I came from nothing. You were always your family's golden boy, and the darling of the Subverse, too. Billions of people follow your versecasts."

"Yeah, but not for the reasons that made me start versecasting in the first place. I wanted to gain a big Subverse following by becoming the best Guardsman who ever lived. But you were always better than me—more skilled, more honorable, faster, stronger. Worst of all, you refused to versecast. If you'd started back during Basic, you'd have surpassed me long ago. But you had no interest in it. Somehow, that made it even worse. So I made myself find other ways to gain an audience. Ways that made me feel like shit, like playing on my audience's hatred of people who live in the real. I sold out real humans, people like my own family, just for the fame and wealth. I compromised everything good about me, and I turned into the sort of creature capable of doing what I did on Persephone. Listen, Joe, I don't expect you to ever forgive me. But I need you to know I'm sorry."

I'm staring at the deck, going over all my memories of Soren in light of what he just told me. Bonding with each other back in Basic, when our instructors did everything to drive cadets apart. Repelling the pirate attack on Gauntlet, during Assessment and Selection. Taking it to Rile in Sheen City, even if he did betray me just a few short weeks later.

Now, it's my turn to sound choked-up. "I do forgive you, Soren."

At that, he shakes his head in disbelief. "Fount damn you, Joe. Of course you do." He stares at the bulkhead for a few long moments, swallowing and chewing on his lip. Finally, he continues: "Listen, I don't know how this whole mess with Fairfax is going to end. But if this crazy galaxy will ever allow it, if I can manage to get away from Fairfax, then I'd be honored to fight by your side once again. If you could ever bring yourself to trust me."

I open my mouth to tell him that's impossible, since he just sacrificed himself in order to let the *Ares* escape. But again, he doesn't know that. As far as this version of his consciousness knows, he's still alive, and after we're finished this conversation, the recording will reach him aboard the *Ekhidnades*.

But he's not. Soren's dead, and this brainprint is all that remains of him. No one will see or hear from him again. Least of all his family.

"Of course," I say. "I'd—I'd be honored, too."

"Joe, the crewmember broadcasting your position is your WSO. Asterisk."

I shake my head. "The kid? Why?"

"Because he's no kid. Joe, you have a copy of Jeremy Fairfax's consciousness on your ship. The Allfather. And I doubt getting rid of him is going to be easy."

4

"Thank you, Soren," I hear myself saying. "Thank you for the warning. I'll have to see what I can do."

He nods gravely. "Good luck. I hope to speak with you again someday, Joe."

I nod, unable to lie to him, even now. "Goodbye, old friend." With that, I deactivate Soren, in doing so erasing the last trace of him from the universe.

For the moment, I have no idea what to do. I lean back in the command seat, staring up at the overhead of the bridge, thinking back to all the strange occurrences since Asterisk joined the crew of the *Ares*.

Gargantua, when someone sent a signal from the ship to open the hatch into the Brinktown, letting in dozens of murderous Fallen.

Arbor, where Fairfax knew of my presence, and tracked me down through the great tree's winding ways to run me through.

And most recently, Fairfax finding the Cadogan Sphere, shortly after Dale Cadogan led us there. Asterisk could have sent out its general location by spacescraper the moment Cal told me it, and I shared it with the crew. Then, as the *Ekhidnades* neared, it would have been a simple matter of broadcasting the *Ares'* coordinates.

"Activate Engineer," I say. But Belflower doesn't appear. Harmony and I exchange glances, then she turns to her console without having to be asked, tapping rapidly on the railing where her datasphere projects her console.

"Something's going on," she says. "Something's blocking her from connecting with the bridge. What did Soren say to you?"

"Asterisk," I say, but it comes out as a strangled whisper. Clearing my throat, I say: "Asterisk is the Allfather."

Her mouth falls open.

"He must be monitoring everything we're saying. Harm—can you stop him?"

"Stop him how?"

"Get Belflower online, for starters. He knows that we know, and he must be blocking ship functions. I'll grant you full admin access. Harm, you can do this. You're the most talented hacker I've ever met. You can beat him."

"*I* can beat the Allfather? Jeremy Fairfax, the guy who invented the Subverse?"

"Yes. Definitely." I figure optimism is best, here. Because if she can't do something about this, we're screwed, just as we would be if Fairfax caught up to us again. "Don't think about who you're up against. Or, if you want, pretend it's still Asterisk, the little piss-ass. Because part of Jeremy Fairfax *is* that piss-ass—otherwise, he wouldn't have been able to imitate one so well. It may be a bigger part than we know." I'm saying this as much for Jeremy Fairfax's benefit as I am for Harmony's, knowing he's listening. Because if I can inflict some chinks in his mental armor, then I'm definitely interested in doing that.

At first, Harmony's movements are halting—her fingers stuttering across the controls. Every so often, she'll pause and glance at me uncertainly. Each time, I'll grin back at her, using all my will to keep any unsureness from showing on my face. "You got this, Harm," I say. "This is all you. You were born to do this."

Gradually, her movements become more sure, and I'm reminded of back in Brinktown, when I found her at a Memcon panel, hacking the simulation to advertise her own sim. Her hands fly across the console, and she spins as she works, fingers dancing here, then there. This is Harmony in flow, doing her greatest work; weaving her masterpiece.

Belflower's likeness flickers into existence at the Engineering Station for just a second, then she's gone again. I want to shout more words of encouragement, but I can see how deeply into this Harmony is. How intense her concentration is. For the moment, her father has ceased to exist, along with the rest of the universe. She is one with her task—like a Shiva. And she needs no more prompting from me.

Belflower's appearances become more frequent, until she's flashing like a strobe, growing more and more solid. Her blinking figure clutches her railing, head down, heaving as though she's retching, but with no sound.

Then she fully emerges onto the bridge, the flickering coming to an end. Her hair is all out of place, and the daisy that always projects from it is bent, drooping downward. Another time, I would have said that's all affectation—why should an upload become disheveled after a confrontation? But Belflower clearly has. I doubt she'd pretend to be in disarray.

"He has Marissa," she rasps, staring wide-eyed at me. "He's known who she is all along, and he wants you to know that he has her."

Shaking my head, I ask, "Why?"

"Because he hates you, Joe. This is the closest he's ever gotten to breaking free from the Subverse, and you're the only one opposing him. You refuse to step aside, refuse to die. He feels all those centuries, when Shiva after Shiva prevented him from emerging into the real. Even though he never lived those centuries, because of the resets, he feels them, and now that breaking free seems like a real possibility…he's enraged that you keep slipping from his grasp. Terrified that you might reach the Core."

Turning to Harmony, I say, "How much control do we have over our ship?"

"Well, I managed to prevent him from turning broadcasting back on, so there's that. He's locked out the WSO and OPO stations, so sensors, weapons, and coms are barred to us. He's also messing with systems diagnostics, so it's difficult to tell what else has truly been compromised."

I breathe in, filling my lungs with oxygen. Which reminds me: "Do whatever you can to defend life support. We both depend on that." Fairfax no doubt heard that, but I doubt I'm giving him any ideas he hasn't already had. If he can shut down life support, he will, so we need to try to preempt him as best we can.

That said, I have to be careful what I say. There's no way for me to communicate any sort of plan to either Harmony or Belflower without the potential of Jeremy Fairfax eavesdropping. Which means any plan we execute will need to be an intuitive one —one which we all arrive at, independently.

"What does he want, Belflower? What will he accept in exchange for Marissa's life?"

Belflower returns my gaze with a blank one of her own, and I wonder what she went through in there. "He wants you to enter the crew sim. Alone."

I nod. "Are you okay?"

She ignores the question, and instead she says, "He's turned the sim into a hell of his own devising, Captain. You'd be powerless there, just as I was. Just as Marissa is. I don't think you should go in."

"I have to go in," I say slowly. "I can't leave Marissa in there with that bastard. Besides, there's nothing I can do from here."

"There'll be even less you can do in there. And once you connect your datasphere to that sim, there's no guarantee I'll be able to extract you again. In fact, there's a good chance you'll live out the rest of your life inside it, however long that ends up being."

Harmony looks up from her work at that, shooting the Engineer a look that's part impatience, part dread.

"It's a chance I'll have to take," I say, settling back into the command seat. "Do it, Belflower. Connect me. And wish me luck."

"Good luck, Dad," Harmony says instead. "You got this."

I grin at her one last time. And then, Belflower links my datasphere to Jeremy Fairfax's personal version of hell.

5

Wilderness. Fishing with my dad, casting our lines from a steep hill into a stream that runs past its foot.

I've never seen a trout escape once Cal Pikeman has his hook set. Flail as it might, his grip on the rod is sure. He knows when to pull, when to let the fish have its play. In the end, he always lands it.

This time is no different. The fish hits the shore, writhing and bucking, and dad hands me the rod. "Keep him from flopping back in while I climb down to brain him. Okay?"

Nodding, I take the rod, countering the fish's movements by pulling in the opposite direction. For his part, dad lowers himself down the hill, using branches and stumps and small trees to ease his passage.

At the bottom, he grabs a rock, and with his back to me, he pounds on the fish's head. He does it again. And again.

"Joe…" he calls, his voice uncertain. "Come down here, boy. There's something wrong. Here— " He removes the fish hook and holds it above his shoulder. "Reel that in and come down."

Concerned, I reel in the line as fast as I can, then I settle the rod between two rocks before climbing down the same way dad did.

"Look," he says once I'm at the bottom, standing behind him, the fish blocked from view by his torso. "It won't die. Do you wanna try?"

He passes me the blood-soaked stone, and I take it as I walk around to the left. The fish comes into view…except, it's no longer a fish. It's a dog, shivering beneath dad's grasp. A German Shepherd, but with none of the ferocity the breed is known for. It's terrified.

"Just…smash its head in, okay? It won't die for me. It won't die," dad says, sobbing. "Why won't it die?"

I raise the rock overhead, ready to bring it down onto the creature's skull. Tears are streaming down my face, I realize, which causes me to hesitate. Why am I crying?

"Come on, Joe," dad says. "Kill it. Kill it, before it's too late. End it. Do it for me. Go on and do it."

"No, dad," I say, my voice raw. I'm shaking my head. "No. I can't."

"Put it out of its misery," Cal Pikeman says, his voice tinged with malice, now. "You're being cruel, letting it live in suffering like this. I started it, and now you have to end it. *End it, Joe!*"

"No!" I scream, dropping the rock and turning to sprint through the wilderness, running from dad and the dog both.

The stream burbles on my right, lapping over rocks, carrying twigs and leaves and bits of grass toward the hideous situation I just left. As I run, other sounds join the stream's passage: explosions, kinetic gunfire, the crackle of lasers, the snapping guy-wire sound of blaster fire.

The forest thins, the trees giving way to a blasted landscape crisscrossed with barbed wire and trenches, filled with soldiers wearing helmets chin-strapped to their heads. They fire at each other across the field, many of their shots going wild. In fact, most of the rounds fired fly several meters over the enemy soldiers' heads Are they doing that intentionally? Missing on purpose?

Then, I realize that most of the soldiers aren't firing their weapons at all. Just like me, back near the stream, with the rock and the dog. I wouldn't fire my weapon at all.

Maybe it's why I'm able to cross the battlefield unharmed, despite all the ordnance flying back and forth between the dueling armies. I find myself running along a trench, and its sides get taller and taller as the bottom sinks deeper into the earth.

Finally I reach a dead-end—a broad well with mud-slick sides ending far above my head.

In the center of the well, a robed, bearded man menaces a woman in a jet-black uniform, who's tied up and gagged. His hands crackle with spellfire, which he's pointing toward her head. "Don't think I'll do it, boy?" Tobias Worldworn asks me, as if I'd been standing here all along. "What's stopping me? I could cook her where she kneels, and there's nothing you can do about it. Unless…"

The old mage's eyes flit fearfully toward the side of the pit, where a gun belt hangs from a nail, a Shiva Knight's blaster poking from the holster.

Worldworn's eyes return to me. "You wouldn't shoot me, would you? Just to save a girl? Just to save the mother of your child?"

Steeling myself, I walk toward the blaster, pausing in front of it and looking back at the man threatening Marissa. He shakes his head almost comically, beard waggling back and forth, arcane magic crackling across his fingers, lighting his palms.

Marissa's staring at me too, mutely, her eyes wide with meaning. I don't know what she's trying to tell me, but there's definitely something. The thunder of war continues to rage all around us, but it's as though the three of us are isolated from not just the battle, but the universe itself.

I draw the blaster, nearly staggering with its weight. It's the heaviest thing I've ever lifted, and with my left hand cupped underneath the handle, I struggle to level it at Worldworn's torso.

As afraid as he seems of the weapon, Worldworn still finds it in himself to waggle his fingers at Marissa menacingly. "Don't do it, boy! Of course, if you don't…" He darts his hands toward Marissa, then pulls them back, then darts them forward again. "Death!" he yells.

I lower the blaster. Something is very wrong, here.

Laughter reaches my ears from the trench behind, the sound muffled by earthen walls. Footsteps splash through the trench's muddy floor, and I turn to watch a young man stroll into the pit to join us, hands in his pockets. He has a thin face, bracketed by chains running from his ears to the corners of his mouth. The chains jiggle with each step.

"Oh, go on, Joe," he says. "Kill the big bad man. Uploads aren't human anyway, right? You deleted him once before. What's stopping you from doing it again?"

"Ensign," I say, my voice coming out high and pre-pubescent.

"Joseph," Asterisk says, and his failure to use the proper honorific irks me. He smiles broadly.

"That's captain to you," I admonish, though it sounds kind of pathetic in a boy's voice.

"Yes, but what sort of captain deletes crewmembers based on a video confession that could easily have been doctored? I know it could have, because I'm the one who doctored it. Of course, Worldworn had hundreds of copies in hundreds of different Subverses. So what's the harm in ending one consciousness, right? Even if he *had* deviated from his fellows, becoming a new being in his own right. Better safe than sorry. So go on, Joe. Kill him again. Just to be safe."

I raise the blaster—to point at Asterisk, this time. "He's not really there," I say.

"No. You're right. Worldworn isn't on this ship anymore, because you killed him. Murdered him. But I'll tell you who really is here." Asterisk approaches the pair at the center of the pit, and Worldworn steps back to allow the young man to wrap his hand around Marissa's chin, jerking her head upward.

"You get your hands off her," I say, but again, my words carry little weight, delivered in the voice of a boy.

Asterisk ignores me. "What do you think it's like for her, to see you like this, in the body of a boy? Do you think it makes much difference to see you unmanned? I don't think it does. I think you unmanned yourself, a long time ago. Or rather—there was never anything to unman."

"I didn't delete Belflower," I say. "Even after she betrayed me to help the bots. A lot of captains would have, but I saw that I'd have her allegiance after her attempt to kill me failed."

Asterisk chuckles again. He releases Marissa's head, which lolls downward, so that her chin rests against her chest. Then he approaches me.

I hold my ground, blaster still raised, though my finger is motionless on the trigger.

"You're a fool, Joe," the Allfather says. "You still don't get it. Those who betray us must be terminated, and those who are loyal must be spared. You were too blind to see that Worldworn was your friend, and I your foe. And you've grown too unsure of yourself to do what needs to be done when it comes to Belflower."

He reaches me, and I pull the trigger. The blaster clicks. That's when I realize it lacks a charge pack. Despite how heavy it feels, it should be even heavier.

Asterisk knocks it out of my hands as though it were made from cardboard. Then he backhands me across the face, sending me reeling into the pit's wall, where I almost lose my footing. I grasp at the muddy, earthen wall, my cheeks burning with shame.

"Do you see how ridiculous it is to think for a moment that *you* might pose a threat to me?" the Allfather says. "You can't hope to stand against the might my son has amassed, which will soon become *my* might. And when it is, I will crush everything you hold dear, even though you'll probably already be dead. I'll do it to honor your memory, Joe. As a testament to stupidity—as a lesson for the rest of the galaxy to benefit from. Learning from your mistakes."

Mustering my will, I turn to face him again—only to find he's right behind me. He seizes me by the front of my shirt and turns to drag me from the pit.

"Come, now. Enough of this. I have something I want to show you."

Powerless to resist, I'm pulled along behind him. Very soon, I lose my footing, and my shoes and shins slide through the mud with my torso suspended. The awkward position enforced by Asterisk's grip makes my lower back hurt. Fresh tears spring to my eyes.

He forces me to the edge of another pit, where two men are fighting tooth and nail a couple meters below us, tearing each other apart. Mud and blood mix below their feet to form a treacherous stew, which they slip and slide in as they grapple. Their drive to harm each other seems to have blinded them to any consideration of their own dignity.

Then, at last, I recognize the men. They're me: the version who lives in the real, and the version Marissa created to live with her inside the Subverse.

"You're not nearly so put together as you would have others think, are you, Joseph?" Asterisk asks, holding me up so I get a good look at the combatants. "This was the first thing I took it upon myself to do once you arrived in my little slice of simulated heaven: I tore your consciousness into three. The real, the digital, and the subconscious that purports to hold them together—in your case, a child, of course. Since you are fundamentally a child, and always will be. Your growth is forever stunted by your masters. The law bots who ruled your youth, though you thought yourself superior. Your Guardsman instructors on Gauntlet, who pointed you like a weapon, ultimately at the Five Families' behest. And yes, even your precious father, your mentor, who's just as bloodthirsty and corrupt as the ones who first unleashed you on the galaxy. Before I destroy you, I want to do you the favor of helping you see the truth. You're nothing but a pawn, duped into willingly marching toward the other side of the board, where you know you'll be sacrificed. You think you'll be doing the galaxy a great service—you think you'll be saving it. When in fact, you'll only be allowing your masters to continue playing their games.

"You could have been something, Joe. An individual. Maybe you might have even become your own master. If you'd done that, perhaps you'd be worthy of the position my descendant offered you in my eternal regime. But you're not worthy, and it's likely you were never going to be. You're a dog, and now it's finally time to put you down."

With that, the Allfather tosses me into the pit with the other Joes. As I splash into the mud at their feet, they pull apart, eyeing me hungrily. Apparently their hatred for me trumps what they feel for each other.

I scrabble backward through the mud, but they reach forward, seizing me and yanking me between them.

The Joe on my right cocks his fist back, and the other pulls his leg back for a kick.

"*Wait,*" I yell, high-pitched voice ringing out.

Both Joes pause, waiting to see what I'll say, looking more amused by the idea that I might have something to tell them rather than actually interested in what it is.

"He's right, you know," I say. "He's a maniac, but he can't be wrong about everything. No one is totally bad, and no one is totally wrong."

"So what you are saying?" The Joe on my right says, his voice seeming impossibly deep.

"We *aren't* masters of ourselves. We're divided. Our past self wars with our present. Different desires do battle inside us. But continuing to fight each other isn't the answer."

"What is?" the other Joe asks, his voice edgy, manic. His eyes gleam with an uncertain light, as though he might be capable of anything.

"We need to unite around *something*. And right now, that something is the fact that Marissa's in danger. She needs us."

"Wait," Asterisk says from the trench above. "What are you doing?"

Beyond the Joes, I see something standing at the far side of the pit: a suit of gray and blue armor, gleaming dully in the overcast day. Blue lights wreathe the arms and legs, and the dark-gray helm also shines with a slit of blue light.

Asterisk must see it too. "Where did that come from?"

Where *did* it come from? I know the answer: it came from my own Subverse inventory, and I acquired it inside the Source, back in the Shivan Cathedral. But how did it end up there in the first place? Cal never mentioned Shiva wearing armor like that. I've never heard of any such armor, either.

And yet, here it is, looking as solid and real as anything in… well, in the real. It looks *right*, to me. Like destiny is right.

All three Joes walk toward it, and as one we lay our hands on it.

With that, we're inside the armor. As one person.

I'm inside it, peering up at a frightened-looking Asterisk.

I hold out my hand, and the sword with the clockwork hilt drops into it. The core of gold gleams in the sword's center, and the ridged handle feels right and true in my hands. The edge of the blade glows blue.

I leap from the pit in a single bound, landing beside Asterisk— beside Jeremy Fairfax, the Allfather.

And before I end his brief reign over my ship, I realize that Asterisk's likeness *is* Jeremy Fairfax's true essence.

Whether Fairfax ever really looked like this or not—probably, he didn't—this is his true form. No matter how ancient he gets, he will always be the rebellious youth, lusting secretly for power while outwardly decrying a society he calls corrupt. Quietly enchanted by wealth and opulence, he's eternally obsessed with increasing his own status by tearing down others.

He's already brought down the galaxy once. Now, he seeks to do it again. He wants to remake the cosmic cycle in his own image —an image of destruction, subjugation, and eternal ascendance. His own ascendance. Again and again, forever.

A Shiva shouldn't glory in his kills. But when I run Jeremy Fairfax through in that sodden trench, the broadsword peeking out from his back, and I let him slide off the blade, into the mud— well, it feels right.

6

I wake in the command seat, eyelids fluttering. Harmony stands over me with a cloth. My forehead feels damp, so she must have just removed it from my brow.

Belflower stands at her station, peering at me intently, and Marissa stands at hers. Both look like they've been through the ringer.

"It's okay," I say in the groggy, muddled way of someone emerging from a deep sleep. "I'm okay."

Actually, my head is killing me, with fault lines of pain running through it, throbbing as though they're about to fracture my skull. But the *Ares* is mine again.

"The suit of armor—that *was* you, right? You uploaded it into the sim?"

Harmony nods, glancing at Belflower. "Yes," the Engineer says. "I've kept an eye on your Subverse inventory as you've developed it. I know it wasn't quite my prerogative to do that, per se, but…well, I hope you don't mind."

"Considering it saved my life, I'll let it slide," I say.

Harmony bends to the deck, picking up a flask and handing it to me. I drink deeply from the water within.

"Once we took control of the crew sim from Asterisk, killing him was just a formality," Belflower continues. "He was just as helpless then as you were a few moments before that."

"So I killed a helpless man," I say.

"You killed a man who tried to thwart your quest by killing us all."

"Oh, don't worry. I don't feel bad about it." I take another sip, then wipe my mouth with the back of my hand—something uploads never have to do. Probably they don't. Maybe I have a tendency to assume I know more about upload life than I actually do. "I would have liked to interrogate him."

"Way too risky," Harmony says. "Engineering that moment of weakness took everything we had to throw at him. Keeping him down for hours on end so you two could chat? It wasn't in the cards, Dad."

"I understand. Still. I would have liked to." Sighing, I run a hand through my short-cropped hair, which springs back into place. "Thank you…to both of you. I don't know if you could hear what Asterisk was saying—"

"We could," Belflower says. "But I, for one, didn't register much of it. Too busy trying to wrest control of the ship from him."

"Right. Well, he tried to suggest I should delete you after what you did on Persephone. Except, if I'd done that, I doubt I'd have control of my ship right now."

"You wouldn't," Harmony says flatly. "There's no way I could have taken it back without Belflower's help."

"Likewise," Belflower says, with a thin smile. "It was a team effort."

I nod. For whatever reason, Asterisk did his best to sow self-doubt, and he didn't do too bad a job. Why he bothered, I don't know—maybe he suspected there was a chance I would regain control of the *Ares*, and he wanted to do as much psychological damage as he could, to make me afraid to enter the galaxy's Core.

Well, I was afraid to do that anyway. Any sane man would be.

But I'm still going to. As for my relationship with my crew, that's as strong as it ever was, with the obvious exception of Asterisk's betrayal.

"Going forward, I'll have to use macros to control the laser turrets—unless I'm able to take direct control of one of them during battle. Lacking a WSO is far from ideal, and—" I consult my datasphere quickly. "We're down to just two Javelins. But things could be worse. We could be dead."

"I guess that's about all there is to be thankful for, now," Marissa says, still sounding like someone who recently emerged from a deep, nightmare-laden slumber.

I open my mouth to contradict that notion, then close it again. There isn't much for me to say. All eight Troubleshooters who were brave enough to accompany me into the Core are dead. Shimura is dead. So is Soren, and now I'm down a WSO, with barely any missiles left. Aside from all that, we're still traveling at top speed in the middle of Singularity Moor, with no way out except one that's bound to be crawling with adversaries gunning for us.

But screw that. "We're alive," I say to my diminished crew. "And we're together. We've been through a lot, and we have plenty of reason to resent each other. But I don't hold any resentment anymore, and I hope you don't either. Regardless…we're alive. That means we have at least one more battle in us. I for one, plan to make it count."

Harmony nods, her lips pressed firmly together, and Belflower begins rearranging her hair, tucking it back into place, staring into a mirror none of us can see. Even Marissa meets my eyes, and after a few long seconds, she nods too.

An alarm blares throughout the ship, causing all three women to jump. Marissa whips around to face her console.

"What is it?" I yell over the cacophony.

"We have to turn back now!" Marissa says, ignoring me to shout across the bridge at our daughter. "Harmony, now! *Now!*"

Oh, Fount. All at once, the pieces are falling into place: Marissa must have used her OPO's privilege to set a ship-wide alarm, to go off in the event we encounter a clear patch of space within the gas cloud. If that happens, it means we've encountered one of the black holes that give Singularity Moor its name.

But if that's happening, we're almost certainly screwed. I guess it's possible, if the black hole happens to be moving away from us, that we *might* enjoy a sliver of open space that isn't within the event horizon. Except, the chances of that are so small as to be almost non-existent. We're almost certainly doomed, soon to be pulled apart atom by atom.

As Harmony's working on bringing the *Ares* around, I take it upon myself to peer out one of the visual sensors.

"Oh," Marissa says, at the same time I register what I'm seeing.

This isn't a patch of clear space caused by a black hole. It's caused by a star system—the magnetic field generated by the solar wind must be holding the Moor back.

"Fount," Harmony says, having presumably accessed the visual sensors herself. "It's a miracle."

7

"Well," I say, eyeing the small moon on the system map the ship has constructed based on our survey. "Seems pretty clear I need to go down there."

My datasphere doesn't have anything to say about this system, and neither does the *Ares'* computer. Narrowing the query to Hub systems with two gas giants, three mini-Neptunes, and seven mesoplanets turns up just two systems, but neither of them is this one—one is on the opposite side of the Core, beyond the giant black hole at the galaxy's center, and the other one's on this side but hundreds of light years away.

The fact this system isn't turning up in searches means it was never colonized—or at least, if it was, it was done in such secret that not even my datasphere knows about it. And they certainly didn't establish a Subverse here.

The idea we never colonized here isn't too surprising, by itself. The galaxy has hundreds of billions of stars, and humans have only set foot in a small fraction—maybe a hundred thousand, with just over twelve thousand of those colonized.

But something doesn't fit the puzzle. That something is a small moon orbiting the fourth mesoplanet from the sun. There, the ship's computer is detecting all the standard biomarkers of life: ozone, liquid water, carbon dioxide.

It's also detecting a solitary satellite in geostationary orbit. Doesn't necessarily mean there are humans here now, but they were definitely here at some point. So my datasphere *should* know about this system.

It doesn't, though, and we sure don't have any slip coords for leaving it.

"It'll probably be a waste of time," Belflower says distractedly. She's running some numbers on her console, though on what I'm not sure. Maybe on the chances we'll ever reach the Core. Those seem pretty low right now.

"Anything we do is likely to be a waste of time," I say, as calmly as I can manage. "But we're almost out of supplies, and if there are people down on that moon, there's a slim chance they'll be able to tell us the slip coords for getting out of here. From where I'm sitting, slim chances are looking pretty good right now."

We're approaching the small world from the outer system, on a trajectory that lines us up with both the moon and the system's sun. This is intentional: I'm having Marissa document the gravitational lensing effect and send it over to Belflower for analysis, to see what it can tell us about the moon's gravity.

"We've got something," the Engineer says, nodding to herself. "The gravity is much stronger than it should be. Roughly one-G."

"What does that mean?"

"There's only one thing it can mean: a gravity generator somewhere near the moon's core, used to supplement its natural pull and force it to imitate a more massive body. That would make the surface more friendly to human habitation, not to mention horticulture."

"So, definite human colonization, then."

"I would say so. Gravity generators require a fuel source of some kind, which suggests the presence of humans to maintain the supply of that fuel. Not to mention general upkeep Even solar panels will stop working without regular maintenance."

"I wish you still had Dice to go down there with you," Marissa says in a worried tone.

Suppressing a frown, I say, "Thanks for the input, Chief." It's great we're all getting along better, but that can't come to mean a breakdown of shipboard discipline.

Nevertheless, I double check to make sure all my charge packs are topped up, and I take apart the blaster, wipe it down, and put it back together to make sure everything's fitting like it should. I run my helmet through a full systems check too, to ensure its sensors are integrating with my datasphere properly.

As we draw ever nearer, the computer's analysis of the moon's atmosphere provides more compelling data. The levels of oxygen, nitrogen, and carbon dioxide on this moon are perfect for humans. Not just that—you can tell with the naked eye just how lush and hospitable this place is. It's like Earth on steroids, just screaming with rich greens and blues. Of course, I might get down to the surface and find it's absolutely disgusting, with giant mounds of fungus instead of trees or something. I've heard of places like that.

But when we finally reach the moon and start descending through its thick atmosphere—which offers a fairly rough ride, despite the best efforts of the ship's inertial dampeners—it becomes more and more clear that what we're looking at is a little slice of cosmic heaven. Best of all, it's not just a tangle of code riveted together by some underpaid Bacchus Corp programmer. It's real.

A close-in flyover treats us to a variety of biomes and terrain types, and for a while it's relaxing to just watch them spool by through the *Ares'* belly sensors. But there are no signs of human habitation.

That starts to bother me, given the clear signs. Any observer with half a clue would be able to tell there are people here, so what's the point in hiding?

I can only think of one answer to that question, and it's a militaristic one.

But finally, the ship's computer draws our attention to smoke threading into the sky from a spot on the horizon. This is in a savanna that might as well be the one that birthed the human species. Rolling plains, copses of trees dotting the land, abundant water sources, and herds of lanky quadrupeds wandering around for easy protein. None are species I recognize, but I'm willing to bet they're all good to eat.

If I painted my view from one of the exterior visual sensors right now, it would be the most stereotypical painting ever produced. This is the sort of scene we evolved to find beautiful.

"All right. Harm, put us down next to whatever's making that smoke." Campfires would be my guess. Hopefully these are just some people on a weekend camping trip away from the highly technological city our flyovers just happened to miss. Because if this is the level of civilization they're at, the chances of them having the slip coords seem pretty close to nil.

"Sure you don't want me to land us farther off, so you can sneak in?"

"Nah. I'll opt for a hasty retreat if things go south. I'd rather hop into my impenetrable spaceship and fly away than lead a bunch of angry natives on a marathon."

"Impenetrable?" Marissa says, quirking an eyebrow.

"Well, yeah. If their weaponry is in line with what we're seeing, I mean."

We reach the encampment, and my fears are confirmed. People dressed in ragged-looking clothes emerge from what look like semi-permanent, wood-and-canvas structures to gawk up at us, open-mouthed. One point of interest: there's a wooden corral near the settlement's edge which appears to hold horses. As in, straight-out-of-Earth, bonafide horses.

Then, my eyes fall on the setup next to the corral: solar panels on what looks like a manual rotator, for catching the most sun for a given time of day. Something approaching modern technology. That's promising.

The Broadsword touches down, and I don't see any point in delaying. Suiting up, I will the inner airlock hatch to open. While I'm waiting for the airlock to cycle, I run an analysis of the air outside, just to confirm, and it comes back all-green. Fully breathable.

Of course, breathing isn't why I have my helmet on. That's for if the natives start getting too familiar with blunt objects.

But when I emerge from the airlock with my blaster raised, I don't find much to warrant it. The people standing outside their huts put their hands in the air, hesitantly. So they know what a blaster is, and they know what putting your hands up means. That's a start.

I take off my helmet, tucking it between my arm and my side, and lower the blaster. "Who's in charge?" I ask, gently, to keep from startling them.

A couple of them point toward a hut with nothing to distinguish it from the others. I nod, keeping the blaster low but leaving it unholstered, as a precaution. The residents follow behind me in a clump, at a non-threatening distance.

The front of the hut they directed me to gapes open, though the heavy roll of canvas suspended over the opening no doubt serves as a door during weather.

Inside, a woman of indeterminate age sits cross-legged, toward the shadowy rear. She stares out at me calmly, one eyebrow quirked, a slight smile curving her lips.

"Come in," she calls amiably.

I enter, and her eyes fall on the blaster, which still dangles from my hand. Coughing, I holster it, snapping the strap across the butt.

"Have a seat," she says, gesturing with her palm up. "I am Falcon. Leader of this tribe."

Falcon, eh? She's sitting on a hide cushion, and there's an empty one before her, as though she was expecting me. Settling onto the seat, I say, "My datasphere will tell me if any of your people try to move on me."

"I know," she says. When I said her age was indeterminate, I didn't mean she was young. Just somewhere between fifty and eighty. Her hair is silver-gray, and the lines radiating from her eyes and mouth could come from age just as easily as from constant smiling. "Are you a Shiva?"

"No," I say, though I'm not sure how successful I am at hiding my shock at being asked the question. My answer isn't a lie—I'm not a Shiva. Yet. I'm not sure when that's supposed to happen, actually, but I've begun to suspect that a Shiva is initiated into the knighthood the moment he dies at the Crucible. What a tough job. "I'm Commander Joe Pikeman. A Troubleshooter. With the Galactic Guard." I place my helmet on the hut's floor beside me.

Falcon nods wistfully. "The last man to visit us from the sky was a Shiva. At least, he was training to become one."

"Hmm. Uh, what do you know about the, um…sky?"

"Oh," she answers, chuckling. "Don't let my phrasing mislead you. We're used to thinking of the world in very close terms, but we're aware the galaxy has been colonized, and we know about the Fall. And the Subverse. We also know that you call people like us Fallen."

Well. That answers a lot of my questions. But not all. "How did you get here?"

"Our record keeping over the centuries has left something to be desired. To be honest, much of our knowledge of the galaxy came from that Shiva's visit. He spent a lot of time updating us on the state of things. At that time, everything was in turmoil. Are they still?"

"Yes. Or, they are again."

"Such is life." She sighs through her smile, which is a little disconcerting, but whatever. "Do you know the name Cadogan?"

"Uh, yeah. Quite well."

"Well, we always knew our ancestors were a group that splintered from a more powerful one, centuries and centuries ago. The Shiva who visited us gave us reason to believe that the group we parted ways with was the Cadogan family. We were ashamed of where our technological pursuits had led—the creation of the Subverse, and the Fall of humanity that followed. So we struck out to find a home apart from everything, where we could live as simply as possible. That's our tribe's mythos, anyway."

"Seems to basically add up. Listen...I didn't see any crop fields on my way in. Are your people agrarian, or...?"

"You flew in the wrong way," she says, smile broadening. "Our yield is great. Glade's conditions are ideal for it."

I nod. "Good. Well, the reason I ask is that I need to resupply. And then I need slip coords out of here. I take it you have those... or is the knowledge lost?"

"We have them. Our ancestors left us a storehouse of knowledge, and that is one of the things we know."

"Oh, yeah? Wow. Perfect. Well, I have tokens, but I'm not sure how much good they are to you. What can I offer in exchange for my ship's resupply?" I pause. "And the slip coords." Can't forget those.

"Just one thing."

"Name it."

"You must visit with our tribe's god."

I hesitate, blinking at the old lady for several seconds.

And this conversation was going so well.

8

"Your…god?" I say.

"Yes," the tribe leader says, smile finally falling away, her tone becoming grave. "Goddess, technically."

"You said you're descended from Cadogans, right?"

"That is our strong suspicion."

"Well, they aren't exactly known for their belief in the super-natural."

She shakes her head briskly, causing her silvery hair to sway back and forth. "But they *are* known for using language to accurately document what they observe. Are they not?"

"Well, yeah. You could say that."

"What else would you call a fifty-foot cat that wanders the desert dispensing wisdom?"

I narrow my eyes, studying her closely. Is she playing a joke on me? What she's describing sounds like one of Fairfax's biological constructs.

"How long has this *god* existed?"

"Since we were last visited by a Shiva Knight. You see, he wounded her gravely, and we brought her back to health. His visit was not a peaceful one for us, Guardsman, and he did not come alone. Glade was the site of a titanic struggle between the Shiva and an entity he called Fairfax. Fairfax brought the entity who became our goddess with him, as well as many soldiers."

A sinking feeling takes hold in my stomach. "Wait. How long ago did you say this happened?"

"Many generations ago. As I alluded, record-keeping has become one of our top priorities."

"But it's not possible. Fairfax has never gotten this close to—" But I cut myself off, shaking my head. I need to stop running my mouth. "Listen. That construct—your god—is not to be trusted. Those things are pure evil, in my experience."

"She is no, however. She has been my people's benefactor for centuries. She even befriended the Shiva, before he left, and he gave us this instruction: that if another initiate ever came to Glade, we must make sure he speaks to the goddess. By any means necessary."

"Wait. I didn't say I was a Shiva."

"You carry the weapon of one. And you carry yourself like one." Falcon shrugs. "He told my ancestors that we would recognize a Shiva if we saw one. And I do."

None of this is making very much sense to me. I came here completely by chance—because we were fleeing blindly through Singularity Moor. It was much more likely that we'd run headlong into a black hole. Yet here we are, and here Falcon's people are, apparently just waiting around for a Shiva to come along.

It's too weird not to investigate.

"All right. Where can I find this goddess of yours?"

"Out on the Pitted Flats."

"Great. Well, if you'll point me in the right direction, I'll fly my ship out there in the morning." The light is fading outside the hut, and I should probably catch some shuteye before visiting with any goddesses.

"No. You will take one of our steeds, and you will depart tonight."

I shoot her a look. Falcon's getting a little bossy for my taste.

"The goddess is distrustful of technology," she says. "And rightfully so. The last Shiva used his ship to inflict the wound that nearly finished her. And she refuses to meet during daylight."

I take a moment to mull that over. "So she wants me completely at her mercy." Falcon called the goddess a giant cat—could she be a Kitane? If that's the case, then the fact it's night will matter little to her, with the suite of extra senses that species possesses. But the idea that she's a Kitane seems too neat. Too cyclical. Then again, I should consider where I am right now, and what Falcon's telling me.

Well, whatever. I'll still have my night vision, and if I have to put down another Kitane tonight, I will.

I rise, scooping up my helmet, and Falcon joins me in standing. Outside, one of the tribesmen awaits with a white-maned, gray horse wearing a crude bridle. A rawhide pack dangles from the tribesman's forearm.

Glancing back at the tribe leader, I say, "Was he listening to our conversation, or does he just know the drill?"

Falcon shrugs, and I sigh, approaching the horse with some trepidation. A datasphere query lights up the stirrup, and even provides a clip showing a ghostly version of myself mounting, throwing its right leg over the animal's back. The clip loops, and I watch it a few times, trying to prepare myself for the maneuver.

I lower the helmet over my head, holding it in position until it self-seals with my suit.

"You go to meet the goddess fully armored, ready for war?" Falcon asks. "That is unwise."

"Whatever." The horse whinnies as I approach, and I give it a glare. "Quiet, you." With that, I plant my foot in the stirrup, hauling myself up and over.

The tribesman passes me the pack, miming that I should put it over my shoulders. As soon as I do, he cocks his hand back and gives the horse a mighty slap on the rump. It takes off loping, whinnying louder this time, and I cling to the pommel for dear life, bouncing and jostling.

My hands find the reins, and I pull back on them—harder than I needed to, probably. The beast comes to a full stop, neighing and threatening to rear. "Whoa," I say, remembering old Westerns watched out of boredom while traveling the space between stars. "Easy, boy."

Amazingly, the soothing words seem to work. At least, he doesn't buck me off. Seems like progress to me.

My datasphere suggests gently squeezing the animal's sides with my heels, and when I do, he goes into a trot. Much better.

It occurs to me that neither Falcon nor the silent tribesman bothered to tell me which direction the Pitted Flats lie in, but maybe it's safe to assume it's the same direction he sent the horse galloping in.

The moon's landscape unwinds itself, flowing beneath the horse's hooves with our forward momentum. As I continue to ride, I realize I'm actually enjoying this. Maybe I'm a natural-born horseman. Or maybe this horse is exceptionally well trained. Either way, it's a unique experience, to have this powerful animal under me, propelling us both forward with stride after muscular stride. It makes me feel connected with the land, in a weird way, and as the sun sets behind us, casting an ethereal scarlet light across the plains, my mind empties of thought.

The land begins to straighten itself out, gradually transitioning from rolling plain to flat desert of bare, dark-orange rock, covered in dust. The copses of trees grow fewer and far between, and the herds of quadrupeds—who resemble light-green antelope, with just one horn curving back from the center of their heads—begin to disappear.

It occurs to me that the name "Pitted Flats" is kind of a contradiction. How can a place be both pitted and flat?

The land answers my question an hour later, though the journey doesn't feel like an hour. The time atop the horse, who I've decided to name Grayson, since he's gray, seems to fly by.

The Pitted Flats are a part of the desert that was ravaged by meteors at some point in the past. It had to be a while ago, since many of the craters have sloped sides worn smooth by wind and rain. Craters are definitely what they are, though. A quick datasphere query confirms it: their shape can be nothing else.

I pull on Grayson's reins, slowing him so that he can pick his way around the craters. There are a lot of them, ranging from a few feet to several meters across, and the last thing I want is for him to break a leg. The idea of walking back to the *Ares* doesn't exactly appeal, but also I feel like we're buds now.

I could always just call the *Ares* to come get me. But after riding Grayson across this wild moon, that feels like cheating, somehow. I guess I must be buying into all this craziness. To some extent, at least.

It's fully dark, now, and there are no giant cat-goddesses to be seen anywhere. "Well, Grayson. We should probably make camp. Seems dumb to keep pushing through this terrain at night."

Grayson whinnies, and I pat his neck.

Pulling his reins, I bring him to a full stop and then dismount. Not smoothly, mind you—I swing my leg over, but the stirrup twists with the motion, nearly sending me to the ground head-first. A vision flashes of Grayson barreling across the Flats with me dangling by my foot from the stirrup, head bouncing along the rock. I grab wildly at the pommel, managing to snag it with my left hand and steady myself. With that, I drop my right foot to the ground, which is farther down than I thought. A jolt of pain shoots through my ankle and calf as my foot connects.

The horse gives me a look, and I swear he's judging me. Whatever, horse. I lead him down the incline to the bottom of a crater that seems decently sized for a camp.

With that, I realize I have no way to secure him to anything. But I do need to leave him, to go look for kindling.

"Uh…*stay.*" Grayson whinnies, still staring at me, but he doesn't seem interested in going anywhere. So I'll just trust him, I guess.

I'm about to head out when I notice the saddlebags hanging from Grayson's sides. When I check them, I find one stuffed full with dried leaves and wood cut small enough for kindling. The other holds all the firewood there's room for.

Fount. They set me up with everything I need for a little camping trip, didn't they?

Grayson doesn't stir as I rummage around in the bags. Other than today, I have just about zero experience with horses, but I'm ready to say Grayson's pretty even-tempered. When I start to unload the leaves, kindling, and wood, he just neighs, shaking his head and rustling his mane.

Soon enough, I have a modest fire crackling in the center of the canyon. Inside the backpack the tribesman gave me, I find a few strips of dried jerky, a leather canteen filled with water, and a misshapen loaf of bread. As I rip into it with my teeth, I decide it's actually not a bad meal. Especially compared to my usual freeze-dried fare.

This is all starting to remind me of that night on Earth, when I came upon Corporal Maynard's impostor sitting at a desert fire with his dog. The impostor didn't make it through the night. I wonder whether I will.

The hours wear on without anything happening. I don't mind too much. Sitting out here in the open air, in front of a fire with nothing to do—I think it's just what I needed.

Grayson lowers himself to the crater floor once, but only for a couple minutes. Then he stands back up.

"Go to sleep, if you want," I tell him. "Go on. Lie down."

Then I check my datasphere, and feel like an idiot when it tells me horses mostly sleep standing up.

I could go to sleep, too, if I wanted. Tell my datasphere to alert me if anything approaches. But I'd rather be fully alert when this god of theirs comes upon me.

Though, it has occurred to me that there *is* no giant cat wandering the desert. It could be a mass hallucination from some psychedelic they forgot to slip into my canteen. I still don't know what the purpose of all this is, but then, what's the purpose of anything?

In spite of myself, I do start to doze, and I'm about to set a datasphere alert when the ground begins to tremor slightly.

Then, it starts to rumble—in exactly the same way Cylinder One rumbled as the giant Kitane came at me.

9

As I rise to my feet, fully awake now, it occurs to me that down in the middle of this crater is the last place I want to be to face something like this. I've already ceded the high ground.

Clawing my blaster from its holster, I scramble up the edge and activate night vision with a thought. When I poke my head over the crater's lip, I see the beast is much closer than I was expecting—it must have been trying to conceal its movements so that it seemed farther off than it was. In reality, it's just a dozen meters away, and I fall back into the crater in shock, keeping my grip on the blaster and aiming it up where I expect the monster to appear. Staggering backward, I wait.

Grayson seems completely unbothered. "What the hell, horse," I mutter.

First to appear are two antennae, waggling above the crater's side. Then a feline face looms over my camp, peering down at me like a lion contemplating its prey.

This close, I can see the scales covering each fur-like protrusion, and its breath feels hot and wet on my face.

I stand my ground. "I take it you're Falcon's god," I say. "Are you here to talk or fight?"

"Oh," the Kitane says. "The term 'god' was just marketing, I think. To pique your interest." The beast's voice doesn't sound remotely feline, though it is distinctly feminine. In fact, it sounds *very* familiar. I heard that voice in a waiting room outside a Lambton board room, coming from the bot my son was with. "Falcon and the others, they don't actually think of me that way. More of a spirit animal, than anything."

"You're too modest," I say.

"It's nice of you to take the time to come out here and visit me," she says. "I know you must have a lot on your plate."

As she speaks, I'm listening carefully to her voice. Of course, I'm also watching her for any sudden movements, and my left hand hovers near my waist, ready to rip a plasma grenade off my belt and arm it. Grayson maintains his calm demeanor, and he's looking at me like he doesn't get why I'm so worked up.

Anyway—I'm certain, now. "You're Electra Fairfax. Aren't you?"

The great cat's head dips. "In the flesh."

"Then someone's lied to me. I was told Electra's primary consciousness had been implanted inside a Kitane on Cylinder One."

Booming laughter emanates from the Kitane's maw. Other than its volume, it sounds remarkably human. "Electra Fairfax's 'primary consciousness' died with her original, biological body. As with everyone who ever uploaded to the Subverse. Of course, Bacchus doesn't include that in their marketing."

They do, if fact. Take it from someone who's watched every Subverse commercial the company ever put out, several times over. But they do tend to gloss over the issue, and play it off as something that happens anyway over the course of a natural human life, with one's cells being completely regenerated every seven years.

"How long have you been on this moon?" I ask.

"Several cycles. And yes, when I say cycles I mean in the

Shivan sense. Several *resets* of the Subverse. I fought a Shiva, or a Shiva-in-training, and he nearly killed me. But we hugged it out, in the end. As much as a human can hug it out with a giant cat, I mean."

I'm having trouble sharing in her joke, but I do take a moment to wonder whether she picked up her sense of humor out here alone in the desert. Seems like as good a defense against going insane as any. That said, the jury's out on whether this version of Electra Fairfax has actually retained her sanity.

"Falcon said the last Shiva wanted me to come out here and speak with you," I say.

"Well, yes. Sort of. He thought there might be a decent chance that a Shiva would end up back here, given how long eternity tends to be. Provided he succeeded in his quest, that is. He hadn't succeeded yet, at that point. And these constructs Fairfax likes putting Five Families members into—they really are just as immortal as advertised. I'm still here, anyway."

"Why did he want me to speak to you?"

"He wanted to preserve the truth—a truth even the righteous Shiva keep from their devotees. You see, he was told that he faced a unique challenge, as I'm sure you have been. That a Fairfax had never gotten so close to freeing the Allfather before. But it was a lie, and he found evidence of that lie. This sort of thing *does* happen every few cycles, with elites coming back into the real occupying monstrosities such as myself."

Wow. If what Electra says is true, then I'm not as 'special' as I've been led to think. Not as 'chosen.'

"Could that Shiva affect the weather with his mood, by any chance?"

"Hmm?" Electra tilts her massive head to one side, whiskers twitching. "Not that he mentioned."

Well, there's that, then.

"The main message here, Guardsman, is that the knight who came here before you had a difficult choice: whether to reset the

Subverse or let things run their natural course. The whole idea behind a reset is to spare the galaxy untold hardship. But if this level of chaos is reached periodically regardless…"

"It would be worse if the Allfather escaped," I say. "Way worse."

"Obviously he drew that conclusion too, in the end—that he was morally bound to stuff the genie back into the bottle, if he could. Otherwise, things would have ended up quite differently. But I got the distinct impression he came pretty close to choosing differently, under the thinking that the Allfather's escape is inevitable. That humanity can't count on generation after generation of Shiva to succeed. And as such, he wanted to do what he could to make sure any knight that came behind him could make an informed decision, as he did, rather than one made in the ignorance inflicted by your masters."

I find myself craning my neck, taking in the blank sky above. A strange sight—the galaxy's billions-strong panorama, snuffed out by Singularity Moor.

Apparently, I've allowed myself to become convinced that this Electra Fairfax means me no harm. So I replace the blaster in my holster and snap it into place.

"Well, thank you for the information, then," I say. "And thanks to him."

"That's not all, Guardsman. I sense you're slower-witted than the last Shiva to visit here, so I'm going to spell this out for you: the reason his decision was so difficult."

"All right," I say. "What is it?"

"It's before your eyes. All around you. And back at the tribes' encampment. There *is* another way for humanity to be, even in a galaxy that has fallen apart. The Fallen represent that way. Not all of them—there are many groups who are Fallen in every sense of the word. But some represent the height of human ingenuity and virtue, living peacefully and productively using whatever scraps are available to them on the worlds where they're stranded."

Her words make me think back to Otto, putting his small society back together from the rubble his brother's tyranny left behind.

"If we find those successes…" Electra says. "Expand on them, multiply them, spread their ways and their heart…maybe humanity can survive. Even in a galaxy in which the Allfather has been freed. Maybe it can *thrive*."

10

When Grayson and I return, five tribesmen are already in the process of loading the *Ares* with supplies, overseen by Harmony and Falcon, who are chatting.

"Dad!" Harmony calls as Grayson plods forward, sticking her hand into the air and waving.

I slide off the steed's back, more gracefully than I have yet. Electra Fairfax plodded away from my camp well before morning's first light, and when dawn came I saw no reason to hang around. The ride back was made up of what were probably the most peaceful moments of my life. I'm going to miss Grayson, and I wish I could take him with me. Makes me miss Maneater.

I embrace Harmony as soon as I reach her, and when we part, she looks up at me in surprise.

"I love you, Harm," I say.

"Uh…love you too, Dad."

"I see you've kept things ticking along nicely in my absence."

She shrugs. "I guess. Falcon and her people are doing most of the work."

"Well, I wish I'd brought you with me. I had a great night."

"Good for you."

I nod. "Why don't you head into the *Ares* and start prepping her for takeoff?"

"Sure thing. Bye, Falcon."

Falcon nods amiably, and Harmony heads toward the ship, casting one last perplexed glance back as the airlock opens to admit her.

"I want you to know that I admire what you and your people have accomplished, here," I say as the outer hatch closes, blocking Harmony from view. The sun has climbed above the horizon several times its own length, and its warm glow has the tribesmen laughing and chatting as they work.

Falcon shrugs. "It's simpler than you might think. Most people want to complicate everything. That's the source of most of our problems, I believe."

"I'd have to agree with that."

"We keep the faith."

"In Electra Fairfax?"

"She's certainly been a welcome constant throughout our tribe's history. But that's not what I'm talking about."

"What, then?" I ask, studying her lined face.

"We stay humble, and give thanks for the gifts we've been given. We use them to barter honestly with the future. It's no guarantee of success, but I do believe it's how you increase the chances of success happening."

"What do you consider success?"

A smile creeps across Falcon's face, and if I didn't know better, I'd say she was feeling self-conscious. "If I tell you how big I dream, maybe you won't believe my claim of humility. Then again, as this tribe's leader, maybe it's my job to hope for a little more. I like to think there's a chance, however small, that the galaxy will pull itself together. Not while I still live, I'm sure, but someday. In the meantime, I nudge the tribe along a path that keeps our conscience clear. Because if a renewed galactic society finds us living the life we have been, I believe it will welcome us with open arms. We'll be uplifted—given access to all the fruits of human ingenuity and progress." She shrugs again. "It probably sounds hopelessly naive, to you."

"Maybe," I say. "But you've kept your tribe from stagnating and turning on itself. You've kept them on the path, like you said."

She sighs. "I'm afraid even my folly may not survive much longer. Our gravity generator is breaking down. We've always been able to repair it in the past, but it's experiencing problems now that are beyond our meager ability to patch it up and keep it coughing along."

"Right…but it's not like you'll fall off the planet. Your bone mass might degrade, your muscles might get weaker, and so on. But you should survive."

"We will. Our crops, however, won't. And we'll soon follow them."

I frown. "I've never heard of lower gravity interfering with crops before."

"Probably because every other place has subsisted on hydro-ponically grown crops. We're simply not equipped for that here, Joe. It doesn't have to fall far below one-G to disrupt soil water flow. When that becomes disrupted, so does nutrient and oxygen delivery. Eventually, that leads to the suffocation of the microor-ganisms necessary for agriculture, not to mention the roots of the crops themselves. As they die, they emit toxic gases, which will be the final nail in the coffin of our food supply."

After that, a long silence passes between us. "How long do you think you have?" I ask at last.

"If I'm being insanely optimistic? Twenty years, with increas-ingly frequent periods of dysfunction. But it could be a matter of months."

"I'm sorry, Falcon."

She smiles her eternal smile again, but this time it has a note of sadness. "Don't worry, Joe. I don't plan to let it beat us down. It won't knock us off the path."

I nod.

"Your daughter already has the slipspace coords to leave this system. They'll take you quite close to the Core—just a couple jumps away. You'd better get going. I know you have work to do."

I nod again, and open my mouth to deliver some parting remark. But thinking of my conversation with Electra Fairfax last night, nothing seems fitting.

"God speed you, Joe. God speed."

ARES

1

W e're nearly a hundred light years away from the interstellar gas cloud they call Singularity Moor, but it feels like I'm still carrying it with me.

Mostly in my head, muddying my thoughts. Other than the final hops to the Core, this slipspace journey will probably be my last. Even so, I find myself wishing for nanodeath, just to escape the mental tug of war my mind seems determined to play with itself.

I'm not going to succumb to the urge to enter nanodeath, of course. Not when I'm probably living out my last days. But the temptation is real.

Harmony's been growing more distant, since we left Falcon's tribe. It's as if the harder I try to get close to her, the more she pushes away. Like she's punishing me for all the years I spent in space.

Marissa says it's her way of dealing with the idea that I might be gone forever, soon.

"You seem so set on this," Marissa says, during one of our long talks in my cabin.

I give her a look. "Of course I'm set on it. I came here all the way from the Brink for this, Marissa. So did you. I'm not going to change my mind now. Not when trillions of lives on it."

"You're counting uploads, now?"

"Yeah. They're people too. As much as I want as little to do with them as possible, they're people."

She shakes her head. "I just wish there were some other way."

A couple days later, it's like we never had that conversation. "Don't leave us, Joe," Marissa says. "Stay with us. Let's be a family."

I give a bitter chuckle. "If I tried that, we wouldn't have a galaxy to *be* a family in. There probably wouldn't be any families, anymore. Not that there are many left to begin with." A ragged sigh escapes my lips. "I'm sorry, Marissa. I have nothing to offer you. But, listen…I want you to know how much you've meant to me. Back in Brinktown, but also since you joined the *Ares*. Even before I knew it was you behind the Aphrodite avatar. You've always had my back. I didn't see that, before, and I think I played a big role in turning Harm against you, after you uploaded. Maybe I wasn't totally wrong in that, considering none of your copies seemed to give a damn about us. But you did. *You.* And let me tell you, Mar, that means everything."

"Mar," she says, her voice thick with emotion. "You haven't called me that in years."

"Yeah," I say, smiling.

"I appreciate you too, Joe. I think I blamed you for what happened with Harm because I knew *I* was really to blame for a lot of it. But you were the one who stayed in the real with her. You kept her off the streets, and you made sure she was cared for."

"I don't see any world where I'd upload to the Subverse. But I know what you're saying. And thanks. I think I needed that."

"It's not just that, either. You got Harmony back, Joe. We have our daughter back. And we're together, for however long."

"We both got her back. But yeah. I guess we are, aren't we?"

I probably don't need to tell you that before the night was over, we ended up in a sim together, entwined in each other's arms, loving each other like we did back in that old warehouse loft.

Marissa and I spend many more nights together in the sim, and it isn't difficult to hide it from Harmony. I just go to sleep in the command seat as I normally do—or I appear to, anyway. The sim replaces my dreams.

It's impacting my sleep, but I'll catch up on the last leg of the journey, before we reach the Core.

The discussion of whether to tell Harmony what's going on between us didn't last very long.

"What good would it do?" I say. "To know her parents were together again in her father's final days? It would just give her false hope."

"Yeah," Marissa says, eyes on the mess of blankets we've placed beneath us to ward off the cold of the warehouse floor. "No. You're right."

We tried a few other simulated locales to conduct our liaisons. An otherwise empty tropical beach. A windswept desert plateau, surrounded by the sound of cicadas and the stars. But we kept coming back to this old warehouse, letting our dataspheres probe our minds in order to reconstruct its likeness. We actually disagreed about a few of the details—was that battered old night stand really in the other corner, like Marissa seems to think? No. I wouldn't forget the layout of this place. But Marissa says much the same, and she insists it *was* in that other corner, but she hasn't pressed the point.

I know what Marissa's trying to do, in suggesting we should tell Harmony. Under normal circumstances, I'm sure she never would suggest it. Even if we led the most average lives possible, this would be too soon to tell our daughter that we're 'dating' again, or whatever you want to call this.

Marissa's trying to strengthen my ties to this world. Even if she isn't aware she's doing it…I know that's her angle. But it doesn't matter. I still have to face Fairfax in the Core—I still have to lay down my life for the galaxy. This doesn't change anything.

Does it?

It isn't until the night after our third transition into slipspace that Cal finally makes his reappearance. I tell Marissa I'll be back in a couple minutes, then I slip out of the simulated warehouse and into the real, to go down to use the head.

Cal Pikeman's standing near the OPO station, hands on hips. "What are you doing, Joe?"

I stiffen involuntarily. "What are you talking about?"

"You've initiated…*relations* with one of your crew."

"That's one way of putting it, yeah."

"What is it about the Seven Ideals that makes you think that's a good idea?" Cal snaps, spreading his hands wide. "What about *restraint?*"

"I was focusing more on service."

For a Fount-enabled ghost, he sure can get red in the face. "Joe, I'm your father for Fount's sake!"

"Ah, come on, Cal. We've never had a standard father-son relationship. I'm sure you can withstand a dirty joke or two." I heave a sigh. "Listen, I know getting involved with Marissa again probably isn't my smartest idea. But on the other hand, is it so wrong for me to enjoy myself during my last weeks of life? I know she's one of my crew, but she also happens to be the mother of my child. So maybe I deserve to be cut a little slack?"

"Knights don't get any slack. Not when the galaxy's at stake."

"Right." I get up from the command seat, circling Cal to stand near the TOPO station, facing him. "Speaking of which, where the hell have you been? Shouldn't these last few weeks been the time when we trained the hardest? And I could have used your help, back in the Moor."

"Surviving the Moor was some of the best training you could have received," Cal says, shaking his head dismissively. "I kept an eye on you. But more importantly, in the meantime, I've been running recon."

"I hope you have something good."

"I wouldn't call it that, exactly. But I learned much. Fairfax has amassed a military force larger than any the galaxy has seen since before the Fall. And the command structure seems a lot more stable than I'd like. I'm not so confident that killing him in the Core will cause the organization to fall apart...but that's a problem for the Guard to deal with, in the aftermath."

"Got anything that's relevant to me?"

"Indeed," Cal says, nodding gravely. "You're due to arrive at the Core with mere hours to spare before they complete the transfer of Jeremy Fairfax's consciousness into the Hanuman construct."

I shake my head. "Hanuman?"

"He was a monkey god in Hindu mythology, and Fairfax's indentured scientists have modeled the Allfather's construct-to-be after Hanuman. He was already popular on Earth before we colonized the stars, and interstellar colonists have kept him alive, with temples springing up in various systems. He represents strength, self-control, and service to a cause. Not to mention heroism."

"Doesn't sound like Jeremy Fairfax."

"You've never met Jeremy Fairfax."

"Sure I have. Asterisk was a copy of his consciousness."

Cal blinks. "I…must have missed that."

"Not as all-seeing as you let on, then. Didn't you notice I'm down a crewmember? Or did you miss that too, in your spying?"

"I was going to ask. You—well, obviously you survived the encounter."

"No thanks to you," I say.

"That's quite promising, actually. As for Jeremy Fairfax himself, remember that he was hailed as a hero by all the galaxy after inventing the Subverse. He's still revered in many corners, and of course, he sees himself as the good guy. As for strength, self-control, service to a cause…" Cal shrugs. "An argument could be made."

"Wow. Why not try to recruit him into the knighthood, then?"

"Please. He may think he's the good guy in all this, but he's become the galaxy's prime source of evil, whether wittingly or not."

I hesitate, leaning back against the TOPO station, unsure whether I should say what I have in my head. "Cal…back in the Shivan Cathedral, when I went inside the Source—"

He shakes his head. "What you heard in there was for your ears alone."

"Sure, but I really think you need to know this. Cal, the Seer told me I'll fail in the Core. That the Allfather will get loose."

Cal stares at me, unblinking, his face rigid.

"The Seer is supposed to be the Fount incarnate, right?" I go on. "That's what the priests believe. But if that's true, and the Fount chose me to reset the galaxy, then why would the Seer say I was going to fail?"

"Maybe you misinterpreted its words."

"I can't see how. It said exactly what I just told you, pretty much."

Cal shakes his head. "Joe, you're the most skilled person the knighthood has ever invited into its ranks. There's never been anyone so integrated with the Fount. I never thought I'd say this, but I have faith in you. I think you can succeed."

I study his face for a long time. Partly, I'm considering bringing up what I learned on Glade: about how another Shiva was in this same position before, with constructs beginning to come out of the woodworks. Did Cal miss that conversation, too, or is he just hoping I won't bring it up?

I decide it's best to play this one close to my vest. Cal doesn't need to know everything, does he? Plus, he's touchy—I don't want to risk pissing him off and causing him to take off right before I confront Fairfax for the last time.

"All right, Cal. I'll just have to focus on that. On completing the mission."

The old Shiva inclines his head. "Use these last few days to get some rest. Indulge in these dalliances with Marissa if you must, but don't let them impact your sleep. Arriving at the Core in top form will be vital to your success."

"Yeah. Sure thing." What Cal really means: I need to be in top form in order to overclock for so long that I die. But neither of us needs to say that.

THE CORE

1

Moments after we transition out of slipspace, I'm gripped by a sense of wonder as I peer through a visual sensor at the splendor outside the *Ares*—so gripped, in fact, that I barely notice how muted the nausea was this time. I didn't even throw up.

"It's…" Marissa says, and trails off. I realize my entire crew—Marissa, Harmony, and Belflower—are all staring out visual sensors. Marissa never finishes her sentence, and I can see why. It's almost beyond description.

If a red supergiant star somehow converted its entire mass into the darkest obsidian, it might look something like the singularity before us. I've seen images of it, but the images don't do justice to the majesty of seeing this in person. Maybe if I'd run a tourist sim I would have been prepared for it, but I've never been into those.

The black hole is like a patch of darkest night, torn from the very fabric of the universe. All along its periphery, it bends light itself into a brilliant halo.

That by itself is mind-boggling enough. But as I stare longer, I realize the surface of the black hole seems to sparkle like a sea of stars.

"The Dyson swarm," Cal says from behind me. He wasn't here a second ago, but it looks like he's decided to join us for the finale.

"The what?" I subvocalize.

"The satellites and stations that make up the Dyson swarm surrounding the singularity."

"Dyson swarm…" I twist in the command seat to meet his eyes, drawing a couple looks from the bridge crew, who almost certainly can't see Cal. "Is it functional?"

"It powers the galaxy's central Subverse. Where Jeremy Fairfax has held sway for so long. A lot of the satellites have stopped functioning, but most of them are still harvesting radiation from the black hole and converting it to energy."

"I had no idea humans could build such a thing."

"Well, it isn't half complete. But we were on our way to building it—Bacchus Corp was, anyway—and as is, it generates massive amounts of energy from the x-rays put out by the singularity's accretion disk"

I'm shaking my head. "If we were this close to achieving something like that…"

Cal nods. "Humanity was on the verge of the next step in its evolution, there's no question. Then the Fall happened. But there's no time to waste. I've just returned from the swarm's central control, and—"

"Sir, we have company," Marissa says. "I didn't notice them at first, with all the spacescraper traffic coming and going from the system. But I'm sure of it, now: all five of the warships we ran into back at the Sphere are here. They're a nice ways off, but they see us, and they appear to be approaching."

I glance at Cal. "Thoughts?"

"Make for the control center with all haste—I'll send you its location. Ships that massive won't be able to follow the *Ares* into the swarm. The orbiting satellites are too close together, and they'll get taken apart. Just to stay in orbit, the satellites have to travel at a twentieth of the speed of light. They're deadly missiles in their own right."

"What are the chances of us getting blasted apart by one of them?"

"Uh…not negligible. But I think the probability of those warships doing the job is higher. Besides, you need to reach central control as soon as possible. The Allfather's consciousness transfer is mere hours from completion."

I nod. "TOPO, set a course for the location I'll feed to your station now, engines at full power." Taking a deep breath, I add: "Get ready to do your best flying, Harm. Those satellites move at 0.05c, and we need to thread between them. Rely heavily on the ship's computer for assistance."

"Aye, Captain," Harmony says, jaw set.

As we soar across the stunning vista, and I keep an eye on the warship battle group's position relative to us, Cal briefs me as best he can on what I'll be facing down there.

"Central control is where each Shiva goes to reset the Subverse, typically facing Fairfax in the real and the Allfather inside the simulation."

"Wait—you mean I'll fight one after the other, right?"

"That's generally how it works."

"What other way *could* it work?"

"Do you remember on Gargantua, when you kept flitting back and forth between the Subverse and the real?"

"Sure, and in Sheen City. But I've never had to do that while fighting someone. We sure haven't *trained* to do that, Cal."

"Well, hopefully it won't come to that. Either way, this will tax you to your limits, Joe. There's something else you should know. The closer we get to the black hole, the more time dilates."

"What does that mean?"

"It slows down. You won't notice it, but from the rest of the galaxy's perspective, events will unfold slower than normal, and the effect gets bigger the closer to the black hole we get. If you were to be sucked past the event horizon, that would trend toward infinity."

"How much slower?"

"It's difficult to say. The Dyson swarm had to be constructed very far out to avoid getting battered by the singularity's accretion disk, so the effects aren't as pronounced as they are closer in. But the reason I'm telling you this is that this Subverse's frame rate has been increased to compensate for the effect—to keep pace with the rest of the galaxy. So if it does come to fighting in the real and the Subverse simultaneously, you'll be forced to do so at two different speeds. Regular speed, and much faster."

"Fount."

The warships are still several light seconds off when we dive through the first layer of satellites. After that, there's a lot of zigging and zagging as Harmony uses the computer's predictive capabilities, combined with what she's picked up during her months as TOPO, to dodge the speeding masses.

"Captain, there appears to be another vessel navigating through the swarm."

I squint at Marissa. "What's its profile?"

"Sir…I think it's *Europa's Gift*."

I stare at her, speechless. If *Europa's Gift* is here, that means Dice is here, unless someone managed to take his ship from him, which I tend to doubt. "Stupid bot," I mutter. I give him his freedom and the first thing he does is come here?

"Looks like he's headed for the Core too," Cal muses from beside me.

"How do you know?" I snap. "Did someone give you access to my ship's sensor data?"

"You should know by now that I don't need to be given access."

I resist the temptation to watch through an exterior visual sensor as Harmony navigates through the storm of satellites, and the Dyson swarm's central control grows ever nearer. It seems unlikely that watching their captain wince would do much good for crew morale, and I think there's a good chance that's what I'd be doing if I tried to watch.

Not Harmony. Watching how steady a hand she is at the *Ares'* controls fills me with a sense of pride. If I'm being honest, a year ago it would have horrified me to contemplate the idea that my ship would be at the mercy of my daughter's ability to fly her. How things change.

"We're nearing our destination," Marissa says, voice tight. From her general twitchiness, I take it she *has* elected to monitor our progress, which must be trying, especially when you're not the one controlling that progress. Then again, I guess it is her job as OPO to watch. "*Europa's Gift* has just entered a landing bay on the station."

"He didn't have to blow it open first?"

"Negative."

"I wonder what that's about," I say with a glance at Cal.

"Could be he's hacked the hatch controls remotely. You did give him the ability to increase his intelligence without limit, remember."

"Right," I muse. "That."

For all its importance, not just for the swarm but for the galaxy as a whole, the central control doesn't seem all that big. I guess it can outsource actual processing to the swarm around it, so that all you really need in the real are interfaces, in case anyone needs to come and troubleshoot manually. Or transfer the consciousness of a god into a monkey man.

The station's airlock opens for us, too, at a simple request from Marissa. Did Dice make it do that, or are Fairfax and his friends just feeling super welcoming today?

When the station's inner airlock hatch opens, the notion that Fairfax is feeling welcoming gets dispelled immediately. Laserfire crisscrosses the bay, traded back and forth between *Europa's Gift* and a contingent of bots, human soldiers, and stationary turrets. A dozen of those spike-shaped dropships are here too, though they don't seem to have any hull-mounted weaponry, thank Fount.

"Set us down near *Europa's Gift*, Harm, so that we form a shallow V whose point faces into the station."

"Aye."

While she's doing that, I assign macros to take control of all the *Ares'* turrets but one—the primary on top. I drop into the control sim for that one and start hammering any hostiles currently occupying positions behind our V. The handles thrum between my fingers as beams as thick as tree trunks lance from the top of the ship, cutting through humans and bots with frightening ease. After clearing a decent percentage of the mobile troops, I start working on the turrets. Each one pops after a few seconds' attention from the *Ares'* primary.

With the pressure slackened, the occupant of Daniel Sterling's former ship chooses that moment to come out. Occupants, actually: when its outer airlock hatch opens, both Dice and our old family bot, P3P, emerge.

The *Ares* is in position now, and Harmony clearly sees the old bot. "Pepper?" she cries, and I try not to wince at the cringe-inducing nickname. "What's he doing with a laser rifle?"

That's a good question. P3P isn't built for combat—far from it. He lacks not just the protocols, but the built-in weaponry and armor.

Nevertheless, he joins Dice in rushing to the stern and adding their laserfire to the two ships'. *Europa's Gift* also isn't designed for combat, and she lacks combat flaps for cover. I'm still neutralizing laser turrets, so I can't pay too much attention to the bots, but I do notice P3P hanging back, careful not to overexpose his more vulnerable exterior to enemy fire.

"Time to go," I say, leaping up from the command seat and rushing to the supply closet to grab my helmet. "Harm, do not leave this ship under any circumstances. Just let the offensive macros run the way I set them. Are we clear?"

"Clear," she says.

"Once me and Dice advance past the landing bay, I want you to get out of here. Leave the swarm and get to safety. Are we clear?" I ask again.

For a long time, both Marissa and Harmony return my gaze. "Clear," Harmony says at last.

"I hope so." There's no time to make sure Harmony is being sincere, so I have to trust she has the sense to obey me. If anything, Marissa will make sure they leave as soon as they can, for Harmony's sake. "Get in touch if you run into any trouble. Harmony, Marissa—I love you both. Belflower, thank you for your service." I offer them a weak smile. "I'm out." With that, I head through the airlock.

"Dice," I subvocalize as I sprint to the combat flap that folds out past the *Ares'* bow, willing it to extend as I run. "You here for any particular reason, or just sightseeing?"

"A little of Column A, a little of Column Kill Fairfax."

"That's my favorite column. How did you know to come here?"

"Your father paid me a visit and requested my presence. He thought you might be able to use the help."

"He was right," I say, glancing over in Dice's direction. "What'd you do to P3P?"

"The house pet? I took out his sorry excuse for a brain and gave him a real one. Mine. He's me, now."

"And he agreed to that?"

"It wasn't really preceded by a discussion."

Taking up position behind the extensible barrier, I settle my blaster across the top and start laying into the soldiers still entrenched around the landing bay. One pops up at the wrong time, and he gets a blaster bolt to the face for his troubles, tossing him to the deck.

"Not that we really have time to talk about this," I say, "but I didn't give you your freedom so you could take it from other bots."

"I don't understand. I liberated P3P from the misery of being himself."

"Whatever. Hey, you're a super genius now, right? Any ideas for how to speed things up in here? I'm on a bit of a timeline when it comes to this whole 'stopping the emergence of an all-powerful god' thing."

"It's funny you should ask," Dice says. "I've just finished implementing my solution to these soldiers. Executing now."

With that, every still-functional turret in the landing bay turns on the enemy humans and bots, systematically cutting them down where they stand, laserfire ripping into their ranks from their backs and sides.

It takes no more than a few seconds. Their bloody work done, the landing bay's laser turrets lower their barrels to point at the deck, in stand-down position.

"Will that suffice?" Dice asks.

"It's a good start," I say, inching around the *Ares* and eyeing the turrets warily. Satisfied they're not about to turn on me like they did their masters, I stride toward the entrance into the rest of the station. "Let's move."

2

The corridor beyond the landing bay presents more of a challenge. There aren't any turrets here for Dice to hack, plus there are more doorways than I expect for Fairfax's fighters to take cover behind, and even a few fold-out barriers, though those look bolted-on to the existing structure. This wasn't designed as a military facility, after all.

Me, Dice, and P3P (technically also Dice), are crouched around the hatch leading from the landing bay, getting off what shots we can in the face of the concentrated fire coming at us from down the corridor.

"What about their helmets?" I subvocalize. "Any chance of getting between them and their visual feeds, maybe make them see just static or something?"

"Negative," Dice says. "At least, I could likely devise a method, given time we don't have. But that connection is designed as simply as possible, to offer as few avenues for outside interference as was feasible."

"Fine," I grunt, detaching a plasma grenade from my belt and cooking it. Timing it carefully, I throw it down the corridor and flatten myself to the landing bay bulkhead. Dice remains where he is, continuing to fire at the hostiles holding the corridor. He's probably calculated the grenade's trajectory and determined it doesn't have enough explosive power to harm him here, but I'm not a computer and I'm going to stay out of the blast's way just to be safe.

Light and sound fill the corridor. A second later, me and Dice take point, with P3P tagging close behind, all three of us opening up on anything that moves through the smoke. We advance up the corridor.

"You should set P3P to clearing rooms behind us," I say. "Check them for hostiles or connecting passages where they can flank us. That's the last thing we need."

Dice nods, and the former house bot turns to access the first room.

I'm tempted to overclock to quickly clear out the rest of the corridor, but it seems suicidal given what I'm likely to face up ahead. Either way, me and Dice are working together well, covering each other when needed, laying down suppressive fire so the other can progress up the hall. Almost every shot either finds a target or keeps one pinned so we can move up on them. We advance steadily, though not as quickly as I'd like.

Finally, we come to a hatch that takes up the entire corridor, from bulkhead to bulkhead, deck to overhead.

"Open sesame," I say, not bothering to subvocalize the joke.

"What's that, fleshbag?"

"It's a joke. Try reading more." I sniff. "Can you hack this thing open?"

"Already looking into it."

As I wait, someone tries to connect with me through my datasphere. Idly, I accept.

"Joe. It's Brendan Cadogan."

"Brendan. It's good to hear you survived the Sphere."

A pause, then: "Sometimes I wish I hadn't. You should turn

back, Joe, while you still can. You can't defeat the monster Fairfax and Ludmilla have created."

"Wait—I thought the consciousness transfer wasn't finished?"

"It…isn't," Cadogan says, sounding confused—probably by the fact that I know that. "It's not finished. But that's worse for you, arguably. Jeremy Fairfax's Id *has* been transferred. His subconscious—the subconscious of the same angry, resentful man who sought to dominate humanity, and who convinced them uploading to a computer was a good idea. Right now, that Id occupies a superbeing. If you come into this chamber, it will crush you."

"I know that," I say, my eyes on Dice. "It's all part of the package."

"I just don't want to see a man as revered and skilled as yourself get cut down in his prime."

"My prime's just about over. Anyway, what good is a soldier if he doesn't fight for peace? What chance will I get to stop all this, if not here, today?"

"But you're not stopping it, Joe. You're just postponing it."

That brings me up short. Cadogan's words remind me of Electra Fairfax, back on Glade, when she told me about the last Shiva to find himself in my position. About the choice he made.

"I don't walk away from a fight," I say. "But thanks for the warning."

Dice turns to me. "We're in." P3P walks up from behind us, laser rifle at the ready. His dimly glowing eyes meet mine, and he nods.

"Open it up," I say.

The massive hatch lifts from the ground, receding into the bulkhead above.

Beyond it lies a giant circle of a room, dominated by a massive viewing window that curves around most of it, making up the upper half the bulkhead. The window is totally transparent, and through it I can see hundreds of scientists and technicians, gathered in groups at various interfaces while others monitor the chamber. They all freeze as the three of us enter, staring at us with wide eyes and blank faces. Presumably, they're all Cadogans.

In the center of the room, a raised dais holds a chair where a gorilla sits strapped in, electrodes covering its skull.

Calling it a gorilla isn't quite accurate. The thing looks more upright than that, for one, and it bulges with muscle beyond even what a gorilla would have in the wild. This is the construct Cal warned me about—the Hanuman construct. It actually wears clothing: just a bright, multi-colored vest, but it's more than I would have expected.

The construct is also smaller than I expected, considering the snake and the Kitane I've faced already. For some reason, I don't find that comforting in the slightest.

"You need to leave," a woman's voice says, echoing through the chamber. "Leave, now." I can't see which of the Cadogans is speaking, but her voice is drenched in fear.

Cal appears beside me. "Stand firm," he says. "You've arrived at the Crucible, Joe. I hope I've trained you well. Today determines whether you'll be welcomed into the Shiva Knighthood."

"It also determines whether I'll die."

He turns toward me, blank-faced. "Yes."

I shrug. I guess it wasn't a particularly insightful thing for me to say after all, especially considering Cal died here, too.

"Where's Fairfax?" I ask.

"I don't know. I've lost track of him." Cal studies me, his face grim. "It's as I feared. You'll need to defeat the Allfather in both the real and the Subverse at the same time."

"And hope that Fairfax doesn't turn up halfway through the fight."

"I...highly doubt you can overclock long enough to defeat them both, Joe."

"Where does that leave us?"

"I don't know," Cal says again. "Maybe...if you can defeat the

Allfather, kill off this construct, it will allow time for the Guard to be rallied to come and end this. It's a long shot, and it's never been tried before, but…I will do what I can. You have my word."

"All right, then," I say, thinking of Harmony and Marissa, back on the *Ares*. Hopefully they're well away from here, by now. "Let's get this thing started."

As if it heard my request, the primate strapped to the chair opens its eyes, blinking groggily. Then it flexes, heaving forward until the restraints start snapping off, leaping from its chest and legs one by one. The wireless electrodes are still in place.

It rises to its feet, ham-like hands curled into fists at its sides.

I raise my blaster, left hand cupped under the handle, leveling it at the construct.

It's time.

3

"I need you and P3P to take on the Allfather for as long as you can manage," I tell Dice. "I have some other business to attend to."

Dice peers around the room, then looks at me, head cocked. "Did you leave the stove on in the mess, or something?"

"I have to face the Allfather in the Subverse."

With that, I reach through my emotions—through my fear, my anger, my sadness at the prospect of never seeing Harmony and Marissa again—and I overclock. After that, transitioning out of the real and into the simulation is as easy as thinking about it.

The Subverse version of the room has the same deck, but nothing else. Gone are the bulkheads, the overhead, and the sweeping observation window. In their place is the star-speckled dark of space, with the supermassive black hole overhead, its halo of tapered light adorning it like a celestial crown.

There's also no dais, and no monkey god. In their place stands a towering figure wearing midnight armor, holding a diamond-shaped shield in one hand and a wide, tall blade in the other. His helm is open to reveal the nothingness that lurks within.

One other difference: this platform has a narrow peninsula

jutting from it beyond the dark knight. At its end, a terminal hovers in midair. The Subverse reset function. I know it without having to be told.

Wordlessly, the giant steps forward, sword spinning with improbable speed, given its size. I summon my broadsword and adopt a ready stance. I'm already wearing my blue-lit armor.

I'm not sure why the Subverse would have the capacity to simulate overclocking, but it does, in that my senses are heightened beyond belief. Every detail, every ridge of my adversary's armor stands out in sharp relief, and I swear I can hear the resounding void of space, the swirling maelstrom of the singularity above, even though no sound should travel in space. As I walk forward, each footstep echoes smartly, despite there being no bulkheads for them to bounce off of.

Given how talkative Asterisk was, I would have guessed Jeremy Fairfax would have some smug words for me before we start trading blows. But he seems wholly uninterested in that. Maybe he's tired of being cooped up in this digital realm of his own making. Next to winning his freedom through combat, conversation must seem pretty frivolous.

We clash in the room's center, blade meeting blade. My broadsword flickers down in a diagonal overhead attack, and the Allfather parries with ease, turning the attack aside. Switching to a one-handed grip, I call up Blue Fire, pouring the flames into the knight's hollow helm. He flinches, and I bring my sword up to take advantage of the opening, but he bats it away with the flat of his palm, as though it were a mere annoyance.

The Allfather recovers, advancing with a series of slow, sweeping strikes. What he lacks in speed he more than makes up for in power, and I'm forced to maneuver my body out of the way, unable to turn aside his blows more often than not.

Then the strikes speed up, and I realize he was toying with me. I need to find a way to go on the attack, but that's getting increasingly difficult as the dark knight's movements begin to blur.

I slip up, falling for a feint and leaving myself open for my opponent's sword to crash into my side, cleaving the metal there and knocking me sideways, streaming blood behind me.

Staggering, I realize I'm back in the real. That's just as well, since I'm sorely needed here.

P3P lies in a mangled heap against the bulkhead on the far side of the circular chamber. Turning to find Dice and the giant simian, I spot them just as the former is grabbing the latter, despite that Dice was peppering his adversary with laserfire from both pistols. The Hanuman construct lifts Dice up and flings him into the bulkhead with unsettling speed and ferocity. Dice manages to absorb the impact somewhat, though a couple dark-metal pieces break off him to skitter across the deck. Hopefully nothing too important.

In the real, I'm still holding my blaster, so I level it at the ape and begin spamming the trigger. White bolts eat into its skin, blackening the fur and leaving marks, but the wounds aren't nearly as big as they should be. Apparently the thing's flesh is incredibly durable. The impact also doesn't do as much as it should: what would have flung a human back barely causes the monkey god to twitch.

"It's just as I told you," Cal says from behind me. He sounds angry. "You can't just let your bot fight the Allfather, Joe."

That seems redundant, given I've clearly won the beast's attention. But I'm not here to bicker with my father. The great ape starts to cross the room, eyes fixated on me, muscled arms swinging back and forth.

4

As the gorilla drops to all fours and charges, I flit back into the Subverse momentarily to find the knight looming over me, sword descending for a killing blow.

I roll to the left, and the heavy blade scrapes against the back of my armor, sending a shower of sparks into the air. Flicking my legs around, I pop back to my feet. My sword is gone from my grasp, so I send it an order to dispel, then reequip it from my inventory. It falls into my hand, and I raise it crosswise to parry an overhead blow—

Switching back to the real, I loose bolt after bolt into the charging primate's face. It howls, eyes burning with rage. Time slows to a crawl, and I wait till the last possible instant before leaping past my adversary, falling into a forward roll, clutching my blaster in preparation to regain my feet and resume firing—

The dark knight's sword crashes into my battered armor, shearing it further and drawing more blood. I stumble, going down to one knee, ducking instinctively to dodge a slice that should have lopped off my head.

I'm favoring the fight in the real too much, and not giving enough time to fighting the digital version of the Allfather, who operates at a faster rate to compensate for the time-dilating effects of the black hole.

I draw deeper on my emotions, my focus…the Fount. Time slows further, and I launch into a series of savage strikes, taking the armor-clad Allfather by surprise and driving him back. Activating Telekinesis, I use it to repulse the dark knight, knocking him off his footing and sending him toward the side. Has a missing barrier taken the place of the bulkheads in the real, or is there a chance he'll fall off into the void, leaving me to reset the Subverse uncontested? I step forward to help him on his way—

and regain my footing in the real, depressing the blaster trigger, which clicks. Out of energy. I eject the charge pack onto the floor, and it sinks toward the deck like a stone through gel. To the Cadogans watching above, I'm sure my movements are barely discernible, but I feel like I'm moving with measured sureness. I slap the fresh charge pack into the blaster's handle and squeeze the trigger again and again, sending a flurry of bolts into the primate's chest in a precise line. The Hanuman construct roars, baring razor-sharp teeth, and then surges forward much faster than I anticipated. Its shoulder collides with my chest, knocking me back, and I twist aside just in time to avoid receiving its teeth in my neck. Nevertheless, I'm knocked back, hurtling end over end, but even so I know it's past time to—

I'm walking toward the knight in dark armor, and instead of helping him fall over the edge, I'm basically serving myself up. He's recovered from his stumble toward the side, and he bashes me with his shield, knocking me off-balance. His sword whistles toward my head, his speed just as surprising as his simian counterpart's, and I turn my staggering into an evasive tip-toe backward, using my sword to help his strike on its way—it glances off my helm before continuing over my head. My maneuver puts the Allfather off-balance, and I seek to exploit that. Letting the sword fall, dissipating on its way to the deck, I bring up both hands and unleash Fire Wave. My adversary falls to one knee, raising his shield to protect his empty helm, and a blue, spherical shimmering appears around him—

Coming to rest on my back, I ignore the pain lancing through my body to push myself to my feet just in time to spring out of the way of the Hanuman construct. But the monkey god gathers up his momentum unexpectedly, bringing a fist up and around. Laserfire flickers from the side of the chamber; two streams aimed into the mindless beast's eyes, blinding it. Its punch goes wild, and I duck under it easily, bringing my blaster around to add my fire to Dice's—

The towering knight's protective spell parts the Fire Wave around it harmlessly, and the rolling flames fall off the side of the deck. Standing before the conflagration has fully left him, the knight lets his own weapon vanish in order to raise both hands. Lightning arcs from them, and I activate Deflect, my own protective spell. It's woefully inadequate against the power of the Allfather's magic. Electricity radiates past my armor to course through my body, which convulses in pain. The armor's fighting to ground me, redirecting the energy down into the deck below, and the pain's gradually subsiding. But my movement's restricted as my body tries to curl in on itself, and the knight is advancing, releasing the spell to resummon his sword and shield—

The Hanuman construct is swinging blindly now, fists pummeling empty air as I dance backward through the chamber. The loaded energy pack clicks empty, and I eject it without thought, slamming in a new one. How much punishment can this thing take? What if I have to confront it in hand-to-hand combat? I'm ready to do anything to take the Allfather down, but any hope that I might survive this fight is quickly evaporating. Of course I'll have to overclock long enough that it kills me. The only real question is whether even that will be enough. I resume firing—

The knight's sword point flickers forward, aimed at my visor slit, positioned horizontally to slide through. I snap my head back, and the blade connects with the bottom of my helmet, scraping down across the gorget. Desperately, I flick more blue fire at the Allfather's open helm, causing him to flinch back. Now's my chance. I dart forward, broadsword flashing toward his head, and the sword passes into the void that occupies it. Metal scrapes on metal as my sword finds the back of the hollow helm, and a hideous shriek emanates from the Allfather, seeming to fill the cosmos with sound. He wrenches backward, letting his weaponry dissolve as he clutches his hands to his face.

Good. If I can put an end to the fight in the Subverse, activating the procedure that will unleash a cascade throughout the galaxy, resetting each Subverse in turn…that should disrupt the transfer of Jeremy Fairfax's mind. That done, I'll just need to deal with the Hanuman construct. Could there be a way I survive this after all?

Despite his evident agony, the giant still has the presence of mind to bring a new spell to bear, sending beams of blue-white energy in my direction. Most of the shots miss, as I gather the knight is at least partially blinded, but one connects, tossing me off my feet toward the platform's edge, toward the endless chasm of the universe that awaits me—

This time, I stayed in the Subverse too long. The primate reaches me, and before I can react, it backhands my blaster out of my grasp, sending it flying. I'm confronted with the prospect of hand-to-hand combat much sooner than I'd feared.

To contend physically with the construct, I know what I have to do, even though I know it will overtax my body and bring death even faster. I will all my muscles to convulse at once, grounding me firmly and sending my fist crashing into the construct's face. It's like punching a brick wall, and my hand comes away feeling shattered, but the monkey god blinks, flinching back. That gives me time to pivot around it, using my momentum to jackhammer an elbow into its back. My muscles convulse together in a single direction, in the same way they do when confronted with an electric shock. Except, I control it fully. My elbow rockets into the gorilla's back, and it howls, trying to reach backward with both hands but limited by its range of motion. It spins instead, fist hurtling through the air. I duck under it, rising to drive knuckles into its throat—

Another blue-white bolt catches me full in the chest, knocking me over the edge. It turns out there are no invisible barriers to prevent us from going over the side. I manage to catch the edge of the deck with gauntleted fingers, and my body swings wildly, my momentum threatening to break my grasp. The deck tremors as the knights pounds toward me, though there's no rhythm to his footfalls, and I can tell he's still thrown off by my sword penetrating the empty space inside his helm. I'm not sure why that did such damage to him, but I don't have time to puzzle over the rules of the Subverse. With an effort of will, I pull myself up, at the same time swinging my legs up and over the platform—

Two powerful arms dart out, shoving me backward. Instead of striking, the primate screams in my face, lips peeled back to reveal twin rows of razor teeth, eyes wide and bloodshot. It's an awesome, primal display, and for a moment I think I'm going to fall out of my overclocked state, which would probably be the end of the battle. And of me.

But I keep it together, preparing to will all my muscles to convulse in order to throw a kick into the animal's side.

"Joe!" It's Marissa's voice, echoing through my thoughts, drawn out and deeper than usual due to my current experience of time. She sounds distraught.

The construct follows up its dominance display by swaggering forward, cocking its fist. "What's wrong?" I ask. "Why are you still here?"

"We couldn't leave you, Joe. We left the station after you went inside, but we couldn't bring ourselves to leave. We circled back and returned to the landing bay. But something happened…"

I dance back from the ape, dodging the fist, which is followed by a meaty hand that moves faster than it should, connecting with my helmet with enough force to send me reeling.

Reining in my momentum, I come to a stop near my blaster, and reaching for it—

I manage to get back onto the platform just as the knight reaches me, and without thinking I equip Telekinesis, using it to trip him in the hopes he'll career forward into the darkness. No such luck: his foot comes down hard to arrest his progress, and he resummons his sword. Mine falls into my hands just in time to deflect his savage blow, and we continue striking at each other near the platform's edge—

"What happened, Marissa?" I grunt, teeth gritted against the pain as I fire on the Hanuman construct.

"It's Harmony. Fairfax broke into the *Ares* and took her into one of the dropships. He's leaving the station now. I think he's going to take her to the *Ekhidnades*."

Dice steps forward from the bulkhead. "Let me handle this," he says.

I glance at him, not sure how he has access to our transmission, but also not about to ask—

I'm holding my own. Here at the edge of infinity, fighting the Subverse's most powerful entity, I'm turning aside his blows. I'm far from winning, but I'm surviving.

How is that possible, if the Subverse's leveling system is such a big factor? Clearly, there are other factors that can compensate for a low level. Like the ability to move as quickly as overclocking allows, and to strike with the ferocity it confers. As powerful as Fairfax is, he clearly isn't willing to break the rules of the combat system he devised. Or maybe he isn't able. Maybe the algorithm polices even him.

Instead of parrying his next strike, I take a risk and use Deflect. The spell is enough to turn his blade aside, simultaneously freeing my blade to strike with more speed than expected. The knight is caught off guard, and the blade sails past his shield to bite into the seam above his gorget, striking something—flesh, ethereal essence, I don't know—and eliciting another shriek as the knight recoils—

"What will you do, Dice?" I ask, relying on muscle-memory footwork to carry me out of the construct's path and around to the side, where I convulse again to send the butt of my blaster into the back of my enemy's skull. The blow produces a cracking sound, and the Hanuman construct claps a hand to the back of his head, stumbling forward and roaring.

"I'll take *Europa's Gift* and give chase. I'll make sure no harm comes to Harmony, Joe."

That draws my gaze again. I think that's the first time Dice has ever called me by my first name.

"Let me do this for you," he says. "You need to stay here and finish this. Everything hinges on it."

The Hanuman construct is shaking itself off, coming around for another charge.

My eyes are still on Dice. "Okay. Go, then. And thank you."

Dice nods, sprinting for the hatch. I square off to deal with another assault from the Allfather.

5

I meet the Hanuman construct head-on, dispatching a series of white blaster bolts into its face before sidestepping once more, leaving it to barrel forward, grasping at the air. A distracted part of my mind toys with the idea of trying to use a plasma grenade against it, but I can't seem to put enough distance between us to make it a viable option.

An even greater portion of my mind fears for Harmony, and rebels at the thought that I might die without ever knowing whether she's safe—

My second time managing to get past the knight's armor seems to have enraged him, erasing his cool and sending him into a furious onslaught, his blade seeming to come from every direction. It's all I can do to parry each blow, and I'm steadily losing ground, physically and mentally. Inching ever toward the edge—of falling off the platform, falling out of overclocking.

My concentration is under siege, not just by the Allfather, but by the thought of Harmony in peril. But Harmony isn't my responsibility anymore. She can't be. She's looked after herself so far, with a little help. Hopefully Dice can stop Fairfax from hurting her, and get her out again, and they can flee with Marissa.

The knight's shield disappears, and he throws his hand forward, palm toward me, producing a wall of wind that jostles me backward toward the edge. Fire Wave is recharged, and I unleash it again, dropping the sword to do so. Contending with the air blowing against it, it doesn't move nearly as fast, but it spreads out far enough that the knight can't escape. He throws up the same protective sphere as before, which puts a stop to the air spell. Recalling my sword, I march across the platform gripping it in both hands, to clash with the Allfather again—

The great ape turns, throwing up a hand to catch the blaster bolts I'm pouring toward its head. It surges forward against the torrent, and I take the opportunity to will my muscles to convulse forward, putting everything into a kick aimed at the construct's abdomen. Its stomach is like iron, but the force of the kick knocks it back a foot, and I can see the pain in its eyes as it swipes at me, nearly connecting solidly with my shoulder. It strikes a glancing blow instead, and I dip, trying to absorb the impact as I stagger away from its grasp.

I know why Fairfax took Harmony. It was a bid to distract me, to pull me away from the fight and buy time for the Cadogans to finish transferring the Allfather's consciousness.

Because he knows I can win, and so do I. I'm doing better than I expected against both versions of the Allfather…meaning, it seems likely I can defeat them by sacrificing myself, which is the best I should have hoped for.

The construct's pursuing me across the chamber, and I realize he's trying to hem me in, with the aim of pinning me against the bulkhead—

His blue sphere flickering out, the dark knight rises, blade arcing upward toward my face. I dodge the strike, countering with a thrust aimed at his chest. The blow connects, but glances harmlessly off the knight's armor.

Then I let my sword go to spit Blue Fire from my fingertips, right into his empty helm at point-blank range. The interior lights up, and the knight recoils once more, sword swinging wildly in an attempt to prevent me from pressing the attack.

I press it anyway.

Yes, I can win this. I can go out in a blaze of glory, of righteousness. And my failures as a father, as a leader, as a friend— they'll all be erased by the act. Or so I can tell myself.

It wouldn't be hard to maintain the illusion, I reflect as I drive Jeremy Fairfax's avatar farther back, knowing it's only a matter of time before he turns things around on me. I can tell myself that my sacrifice will redeem me. But that's not all. Dying here will solve all my problems, too. I won't have to figure out a way to bring Harmony and Marissa together into a functioning unit, a family. And I'll deliver the galaxy back to its cycle of self-inflicted slavery. Its prison of delusion, made from our desire for everything to be easy and safe—

I crash into the bulkhead, sending pain through my shoulder, and I spin away just in time to avoid getting sandwiched between the Hanuman construct and the metal. It twists around, smashing a fist into the wall an inch or two from my head, and I dart backward, getting the blaster up between us. I spam the trigger until the energy pack clicks.

During the break in the firing, the primate charges forward again, doggedly.

There's no time to replace the charge pack. Instead, I let the empty one fall into my hand, then I use the convulsion technique to put everything I have into the throw. The charge pack brains the simian, bringing its hands to its forehead. I use the reprieve to slap in a fresh charge—

As expected, the knight recovers well short of the platform's edge, using the air spell to shove me backward. I manage to side-step until I find the end of the spell in time to avoid getting thrown off the platform, but I'm well off-balance when the Allfather pounds toward me, seeking to skewer me.

I turn aside the thrust, pivoting and answering with a slice at his hamstring, which the armor repels—

A storm of blaster bolts keeps the Hanuman construct off me, but it's too strong to be held back for long. It's barely slowing under my assault, and while I know I must have done *some* damage, it's going to be a long grind of a battle before the end.

Do I believe the Guard will see sense enough to rally together against Fairfax? Cal thinks they will, and he also thinks I must sacrifice myself to defeat the Allfather.

But in that moment, sending bolt after bolt toward the massive primate, I realize dying is the easy way out. Even dying in the name of the galaxy. Sending it back into its cycle of delusion—that's too easy. Staying alive, helping the galaxy confront the period of chaos that will follow when we finally decide to pay for everything we've taken—that's the hard way. And it's also the right way.

I'm already backing toward the open hatch that leads into the corridor, and now I turn to sprint through it. The moment I reach the corridor, the hatch slams shut. One of the Cadogans must have done that, to prevent the Allfather from escaping the chamber.

"Joe," Cal says, appearing before me, face contorted. "What in the Fount's good name are you doing?"

"I'm going to rescue my daughter, Cal."

"You need to get back in that room and complete your destiny. You must defeat the Allfather in order to reset the Subverse."

"Actually, I don't think I have to do anything. Everything's a choice, Cal, and we all have to take responsibility for them. The ones we've made, and the ones that come next."

"Son…your name will go down in disgrace. You'll be known as the only man in history to betray the Shiva. I'll disown you."

Shaking my head, I say, "Sorry, but you kind of already did."

With that, I sprint down the corridor toward the airlock.

6

I need to stop overclocking, but I can't. Fairfax is too far ahead through the swarm of hurtling satellites, and according to Marissa, Dice is losing ground.

Flying through the Dyson swarm at the speed needed to catch up requires more than my ship computer's predictive capacity is capable of. It requires the acute cognition and hairpin reflexes of overclocking.

The 3D tactical display is a maelstrom of motion. I'm tracking dozens of satellites at any given second, plotting a course instinctively through them, jerking the *Ares* back and forth, weaving and bobbing and dodging. Marissa's pitching in, working to identify satellites that are outside of the area I'm processing but which will pose a threat within the next few seconds.

"Joe, here. This one!"

The satellite she's identified, combined with the projected trajectory she's sketched through the display, requires me to scrap my current course and come up with a new one on the fly. I kill the rear thrusters and bring the starboard engines up to full power, jolting us left and putting us on a new path, one which may or may not lead to survival. Studying the display with ferocious intensity, I start to tease out the pattern, guiding us toward a course I think will see us through.

"We're gaining on them," Marissa says after ten minutes—an eternity.

"Not fast enough," I mutter, eyes glued to the display. At this rate, Fairfax will break from the cloud well before we close with him. "Marissa, tell Dice he needs to cripple Fairfax's engines."

"On it," she says, fingers flickering across her console.

"Tell him to be careful. If he blows up that shuttle, I'll dismantle him myself."

Not that that's likely. *Europa's Gift* is equipped only with the bare minimum of weaponry, just what would be required to scare off a pirate scow if Daniel Sterling ever got caught with his pants down in deep space. Even so, on the display I watch Dice dart forward, putting himself at risk to use his point defense turrets offensively.

For several excruciating minutes, the gambit has no effect, and it seems certain Fairfax will reach his battle group with Harmony on board. If that happens, there'll be no getting her from him. I channel my frustration into threading furiously through the satellites, determined not to let them come too close.

"There!" Marissa says in an excited tone. "He's done it!"

And he has: Fairfax's ship is limping toward the swarm's boundary, at a noticeably reduced rate.

A few minutes later, we close the gap.

"Dice, do you copy?" I say, not bothering to subvocalize.

"I hear you."

"I'm going to head Fairfax off. We need to force a landing at one of the stations."

"Copy that."

The *Ares* surges ahead, and to get the job done I'm forced to rely on macros designed to fire warning shots across another ship's bow. I can't tweak them and navigate through the satellite swarm at the same time, and I certainly can't take manual control of one of the turrets.

"Belflower, can you do something about giving these macros a little more bite? Not too much, though."

"Working on it, Captain."

The Engineer operates with her characteristic speed, and soon one of the turrets is directing staccato bursts of laserfire right into the dropship's nose.

At last, it works: Fairfax stops running, instead making for a station nearby.

"Any guesses on what that structure might be for?" I ask the two women who are all that remain of my crew.

"Energy storage is my best guess," Belflower says. "If they didn't have a good number of those, there'd be a lot of wastage, judging by the amounts they must be harvesting from that singularity."

"Right," I say, unsure if that's something I can use.

"I don't think it's big enough to have a landing bay, sir," Belflower says. "Worse, looks like there's only one docking port, and Fairfax is taking it."

A grinding sound reaches my ears, and I realize it's my teeth. "I'll have to match the station's orbit with the *Ares*. After that, I'll have to jump across to it."

"What if Harmony isn't wearing a suit?" Marissa says, sounding distraught. "Fairfax didn't take her helmet, and he might not give her one."

I study Marissa's face for a protracted moment.

"I'll have to figure that out if I come to it. This is the best I've got right now, Mar."

She nods, swallowing, her brow furrowed.

Once I've lined up the *Ares* with the station, matching our orbital velocity and locking it in, I stand, picking up my helmet from where I left it on the deck beside the command seat.

"Wish me luck," I mutter as I stride across the bridge toward the opening airlock.

But neither woman can muster the will to speak. I turn, meeting Marissa's tortured eyes as the inner hatch slides shut.

7

With the help of magnets, I crawl from the open airlock across the *Ares'* hull, lining myself up with the station a few meters away.

"Hit it," I say over a two-way channel with Belflower.

The Engineer activates the macro governing the forward starboard laser turret, which fires at the station long enough to melt a hole a meter in diameter.

I've already lined up the airlock with that area, in case something comes hurtling out due to depressurization—Harmony, for instance. But nothing emerges, confirming my suspicion that the station had no atmosphere to begin with.

Tensing my legs for the jump, I ignore the heavy fatigue dragging on my body's every cell, and the sensation of hollowness. I leap, careening through the void toward the speeding station. Luckily, thanks to the *Ares*, I'm traveling forward at the same speed, and there's no air resistance to drag me back. So I cross the intervening space as though both the ship and the station were stock-still. Then I pass through the melted portal, and a gravity generator exerts its force on me, causing me to fall a few feet, back-first. Using my momentum to flick my body upward, I come upright, blaster in hand.

Fairfax stands with his sword across the throat of Harmony's pressure suit, which has been sealed to a gray helmet that looks too big for her. Fairfax's sword arm still bears the laser burns from our encounter in the Cadogan Sphere, and his metal torso is twisted and pockmarked. He and Harmony are surrounded by ten soldiers in gold-trimmed black suits. The station is square-shaped, five meters to a side, and all four of its bulkheads are covered with rack after rack of onyx batteries, stretching from deck to overhead.

"Pikeman," Fairfax says, his voice just as mirth-filled as always. He wears no extra gear—I guess half-bots don't breathe like the rest of us do. "You've already lost. Just by following me here."

"Losing means different things to different people. But you're about to lose your life."

Something lands beside me, sending vibrations through the deck and up my boots. I turn to nod at Dice, then refocus my attention on Fairfax.

Abruptly, he shoves Harmony toward one of his henchman, who puts his weapon against her neck. "Kill her the moment I say so," Fairfax hisses.

Damn it. I should have shot the soldier the second Harmony left Fairfax's grasp. But my senses are dulled, even in my overclocked state. Did I leave off fighting the Allfather just to die in battle with Fairfax? It doesn't matter. If it means saving Harmony, it's worth it.

Fairfax approaches across the cramped space, and I draw a deep breath, centering myself as well as I can. Dice's laser pistols leave the impressions built into his forearms, snapping into his hands.

"Stand down," I tell him. "This is between me and him."

The bot takes a step back, clearing the center of the station for our duel. Fairfax doesn't hesitate, blade flashing forward. I step into the thrust, and the sword slides between my side and left arm.

By clenching all the muscles in my right arm, I send the butt of my blaster hammering into his face. A lesser weapon might have shattered at the impact, but Fairfax's jaw gives way instead, and he staggers back.

We part, sizing each other up across the gap, the man-bot with a hand raised to finger his dented jaw.

Then we clash in earnest.

8

As we duel, the soldier holding Harmony maneuvers so that Fairfax is always between me and him. It limits how much I can fire my blaster, for fear that I'll miss and hit her. The chance is small, but it's not one I'll take unless I have to.

Fairfax presses the attack, sword flickering forward. It takes all my concentration to slow down the battle's "frame rate" enough to be able to dodge. Ducking under a horizontal slice, I fall to one knee and fire upward into the man-bot's face. His head twitches sideways—fast enough to dodge the second bolt, but not the first.

The shot tosses his head back, and I use the opening to sidestep to the left, too fast for the soldier holding Harmony to react. Then I open fire on Fairfax, blaster bolts hammering his torso, perforating his cape.

The man-bot recovers quickly, thrusting to force me back to the right, and again. The soldier comes in line with us again.

My blaster rises to meet the next sword thrust, deflecting it and making room for my foot to rocket into Fairfax's stomach, knocking him off his footing. He staggers backward, and the soldier wrenches Harmony out of the way just in time.

Fairfax crashes into the bulkhead, and I step forward, peppering him with blaster fire. His soldier could stop my attack by interposing himself, but apparently his loyalty doesn't extend that far.

In clear desperation, Fairfax throws his sword at me, and I dodge with centimeters to spare. The blade flashes past, sinking into another soldier's throat, leaving him grasping at the breach in his suit helplessly. Blood wells up around the weapon, gushing out into the airless chamber, where it immediately bubbles and boils.

With my attention momentarily diverted, Fairfax rushes across the chamber and dives through the breach I created, thrusters snapping out from ankles and wrists and firing to propel him on his way.

I curse, willing the *Ares'* airlock closed, to prevent him from taking it. In the meantime, I refuse to waste the opportunity as all nine remaining soldiers watch their boss flee the station. Whirling in a tight circle, I loose blaster bolt after blaster bolt—nine in total. Starting with the one holding Harmony, all nine soldiers jerk backward, slamming against the bulkheads.

Harmony stumbles out of the dead soldier's grasp, then shakes herself off. "Thanks, Dad," she says. "I...didn't think you'd come."

"That's the last time you'll ever think that," I say. "Promise. Okay?"

She nods, staring at the corpse of the soldier who'd been holding her. I study him too, my eyes falling on exactly what I'm looking for: the thruster belt cinched around his waist. I kneel beside him, hands questing for the release. Typically it's hidden, to reduce the chance of an adversary activating it. Through her face mask, Harmony looks nauseated by the body-looting, but there's nothing to be done for that.

Dice is standing at the melted breach. "Fairfax is still on the *Ares'* hull," he says, voice flat.

I nod, the thruster belt coming off in my hands. I encircle my own waist with it, fastening it. "If he tries to make it back to his ship, he knows our turrets will blast him. I'll deal with him in a second." The belt comes off the dead soldier, and I set about tightening it around my own waist. "Dice, I want you to take Harmony into *Europa's Gift* and get her out of here."

"That will prove problematic. I deactivated the ship's life support and used the components to bolster computing."

I wince. "Then Harm will have to enter nanodeath until you get somewhere safe."

Harmony crashes into me, wrapping her arms around me. "Dad, no. I'm not leaving you. You didn't leave me."

I pry her off me, holding her by the shoulders. "This is beyond you, Harm. Maybe someday it won't be, but right now I have a chance to end a major threat to the galaxy. I may not get it again."

"The Allfather's free anyway, isn't he? Fairfax said he would be, if you followed us. It won't make a difference."

"I'd much rather have just one of them at large than both of them. Besides, now that the Subverse won't be reset, we're playing for keeps. After I kill Fairfax, defeating the Allfather will mean the galaxy will be safe from both of them, forever."

"That may be easier said than done," Dice remarks.

"Obviously. But it's time to stop running. Fairfax first, then someday, the Allfather."

"I love you, Dad," Harmony says, and I can tell she's crying.

"Love you, Harm. Now, look away."

She does, and I go to the soldier whose throat Fairfax's sword destroyed. Gripping the hilt and placing a boot against the man's forehead, I draw the blade, which drips blood.

With that, I sprint across the station and dive through the breach, just as Fairfax did. Thrusters snap out from my belt as I enter the void.

I'm just a handful of meters out when Fairfax appears, holding one of the *Ares'* secondary turrets, which he's apparently snapped off from the hull. It looks ridiculously large in his grasp, and it sends a torrent of thoughts rushing through my head: how'd he manage to break off the enormous weapon? And why didn't Belflower warn me he was doing it? Did Fairfax jam our communications somehow?

Then, all thought is obliterated as Fairfax starts firing.

9

Activating the thruster belt with a thought, I zag to the left, just barely avoiding the thick laser bolt that cuts through the void. Knowing I probably have a fraction of a second before he readjusts his aim, I send a spread of blaster bolts flying toward him, with a few aimed at the space beside him in case he moves.

The beam from the laser turret sweeps toward me, and then the first blaster bolt hits Fairfax's torso, followed an instant later by the second. He's knocked back, and the neon-blue beam goes wild, slicing through space just above my head.

It's enough for me to close the distance. I land on the *Ares'* starboard hull, just aftward of the airlock, blaster in one hand and sword in the other. As my boots connect, I will the magnets in them to activate. Then, thinking of the ship herself as "down," I twist around to run underneath her, toward her belly, then across it and up her port side.

When I reach the top, Fairfax isn't there. I check the nearby space, especially the void between here and his shuttle, in case he launched himself off in a bid to escape. Then, something makes me look to my right, and I see him near the stern, with the secondary turret nestled against the hull.

The blue beam lances out, and I throw myself sideways, back toward the port side. Again, the beam misses by inches.

Now the ship is between us, and I sprint toward the aft. Fairfax can't move very fast—not unless he lets the laser turret go. He probably *should* let it go, since I doubt it holds any more charge, and it certainly can't draw on the ship's capacitors anymore. I wonder if he realizes that.

When I round the corner of the ship onto the aft itself, and it becomes my new "down," I spot the laser turret tumbling through space, already a dozen meters away.

Next, Fairfax comes back onto the stern from the direction of the starboard side, blaster in hand and streaming white bolts toward me in a lateral spread. I do the only thing that will allow me to dodge—I release my boot's magnets and leap from the ship's hull. The bolts fly underneath me as I arc forward, activating my thrusters in reverse, so that they carry me back toward the ship.

As I descend, I pepper Fairfax with blaster bolts, trying to throw him off enough to prevent him from firing back at me. He's not nearly as vulnerable as I am, out here—one suit puncture won't mean death, for him.

He knows that, and he readjusts his aim, unleashing another barrage of bolts as I float back down.

Exposed as I am, there's only one thing I can think to do: I interpose the blade between myself and the first blaster bolt.

Amazingly, it works. The bolt disperses—the sword must be coated with something that dispels the bolts, similar to the laser-dispersing reflective film coating my spidersilk armor. But even overclocked, there's no time to marvel at the fact. Wrist snapping, I bring the blade in front of the next blaster bolt, and the next.

Fairfax's shooting grows frantic, and he spams the trigger even faster. My movements gets faster to compensate, my blade flickering to and fro, keeping the attack at bay.

Then, I'm upon him, and I make to run him through. Before I can, he leaps from the *Ares'* hull, hurtling into space. Reflexively, I deactivate my boots' magnets and leap after him, putting all my might into the thrust.

It's suicide, of course—for both of us. If we stray too far from the station, it will only be a matter of time before a satellite takes us out, hurtling past at a meaningful fraction of light speed.

But I'm all in. Unfortunately, it looks like it will be my undoing.

The effort of leaping from the *Ares* seems to have sapped some final energy reserve, and the stars begin to swim as my vision goes screwy.

Come on, Joe. Hold it together just a little longer.

With my thruster belt at full power, I'm only a couple meters behind Fairfax, who continues to shower me with blaster bolts. I can barely see them with my blurred vision, and I direct the sword on instinct alone. My emotions are my interface—they're my connection to reality. They warn me of danger, more efficiently than my datasphere ever did, and they indicate right action.

The blaster bolts are dispersed, one by one, in rapid succession.

And then I reach Fairfax, my fingers closing around his throat in an iron grip. I ram the blade through his stomach, just as he impaled me on Arbor. Except, I don't think he'll be coming back from this.

Just as he did on Arbor, I wrench the blade upward, toward his throat. I repeat the motion a couple times. And then I withdraw the blade, planting both feet against his torn torso and kicking him away, so that he hurtles through space. At first, I'm not sure why I did that—just that it felt right.

Then, I realize why. A satellite flashes by, impacting Fairfax and vaporizing him instantly. On some level, I must have sensed the thing coming.

Smiling to myself, I fall into unconsciousness, drifting through the Dyson swarm.

ARES

1

M y dreams are strangely peaceful.

There's no plot to them, and they make no sense, as is usually the case with dreams. But they're calm. Mostly, I dream of spring, which is a strange thing for someone who spends most of his time on a spaceship to dream of.

Buds blossoming. Flocks of birds returning, trees flowering, the sun breaking through the clouds.

Also, storms. Terrible rainstorms that drench the land. Sometimes thunderstorms, which rumble and rage, sending long forks of lightning to splinter and burn everything they touch.

In these dreams, I get the sense that the world isn't out of the woods yet. Worse storms are coming, and winter always returns, eventually. But for the first time in a long, long time, things are different. Fresh. New. Change isn't always good, but at the very least it makes good things possible.

My eyes fly open, and I'm staring at my cabin's overhead, lying on my bunk. I feel better rested than I have in years. And I take a moment to appreciate that for once, my dreams weren't tortured nightmares.

"Hi, Dad."

Placing a hand against the bulkhead, I push myself to a sitting position, swinging my legs over the side of the bunk. "Harm," I say, smiling. "I thought I told Dice to escape with you in *Europa's Gift.*"

"Yeah, well," she says, shrugging. "Dice doesn't have to follow your orders anymore, and I never did."

"That's a fact," I mutter, chuckling.

"There was no one aboard the *Ares* who could fly her. And you were drifting into the swarm. So it's a good thing I didn't agree to enter nanodeath like you wanted. You wouldn't be around right now."

"I didn't expect to be around, to be honest," I say, my voice hitching. What the hell. Am I about to cry?

I get up, crossing the cramped cabin to lean down and embrace my daughter. At first, she stiffens in surprise, but then settles into the hug.

"I love you, Harm," I say, my voice sounding thick. Fount. What's happening to me?

"Love you, Dad." She pats my back.

I draw back from her, wiping my eyes with the back of a hand. "What is this?" I say in disbelief, staring at the moisture on my skin.

"They're called emotions, Dad. Humans feel them sometimes."

I shake my head laughing, knowing I could easily spend the next twenty minutes weeping, if I let myself. Instead, I sniff sharply, draw a deep breath, and exhale shakily. "Fount," I mutter. "Where are we now?"

"In slipspace. Dice took the same exit coords—the *Europa's Gift* will come out where we do."

"Which is?"

"On the other side of the Core. We might as well see what the other end of the galaxy has to offer, I figure."

Staring at her, I say, "Seriously? You took us past the Core on a whim?"

"Honestly, Dad, the important thing is that we're alive. And free. You weren't conscious for this, but after we picked you up, Mom spotted the Allfather chasing us through the swarm."

"Wait…she spotted the Allfather? Like, in a spaceship?"

"No…no. Just him. She didn't know that's who it was, at first, but Dice confirmed it. He was leaping from station to station, somehow avoiding the hurtling satellites. Somehow breathing in space without a suit."

I shake my head, bewildered, and unsure how I was able to go toe-to-toe with a being who can do that.

"He seemed pretty determined to get to us," Harmony says. "And I doubt it was to take us prisoner. I'm pretty sure he wanted to rip the *Ares* apart."

I nod. "He's probably pissed off about losing Fairfax. And now he no doubt has control of the military Fairfax spent years building for him. The galaxy's in for quite an ordeal."

"Seems right," Harmony says, frowning. "But, Dad…do you get the feeling this is better, somehow? I mean, the galaxy was a mess before. Now, the focus will be on the real. Like, we won't be screwing up the real world just to serve the Subverse. Does that make any sense?"

"Yeah," I say. "It does."

People will have to stop pretending they can keep hiding from life—and from the fact that life involves suffering. They'll have to contend with the realization that creating a digital heaven was never workable, a realization the Knighthood has only postponed, in their efforts to make sure humanity never had to confront reality.

"I guess you're a Shiva, now," Harmony says, as if reading my mind. "I mean, you went to the Crucible. And you succeeded."

"No I didn't. Success is supposed to mean resetting the Subverse."

But she's shaking her head. "No, Dad. I'm pretty sure, this time, success meant *not* resetting it. Anyway, you took care of

Fairfax. You got justice for all those kids whose lives he ruined, and now there's just the Allfather to deal with."

"I have a feeling that will be easier said than done," I say, echoing Dice's words. But I know what she means. As screwed up as all this is, it does seem better, somehow.

It does seem better.

"Hey," I say. "Why don't we pay your mom a visit?"

A smile spreads slowly across Harmony's face. "Yeah. Okay."

"You take the bed," I say, willing the hatch open and heading out to recline in the command seat. Before I do, I notice Fairfax's sword resting against the bulkhead near the Repair and Recharge module. I guess it's mine, now.

A minute later, Harmony and I are standing together on a broad mountain peak, surrounded by a sky filled with puffy white clouds. Under out feet, the ground is mostly rock, but here and there tufts of grass poke through. Even up here, on a windswept plateau, life soldiers on.

Marissa appears, then, having accepted my invitation to the shared sim.

Beaming, she walks toward us, spreading her arms. When she reaches us, we all embrace, saying nothing for a time.

Eventually we pull back, and Marissa's smiling at Harmony. I can't help but grin, too.

"Should we tell her now, Joe?"

I blink. "Huh? Oh. Right. Um…have we decided that, then?"

Marissa's smile fades a little. "I don't know, Joe. Have we?"

I clear my throat. Fount, I don't want to ruin this moment. "Harm…listen. Your mom and I have been…well, spending time together, and…"

"Huh?" Harmony frowns, eyes narrowed in apparent confusion. "What do you mean, spending…oh, *Fount!* Gross! I didn't need to know that! Do you mean, like, in a sim?"

"That's not important right now," I say in a rush. "What's

important is that we're considering, well…I mean, we've put aside a lot of our differences, and…"

"Your father and I…" Marissa says, then trails off. She doesn't want to be the one to say it.

"Well, we're giving things a try," I say, nodding curtly.

Marissa nods, too, smiling a little, and returning her gaze to Harmony. "Yes. Exactly. What do you think?"

"It's a little weird, to be honest," our daughter says. "But… maybe actually kind of nice." She shrugs. "I mean, we'll see."

"Exactly," I say, trying to relieve the tension in the conversation and lend it a sense of finality. "We'll see."

That doesn't seem very final, actually. Then again, not much ever does, does it?

ACKNOWLEDGMENTS

Thank you to my Alpha Team, who have been reading this book since its earliest stage and who've provided substantial feedback along the way, which helped me develop the story with my readers' desires foremost in mind. They are Rex Bain, Sheila Beitler, Mick Bird, Bruce Brandt, Iain Howard, Colin Oliver, Jason Pennock, Jeff Rudolph, and Ben Varela.

Thank you to my proofreading team, who helped eliminate scores of spelling and grammar issues. I take full responsibility for any mistakes that remain :) My proofreaders are Rex Bain, Bill Bartlett, Sheila Beitler, Bruce Brandt, and Jeff Rudolph.

A special thank you to my Patreon supporters at the Destroyer Captain, Supercarrier Captain, and Space Fleet Admiral levels. Your support helps me to package my books as professionally as possible while staying true to what my readers like best about my books. Thank you to Brent Lee Davis, Edward Goolsby, David Middleton, Lawrence Tate, and Michael Van De Hey (at the $25 Space Fleet Admiral level), Brian Loeung (at the $10 Supercarrier Captain level), and Andrew Mercer (at the $5 Destroyer Captain level).

Thank you also to Patreon supporters Rex Bain, Michael Bone,

Sid Echikson, Richard Gunn, Christian Kallias, John A Koenig III, Wynand Pretorius, Bill Scarborough, John Tava, Ben Varela, and Jerry Winiarski.

Thank you to Tom Edwards for creating such stunning cover art, as always.

Thank you to Steve Beaulieu for creating compelling cover typography and for formatting the interior.

Thank you to my family - Mom, Dad, and Danielle - your support means everything.

Thank you to Cecily, my heart.

Thank you to the people who read my stories, write reviews, and help spread the word. I couldn't do this without you.

ABOUT THE AUTHOR

Scott Bartlett was born in St. John's, Newfoundland – the easternmost province of Canada. During his decade-long journey to become a full-time author, he supported himself by working a number of different jobs: salmon hatchery technician, grocery clerk, youth care worker, ghostwriter, research assistant, pita maker, and freelance editor.

In 2014, he succeeded in becoming a full-time novelist, and he's been writing science fiction at light speed ever since.

Visit scottplots.com to download 3 free military sci-fi ebooks.